THE EDINBURGH SEER

Edinburgh Seer Book One

ALISHA KLAPHEKE

Text copyright © 2017 by Alisha Klapheke
Cover art copyright © 2017 by Damonza

Visit Alisha on the web! http://www.alishaklapheke.com

Library of Congress Cataloging-in-Publication Data
Klapheke, Alisha
The Edinburgh Seer/Alisha Klapheke. —First Edition.
Summary: A candymaker's daughter conceals her sixth sense to avoid the firing squad until her father is kidnapped and she must use her ability to track him through a trail of ancient artifacts.
ISBN 978-0-9987379-6-6 (trade)
ISBN 978-0-9987379-7-3 (ebook)
[1. Fantasy. 2. Magic—Fiction.] I. Title.

Printed in the United States of America
10 9 8 7 6 5 4 3 2 1
First Edition

ISBN: 978-0-9987379-7-3

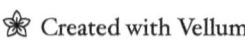 Created with Vellum

To my Uncommon Crew and my Reading Rebels
May the goats be with you

CHAPTER 1
CANDYMAKER'S DAUGHTER

Summer, 2017, Fifteenth Year of John III's Reign

THE MORNING SUN HAD JUST MANAGED TO PAINT A PALE yellow light over Edinburgh's Old Town, and, as usual, Aini MacGregor had already run three errands and set up her father's candy lab for the day's work. Pots, scrubbed and warmed, on the stove. Measuring spoons shined to make the morning sun jealous. Bags of powdered sugar and vials of hormones and chemicals standing in place like disciplined kingsmen. Everything was exactly where it needed to be.

The tower was chilly this time of day and goosebumps hurried over Aini's skin as she unscrewed a jar and shifted the newly purchased cinnamon into its tidy home. She inhaled the lovely scent. Tears burned her eyes—not because of the many spices she had at her fingertips, but because of the rasping voice carried on the wind through the cracked, leaded window above her head—the voice of Nathair Campbell, the very powerful man who would shoot her dead if he knew what she was.

A sixth-senser.

Demanding her skittering heart to quit distracting her, Aini continued about her work. Today would be a great one for her father, Lewis MacGregor, crafter of the nobility's beloved sweets. Together, with the apprentices' help, they shaped goodies that not only tasted divine, but gave the eater certain short-term abilities usually enjoyed by birds or insects, or only dreamed up by wild imaginations. They'd been a hit at the king's last birthday party. The British king was a terrible man—Aini couldn't change that—but at least his parties helped with business. With the vision-inducing gum they were about to craft and test, the MacGregor business, Enliven, was poised to rule the boutique sweets market. If only the stupid thugs, the Campbells, would leave well enough alone.

Clan Campbell worked for the king, maintaining his rules here in Scotland. But lately...they seemed to have become very full of themselves and were taking on projects that Aini was certain the king himself knew nothing about.

"Who is shouting to wake the dead in the Grassmarket?" Neve demanded in place of a *Good Morning*. Father's female apprentice padded into the room. When she wasn't working in the lab, Neve took tourists around Scotland with Caledonia Tours. She knew her history, that was for sure.

With quick fingers and a smile, the Edinburgh native pulled her hair into two high buns and secured them with pins. All the girls here wore their hair like that. Aini tugged at one of her own heavy, black locks. It refused to be tied up, but even though it made her stand out—not many half Balinese girls in Scotland— she couldn't hate it. It reminded her of her mom, a woman who hadn't been perfect, but who'd loved her completely.

Aini straightened her lab coat and eyed the king's rules hanging on the wall. An identical list of "Scottish citizens cannot do this" and "All citizens and colonials must do that" were posted in every pub, home, and store in the entire British Empire. Even across the pond in the rebellious Dominion of New England colonies. Aini wondered if they'd ever get over their 18th century loss. They were nearly as bad as the Scottish rebels here.

Blinking, she remembered Neve's earlier question. "Nathair Campbell is down there, dirtying the morning."

Neve made a Scottish sound of disgust in the back of her throat. Aini couldn't have agreed more. "I'm excited about that new gum recipe," Neve said.

Perfectly on time—because Aini perfectly timed it—the gum base started to bubble on the stove.

"Your white pepper idea for the gum is going to work. I can feel it." Aini wiped her hands on a towel, breathing in the sweet smells. "I really think it'll trigger the chewer's schema for fire."

Neve grinned, and Aini realized her Dominion of New England accent was blazing again.

Thane loped into the lab, and Aini's heart whirred like a broken taffy puller and pushed every other thought out of her head. At six-foot-four, the Scotsman dominated the room, all broad shoulders, gray flashing eyes, and downturned mouth. He pulled his glasses out of his messy, honey-colored hair and headed toward his lab coat on the far hook. Mud caked the toes of his boots, and a silver necklace winked from his collarbone.

Because of who Aini was, and *what* Aini was, Thane with his late nights and penchant for whisky was the very definition of *Look, but don't touch*. She had to be careful. Do nothing danger-ous. Never break any rules.

"Good morning, Thane."

Just because he wasn't for her didn't mean she had to be rude. After all, he was Father's favorite, besides herself, of course. Thane had developed the original formula for the vision gum. Aini wished she had half the brains he did.

"We're almost ready to mix," she said.

His gaze slid over her fingers and up her arms, and he gave her a nod.

As Neve measured out the pepper, Aini held a hand toward the bubbling broiler. "A little help?" she asked Thane. Her face heated. Why did her cheeks have to flush so easily?

"Aye. Course." Thane's thick, West Scots accent wrapped around every O and tripped over each R beautifully.

Tugging his coat on, Thane slid his glasses onto his slightly overlarge nose. Tattoos of chemical formulas snaked down his fingers in black letters, tiny numbers, and mathematical symbols. Aini leaned forward a little. NaCl was salt. Another finger had a V over a t and—*oh*—it was the formula for viscosity. But the other markings? She could never quite get a good look at them.

Father walked in, wearing his usual style—all black under his lab coat, and every item ironed into full submission. He winked before readying the powdered sugar at the lab's silver table. He still wore his wedding ring, though the divorce happened long before Aini's mother died two years ago. She sighed, wishing she could do something about that pain.

"I was thinking," Father said to Thane, "if we used a pressure cooker to force the Maillard reaction in tomorrow's Dulce de Leche recipe..."

Thane's face brightened. "We could decrease the cooking time by perhaps six times." Thane lifted the pot as Aini stirred. His arm brushed hers and she swallowed. "Genius, Mr. MacGregor," Thane said.

"Will you never stop with the Mr. MacGregor? Just Lewis, please."

Thane smiled at Father like he was his own, like Father could somehow heal the hurt that clouded the uni student's eyes. But it was all right. She wasn't jealous. Aini knew Father was good at providing a stable life, a simple and scheduled way of living, something maybe Thane hadn't experienced before apprenticing here.

"Neve, will you please warm up the mixer?" Father wiped a spot of sugar off his nose and set his planner on the desk near the far end of the lab. The green and blue sugar, in the jars he'd mounted on the whitewashed wall, sparkled. He frowned like there was something unpleasant about them. Aini touched her chin. She'd always wondered why he displayed the jars like that. They'd never used those colored sugars and surely it would be better to have them with the other ingredients, organized by the lab table. She'd look into it later.

Father shook his head and went to help Thane pour the steaming gum base into the powdered sugar.

The lab's landline rang and Aini picked up. A familiar, rough voice asked for Lewis MacGregor. Aini gritted her teeth. Not *them* again. Her grip on the phone tightened.

"Hold please." She looked to Father. "It's for you."

He stared at the ceiling, eyes pressed closed, before finally taking the call.

While Neve dealt with the mixer's perpetually moody switch across the room—all while humming a song loved by Father's other male apprentice, Myles—Aini took Father's place beside Thane.

Plunging her hands into the gum blend, she kneaded the sticky stuff. The mix was ready for flavor. The powdered sage, white pepper, and smoky nutmeg did nothing to improve the color of the chewing gum, but she was pretty sure Neve was on to something with this flavor choice. The herbs and spices, along with the medieval art packaging that Myles had drawn up, might just get people seeing ancient castles and feasts in great halls. Chemistry crossed with suggestion. It was how the human brain worked.

"No." Father's knuckles whitened as he squeezed the phone. "I'm not going to weaponize my products. Not until I see the royal approval. I'm finished talking about this." He punched a button and threw the phone to his desk where it banged against his laptop. "Campbells. Pushing and pushing. Playing both sides, and I know very well I'm not going to be the winner no matter how..." Muttering, he stalked back to the table. "I need to get something from my downstairs office. Give me a shout when we're ready to test." He disappeared down the staircase, growling about being left in peace.

The Campbells made up the majority of kingsmen stationed in Edinburgh. Normally, they were the law, acting as the king's agents, along with the other kingsmen. But since that public execution of those rebels last month, things had been different. Nathair Campbell had executed Scottish subjects without a trial of any kind. The king had excused him, blaming overzealous loyalty to the crown, but Aini wasn't so sure. Clan Campbell was less an arm of the king and more of a criminal gang these days. Aini couldn't believe they were pressuring Father to develop products that could covertly paralyze and poison without the king's seal of approval. Even if it was to fight the rebels. It was unfathomable.

Thane breathed hard through his nose like an angry horse.

She eyed the gum, looking for dry spots or uneven spicing. "What is it? What's off?"

Vine-like muscles twisted below Thane's rolled coat sleeves.

He dusted his hands off and pushed his glasses into his hair. "If your father would agree to aid the Campbells, he'd be helping Scotland fight the rebels."

"He doesn't want to twist our craft into something sick and evil." She put her hands on her hips and powdered sugar puffed like little clouds. Flushing, she brushed herself off. "He's worked long and hard to establish Enliven. It's a boutique candy supplier. Not a government laboratory. Besides that, why can't the Campbells go through the official channels and find their own chemists if they're so set on this?"

Neve gathered the pre-blended gum mix. "Because Mr. MacGregor is the best chemist in the empire and they know it."

"Well, we're going to follow the official rules." Aini crossed her arms. "The king could shut us down and you know it."

Neve opened her mouth and closed it again. She hurried to the mixer and dropped her bundle into the metal bowl.

Aini chewed the inside of her cheek. She didn't want to be hard on Neve, but the rules were the rules.

"The Campbells and the king have the same goal, don't they?" Thane frowned. "What difference does fussing about with royal seals make?"

"If my father skirts the law like the Campbells want him to do, the Campbells might get away with it, but I seriously doubt he will."

An image flashed through her memory—an executed sixth-senser.

The woman had been about her mother's age. Aini remembered the lady's wispy, auburn hair. The black band across her eyes. Her body jerking as the bullet hit her chest. The red blood against her striped dress. Her clothing said native Edinburgh, the style Aini tried to imitate. But even fitting in hadn't saved her.

If Aini was found out, the Campbells would assume Father knew about her ability, which he didn't. She squeezed her hands together. She couldn't even think about him rotting in a dark cell.

When the gum was mixed and cooled, Thane cut the ropes into small pieces and Aini called her father back up to the lab. It was time to see if the gum really worked.

THE LIGHT THROUGH THE LAB'S WINDOWS CAST A NET OF GOLD around Aini's father as he peered at his watch. He handed Aini the clipboard of notes they'd destroy as soon as the trial was complete. They couldn't let anyone outside of Enliven get a hold of the information. The competition would leap at the chance to outdo them. Because of this, Aini and the rest had become very, very good at remembering recipes.

Neve and Aini found seats and Thane took a stool, ready to try the gum.

"Where is Myles anyway?" Neve asked.

Aini was actually glad Father's second male apprentice wasn't here. "Buying new paints for his adverts." Myles was great fun, but he could really be a distraction during tests like this.

Father stared at Thane. "I want to know the very minute—the exact moment—you see something." He started the timer on his watch.

"Aye," Thane popped the gum between his lips and chewed, rubbing a hand over his sharp chin.

"How's it taste, then?" Neve scooted forward on her stool.

"A bit fiery."

"Fiery?" Aini asked, pen poised over the clipboard. "Be more specific. We need details for the investors."

"Any visions yet?" Father inched closer to Thane.

Stumbling back, Thane's mouth dropped open, the gum on his tongue.

Aini laughed.

Father practically hopped on Thane. "What do you see, lad?" He normally hid his accent, wanting to please his many English clients, but excitement drew it right out of him.

Staring at the ceiling beams, Thane paled. "Translucent wings. About ten feet long. He's...he's..." The uni student ducked and laughed once, his Adam's apple bobbing in his throat. "He's breathing fire." He shoved his hands through his hair and knocked his glasses to the floor.

Neve hugged herself. "A dragon."

Father lifted his feet in a little jig and grabbed Aini's arm, pulling her into his dance. Heart light, she did a spin, then squeezed him, feeling safe and loved, as if everything was going to be okay.

"I can't believe it," Thane whispered.

Neve grinned. "I knew that white pepper would do the trick."

"Couldn't have done it without you, my wee squirrel," Father said to Aini. "The king will reward us handsomely, what with his birthday celebration coming up. We might get a tax exemption."

"And the elite will want it at their parties if the king has it at his," she said.

Father shouted, "Huzzah!" and zipped over to his desk to write something up.

Aini couldn't stop smiling. Another candy for their impressive inventory. Another building block for Father's beloved business. Somehow, she had to thank the apprentices for all their hard work. Maybe a special dinner or a big night out. This vision-inducing gum was another reason she loved having all of them here, a part of the family.

Neve peppered Thane with questions about the formula. Over Neve's head, Thane met Aini's gaze. A shadow passed over his face. He was a melancholy sort, but this was more. Something...darker. Aini's smile faded. He had nothing to be upset about today. What could be bothering him? Surely not all this stuff about the Campbells. It would pass. Wouldn't it?

Father tugged Aini into another jubilant hug, and her smile returned. She could maintain this happiness. She would maintain it. No matter what. She just had to keep her sixth sense concealed. Because visions prompted by chewing gum earned money, but visions of another sort only led to death.

CHAPTER 2
LIVING IN THE DARKNESS

In Mr. MacGregor's townhouse common room, Thane pulled a book off a shelf. It was a mystery set in the Dominion of New England, where Aini had lived with her mother, then her grandmother after her mother passed on.

Now Aini and her father were settling in for their nightly poetry nonsense by the stone fireplace, and Thane wanted to give them room. Deep inside, Thane knew their ritual was anything but nonsensical, but he didn't want to think on that. He had to stay cold, stay focused.

"Robert Burns again tonight, squirrel?" Lewis said to Aini as he crossed his legs and opened a book on his lap.

The light scrape of a turning page followed the click of the lamp. Aini sat opposite Lewis, her foot pointed as she drew an imaginary circle on the floor with her toe like a ballet dancer. Thane's neck grew a little too warm. He turned away.

"Care to join us, Thane?" Aini asked, her red lips plump and lovely in the lamplight.

"No. Thank you though."

His heart pulled at his chest as he bid them goodnight and went to the room he shared with Myles. The time Thane spent with his own father was minimal and perfunctory, more about drilling loyalty to the clan into him than any kind of bonding.

Thane pushed the bedroom door open, and the glare of the overhead made him squint. A quilt—stitched with the leaf logo of Myles's favorite band, Mint—lay half on, half off the guy's bed. Myles was still upstairs working on his advert with Neve. At least there'd be an hour or so of quiet before the colonial tossed himself into bed to snore like a Highland cow.

Thane switched the overhead off and lit a wide candle on his nightstand. When in the lab, focusing on chemistry and his mission, bright light was key to staying alert, focused. Alternatively, the golden shadows of a candle told Thane's brain to relax.

Using a paperclip, Thane popped his phone open, revealing the electronic guts. He picked out the small square that fed his calls to Campbell headquarters, set it near the candle, and dialed his mother's number.

She answered on the first ring, as always, her strong voice softened by anxiety. "Thane?"

"Yes, Mother. And how are you today?"

"Oh, it's a joy to hear your voice. How's all with you?"

"All right."

"Liar," she said. "You know I don't sleep at night, thinking about the orders they give you."

He rubbed his face roughly. "Can we *not* talk about that for a bit, aye? How is your new gardener working out, then?"

She made a huffing noise over the line. "I had to let him go." Her voice was sad, but then it lifted and sparked. "The man had no sense of what I wanted."

Thane smiled. "Too much trimming?"

"Exactly that. He wanted it like an English garden."

"Well, that wouldn't do, would it?"

"Certainly not," she said, a laugh in her voice. "I can't stand feeling like I'm in someone's parlor when I'm enjoying a walk." She broke off, coughing.

"Are you sick?" he asked.

"No." There was a sound like she'd switched the phone to her other ear. "I'm..."

"He hasn't hurt you again, has he? Just leave, Mother. Please."

"You know he would find me. Find us."

Thane let the silence speak for a beat. It was an old argument. There was no answer for either of them.

"I should have something to please the clan soon," he said tightly. "It's something to do with my mission here."

"Don't fret over me, Son. I've been managing that man since long before you were a twinkle in his eye."

Managing. Enduring abuse is what she did. Thane pressed the corner of the phone into his forehead until the pain cleared away his anger.

"I'll ring you again soon," he said. "All right?"

With her blessing, he clicked the phone off.

He could picture her folding her arms over herself, the phone tucked under an elbow. She was probably standing beside her bedroom window, looking out on the green gardens she loved so well and wearing her favorite cashmere sweater. Though her hair had gone prematurely white, she stood tall, nearly as tall as he, and her shoulders only slightly bent against the life she lived. She'd tug on her perfectly plucked eyebrow as she planned how next to handle her husband, how to best cover the yellowing bruise on her cheek. If there was a woman who could survive under these circumstances, it was her.

If only Thane could help her get away. But the network of Campbell relatives, operatives, and kingsman, both related and not, was too thick and far-reaching. No one could find their way out. Especially not Thane.

He couldn't truly think of leaving Scotland. He'd been to Paris, Rome, even the colonies and parts of Asia, but no place gave him the same feeling as his own home country. He wondered if others—maybe those who were also descendants of the country's most ancient families—felt the same way. It was like Scotland was a living, breathing being. A person to come home to, who laughed at your jokes and gave you rest when you needed it. The high slopes of the bens, the peat-brown waters, the smell of the air, his feisty people. Scotland beat in his chest like a second heart. It'd kill him to turn his back on the homeland, and he hoped with everything in him he'd never have to do it.

He leaned back on the bed to start on the mystery, but his book sat in his hands, ignored, as Lewis's reaction to the clan's pressure flickered through his mind.

So Lewis thought he could simply say *No.* That Nathair Campbell needed royal approval to actually force him to create sweets that were anything but sweet. Until a month ago, Thane would've agreed his father would wait for the king's go-ahead to pursue this route. But when Nathair ordered those rebels and sixth-sensers shot down in public last month, he'd turned a page in the story of his growing madness. The king had excused Nathair's disregard for following proper execution mandates, saying his head of security was simply overcome with loyalty to king and crown.

Thane knew better.

Nathair wasn't overcome with loyalty; the scarred and vicious leader of Clan Campbell, Thane's own terrible father, lusted for more power.

Unable to read, Thane blew out the candle and pretended to sleep when Myles came in, smelling like paint.

"Good night, sleeping beauty," Myles said, comic sarcasm dripping from his southern colonial accent.

Thane rolled his eyes in the dark. He turned over and began the long wait for a short sleep. He wondered if he'd sleep better if he had a different life to wake up to. Working in the lab was a sick sort of tease. Having Lewis MacGregor as a mentor—such a master chemist and a good man all around. Sharing work space with the others who knew nothing about Thane's real life. It was a dream that would end all too soon, and in a bang, if the past had taught him anything.

THANE WOKE ABRUPTLY, HEART RUMBLING AND STUTTERING. He sat up. The clock on his nightstand said five in the morning. He'd had that strange dream again. The one that had haunted him since childhood.

It began with him simply looking down at his palm. The focus narrowed onto one of his fingers, zooming in, closer, deeper. He seemed to race through the ridges and lines of his own fingerprint. They towered over him like walls of a great valley. Their flesh tone faded. The curves and patterns of his fingerprint grew black as he seemed to rush backward. The sound bothered Thane most. In this last part of the recurring dream, the air reverberated with a shattering boom that made him feel as if his eyes might pop from their sockets.

He'd never told a soul about the dream. When he was young, he didn't want to tell his mother. Running to Mummy was something only wee bairns did. Now, the dream smacked of a sixth sense, so he ignored it as best he could.

One of Myles's ear-cracking snores broke the silence in the dark room, and Thane forced his tired legs out of bed, fumbling for his glasses. Leaving Myles to his dreams, he slipped out of the room, through the warm kitchen, and up the winding, stone steps to the tower lab.

At the low, wide stove, he poured ingredients for Lewis's golden taffy into a huge copper pot. Aini had edged the color enhancing sweet into the day's schedule after she pre-sold a batch to the Earl of Lincoln. With that boiling, and the automatic wooden spoon spinning in the pot, Thane moved on to his real project. If anyone was out of bed this early and surprised him, he could simply point to the taffy as his reason for being here.

The mortar and pestle were still where he'd stored them, behind the blocks of wax they sometimes used for molds. Henbane and nightshade, the dried anticholinergic herbs he'd researched and gathered, hid under the mortar. After setting all this on the table, Thane pulled a vial from his boot.

The small glass container held the substance he'd developed during his first week here. He'd drawn the basics of it from Lewis's aphrodisiac cherry drops. The way Thane distilled the substance increased the paralyzing effect ninety-seven percent and would hopefully, with today's mix, draw the herbal additions through the victim's tongue and into the body.

Dropping the ingredients into the mortar, he ground them until they made a fine powder he had to be sure not to inhale.

The taffy was ready on the stove, so he added the sparkling golden color and orange flavoring, then pulled it off the heat. The mix cooled, and Thane added one tablespoon of Lewis's photoreceptor enhancer, Cone5, into the mix. Those who ate this golden taffy would see the world in an array of colors usually reserved for the Chinese yellow swallowtail butterfly, *Papilio xuthus.* Twenty minutes after consuming, candy-eaters' eyes would be flooded with two extra types of rods that allowed ultra-violet and violet color vision. Thane had never tried it, but it sounded fairly interesting.

Pouring the hot taffy onto a baking sheet and placing it in the lab's oven on two hundred degrees, he'd keep it warm enough to put on the puller when he'd finished his secret project—the altered, intensified cherry drops.

Now for the dangerous drops' flavor—the project for his clan to possibly use on the rebels.

It had to be something unique, not simply cherry. Something that would make any daft fool want to give it a go. Setting the pestle down, he eyed the shelves and jars. What flavor would cover the foul taste the higher levels of the chemical produced?

Above him on a high open shelf, a tall glass container held a cloudy liquid. Coconut extract. He poured two teaspoons into the mortar, his brain latching onto the scent and throwing out mental images of Aini. Ebony hair knotted high and showing off her slim neck. Her ruby lips. That sweet, painfully innocent smile.

"What are you working on?" Aini's voice carried across the lab.

Heart rate increasing, Thane smiled casually, quickly setting the coconut extract on the table and turning to take the warm taffy from the oven.

"Just the taffy you had on schedule."

He laid the baking sheet near the extract, the orange of the taffy rising and combining with the island scent.

Aini gave him a quick smile, then eyed the coconut oil. "And what's this for?"

As she turned, he slipped the mortar and the secret herbs onto the shelf below the table. "I was thinking about a twist on your father's cherry drop recipe. Adding coconut." A little truth turned lies to gold.

"Did you fill out the form for the flavor addition?" Aini touched the mound of taffy on the table, wincing a bit at the heat. With a metal scraper, she began folding the taffy to ready it for the puller. "The king can shut us down for not following procedures." Her hand went to her hip and her eyebrow quirked into a vicious slant.

"Give me the form then. I'm not here to ruin anything." The words stuck a bit in his throat. He certainly wasn't there to make things all rosy.

Lewis walked in, his gaze raging over the lab. "Why is the coconut extract out? Where's the mortar?" He took a breath and looked at Aini, who was ringing her hands. "Can you tidy this place up a bit? I'm shutting the lab down for today. I have to go to the kingsmen's office and have a chat about the Campbells." Lewis's gaze strayed to the battered ring on his left hand.

Thane fisted his hands, his nails cutting into his palms.

"At least I've readied the King's Ointment they ordered..." Lewis pointed to a crate of vials nestled in packing paper. The stuff could heal almost any wound. Expensive and time-consuming to craft though. "Thane, will you take it downstairs?"

"Aye. No bother, Mr. MacGregor."

Pushing the tall bottle of coconut extract over—on purpose —with his elbow, Thane apologized. As Aini and Lewis rushed to clean the mess, Thane bent and cupped the mortar. With the substance behind his back, he retreated, then rounded the table, heading for the vials of King's Ointment. Cloaking his movements with his body, Thane tucked the mortar and herbs into the crate.

His secret concoction hidden, he grabbed a towel and helped with the cleanup.

"Never knew you to be clumsy," Lewis said, frowning at him.

"Didn't sleep much I guess."

Again, Aini raised that eyebrow. She screwed the cap onto the oil. "Did you go out last night?"

"No. Just...my brain would not shut down."

She smiled then, looking sorry for accusing him of sneaking out. It made Thane feel even worse. "That, I understand," she said.

Lewis clapped a hand on his shoulder. "I'm sorry I was so abrupt. I'm a bit...stressed. Please remember, I require dedication, lad, but not more than your mind and body can handle. Why don't you go have a lie down?"

Thane swallowed and his eyes burned. The man was far kinder than any he'd ever known. "I thank you, but no. I'll do."

"All right then."

"Father, why don't we let Thane finish up here," Aini said. "I'll make some oatmeal downstairs and you can be on your way."

Lewis started to pick up the crate of King's Ointment.

"Don't," Thane said. "I'll take it. Don't worry."

Aini looped her arm through her father's and they disappeared down the stairs.

With them gone, Thane had a moment to turn the powder in the mortar into something he could use. After finding a jar of petroleum jelly, he snapped on a pair of latex gloves from his lab coat pocket and lifted the tiny container of healing ointment from its nest. He smeared a nice glob of jelly into the mortar, mixed it, and scooped it into a vial.

It wasn't a clever candy recipe, not what he'd been ordered to work on, but the paralyzing ointment might be enough to please his fool cousin for the time being.

CHAPTER 3
GONE

T o do list:

1. *buy apples*
2. *look for deals on spices/herbs*
3. *purchase the bread Father likes with his stew*

SINCE HER FATHER HAD DEEMED THE LAB CLOSED, AND IT WAS Williamsday, Aini herded the apprentices to the weekly market. If she let them stay home, they'd lie around eating and watching television.

Her mother had been like that; throwing time away as if it wasn't already designated as work hours by the oily man who managed their dance troupe. During their off weeks, Aini tried to get her mom to teach her Balinese or even Scottish history, the story of Lewis's homeland, where Aini had been born. But her mother would only smile condescendingly and claim she needed rest. Aini would retreat to her cot and simmer, frustrated at her mother's nature and the fact that she'd broken up the family for a reason she'd never share.

Visits to Edinburgh were the opposite of Aini's changeable, painfully lackadaisical days in the colonies. With her father's penchant for order, Aini slipped into his type of life happily. He was like her. A goal, a list, the rules—and they were off, conquering.

At the market, the hot and determined sun washed the gathering clouds, whitening their edges and deepening the gray-blue of their heavy middles.

"It amazes me that the days are named after the king now," Myles said, joining everyone under a produce man's tarp and picking up the thread of Neve's conversation about the days of the week.

Aini added another shiny apple to the bag Neve held.

"It shouldn't." Neve used group funds to pay the man.

Thane took the proffered bag of red fruit from Aini, his head brushing the tarp.

"The king can do as he likes." Aini checked off the first chore on the list and enjoyed the momentary shade.

Myles brushed imagined dirt off his purposefully ripped, designer T-shirt. "I know. But I thought I was the only soul arrogant enough to do something like that."

Aini elbowed him. "Quiet." He needed to be careful. Kingsmen patrolled the streets, occasionally stopping people and studying their Subject Identification Cards. "Seriously. Hush."

Myles frowned and pulled at two clumps of his green-dyed hair, lengthening them to resemble horns. Incorrigible. A lot of boys from the plantations of the southern American colonies wore the same style because of that banjo and drum band, Mint. Aini wondered how many of them talked bad about the king like Myles.

"God, look at those poor kids over there." Myles shook his head. "Sucks."

Aini squinted into the sunny marketplace. Children wove around their parents. And yes, they were thinner than she remembered them being. In the colonies, everyone was thin, but Edinburgh had always seemed immune. Until now. The king's new taxes were obviously having a marked effect on those who didn't have a lucrative business like Father's.

The group left the shady produce spot, tall Thane ducking to escape the tarp.

"Give me two of those apples, Neve," Aini said. She slipped away and handed the fruit to one of the scrawny children. It wasn't against the king's rules or the law. They grinned up at her, eyes bright, and ran back to their parents as her heart pinched. If only she could buy them all apples. Even if she had the means, the kingsmen wouldn't like it.

Myles was doing a ridiculous dance, all elbows and raised knees, when she returned. In the craziness of the market, only Neve had noticed her little errand.

"There's that fool with those fancy measuring spoons you like, Aini." Thane pointed across the crowd.

"He's selling cider too, looks like," Neve said, and with a quick smile, she took off.

The merchant accepted money from a foreign woman who'd apparently bought a set of spoons as another tourist reached over her to grab a cutting board made in the shape of Edinburgh Castle. Why people felt the need to buy such silly things was beyond Aini. At least the tourists brought money in. Too bad

Scots were forced to give most of it to the Campbells and the king.

Sweat drizzled down Aini's chest as she trailed Thane and Myles. "This isn't next on our list. I only brought enough money for—"

At the booth, Thane twisted and shoved a cold bottle of cider into her hands. He smiled, his gaze going to her lips. He blinked and looked away. "Hurry. Go on," he hissed at the group.

He'd stolen the cider. Aini blinked, shocked.

As they passed a row of postcard displays, Myles took another bottle from Thane and drank.

Neve looked at the one Aini held. "May I have a bit? It's rough in this sun."

Aini couldn't believe it. Thane had stolen things and right in front of some kingsmen. "But...but we didn't buy these. We can't," Aini lowered her voice, "steal."

She could just imagine what would happen if a kingsman questioned her. If she touched anything sentimental to him—a ring, a bracelet, anything—the memories, they'd swamp her, and it'd be obvious she wasn't normal. It'd all be over for her, for Enliven, for Father.

Thane put a hand behind her back and gently pushed her forward. "Last week you paid eight pounds for one bottle. There's the real crime in this. The man's prices are three times what they should be."

She spun and headed back toward the man's booth. She wasn't about to break the law for some free cider. Ridiculous. She peeked over her shoulder. Thane smiled a little as Neve and Myles finished their stolen treat. This was yet another of the many reasons she couldn't get her head around Thane. It almost seemed like he lived to bend the rules.

～

WITH THE TO-DO LIST COMPLETE, THEY SET OFF FOR THE townhouse, holding their market buys: a bag of apples, a loaf of delicious-smelling fresh bread, a new dress Aini had bought for Neve as a birthday gift (not planned but a good buy none-theless), a tub of honey, and some dried lavender, which was cheaper than Aini had seen it in a while.

Patting the honey crock, Myles wiggled his dark eyebrows at Neve. "In the past, some ladies have dubbed me their little tub of honey."

Pink patches rose on Neve's neck.

Thane pretended to vomit. "You're pure giving me the boak."

A laugh bubbled out of Aini and she took an apple from the bag. "If you'd cook when it's your turn, Myles, instead of talking that girl down the road into doing it, Neve might consider calling you something nicer. Doubt it'll involve food stuffs, but you can hope."

Neve pulled an edge off the loaf of bread. "She has a point, colonial."

Myles raised his hands to heaven dramatically. "*Colonial.* She got that from you, Thane. Now every time she refers to me, she'll be thinking of your handsome arse."

"Only because you've mentioned it," Thane said.

Myles leaned back to view the subject of the conversation. He whistled low at Thane's backside. "It's only my jealousy talking." He twisted to look at his own rear and shook his head sadly.

Laughing, Aini threw an apple core at him, knowing the tourists' carriage horses would enjoy the treat. Thane palmed Myles's head and shoved him away playfully.

A shriek tore at the morning.

Three kingsmen—not Campbells as they didn't wear the tartan—herded a family of four toward the back of a black van. The smallest, a boy missing most of his front teeth, yanked at the kingsman's grip, crying out. Tears ran freely down his parents' dirty cheeks.

"Let him go." Aini was beside the nearest kingsman before she even realized what she was doing. Her body began to tremble. If they questioned her...

The kingsman's ruddy face pinched into an ugly frown. "Their Subject Identification Cards are expired."

"We don't have the money to renew them," the mother said. "Not after the new tax. Maybe if we—"

The kingsman cut her off. "No maybes. You and yours are going in as punishment for your crime."

"But the children..." Neve started forward, pale. She was probably imagining how this could happen to her little brothers.

Aini took Neve's arm and raised her chin, willing herself not to cow to these men.

"The wee ones will be cared for," the kingsman said. "By the courts. Now move on or you'll be the next taken in." He made to push Aini away.

Heart drumming, watching the kingsman's ring, Aini jerked back, bumping up against Thane who swore quietly and stared the kingsmen down. If that man's ring had touched her, she'd have seen something and it would've all come down on her and Father. There was nothing she could do here and not risk her own family. The wee ones wouldn't be properly cared for. They'd be slaves in all but name, cleaning for the courts and never having someone to look after them. But there was nothing she could do without seriously endangering Father's life. She hated her selfishness, but it was what it was. She couldn't risk Father just to argue with these kingsmen only to lose the fight.

"L-let's go," she said shakily to the group.

The boy's crying leaked through the city's sounds of cars honking, sea birds cawing out, and the hum of market crowds.

None of them spoke as a misty rain started and they rounded the corner, nearing home.

The townhouse, as old as everything else in this area, reached toward the sky and endured the squeeze of the neighboring structures. Greyfriars Cemetery with its tombstone labyrinth and lurking ghosts were only steps away. Aini pulled the three keys to the front door's massive locks from her purse.

Neve touched the door. It swung open. "Aini..."

A prickly sensation climbed over Aini. Palms sweating, she pushed inside. "Father?"

Myles and Thane eased past her and Neve.

"Mr. MacGregor?" Myles called out. "Maybe he just forgot to lock it."

"Doubt it," Thane said, his voice very deep and almost...threatening.

The only sound in the house was the refrigerator's hum in the kitchen and the buzz of the computer in the glass-walled office. Shadows hung around the room; day never really lit the place. An odd smell—tangy, metallic—grabbed Aini's nose. The hairs on the back of her neck lifted.

The carved walking stick she'd bought Father on one of his birthday trips to Ireland sat in the umbrella bin beside the door. She picked it up and stalked farther inside, Thane beside her, as she made her way toward the office. Neve and Myles branched out into the sitting room.

"Should I go check the lab?" Neve asked.

The office door's knob was sticky. Her heart in her ears, Aini brought a hand to her nose.

Blood.

Her lungs solidified.

Raising the walking stick over her head, she looked right, left, down, searching the office for more, that prickling sensation running wild over her skin.

"Father!"

Myles ran in. "What is it?"

Reaching up on the wall, Thane flipped the switch, lighting the empty office. A spatter of blood on the edge of the tasseled rug. Three drops of red on the wall. A line across the desk.

The room pulled away, like Aini was suddenly very, very small.

She tore out of the office and toward his bedroom. Pounding through the hallway, into the kitchen, and stopping at the well-worn threshold of his room, she tried to breathe. No air would come.

His room had been ransacked.

The others' jumbled voices ghosted down the hallway.

"I'll go to the local police..." Myles was saying.

"The Campbells own them and you know it," Neve said. "That's who has done this. After all that yelling over the phone and—"

Something crashed and Thane yelled in Gaelic.

"Don't punch the wall. You'll break your hand!" Tears clouded Neve's voice.

Aini pressed hands over her ears, shoulder pressing into Father's doorframe. In the room, his black coverlet tangled around scientific journals thrown from his bedside table. The doors of the armoire hung open to show clothes pulled from their shelves and socks yanked from their drawers to litter the floor. A crack marred the framed photo of Aini and her mother in traditional yellow and red Balinese dancer costumes, taken a month after the divorce.

She started toward it, hands shaking, and her toe caught on something. Father's diary. The cover, what was left of it, was covered in blood.

Her heart was a runaway train. Her vision went blurry.

She spun and ran directly into Thane's hard chest. Her fingers curled into his shirt.

"They've taken him," she said. "There's...there's blood." Her hand, feeling separate from the rest of her, swung in rickety circles at the broken diary and toward the hallway.

"I know. Just—" He started to pull away, but she held to his jacket, her lungs tight, burning.

"What am I supposed to do?" She pressed fisted hands into his chest as the hallway tilted.

"Shh." He pulled her into the warmth of his arms. He ran a hand over her back, his fingers hot. But even though his skin and words were warm, his tone was cold. "You're strong, Aini. Smart. You'll go on."

She jerked away. His nostrils flared and his mouth pinched up.

"Go on?" The door hit the back of her head as she reared away.

Her mind wouldn't work. It couldn't be. Father couldn't be gone. The walls crowded her, choking, smothering. She had to get out of the townhouse, away, away, out, out, out. Away from the smell of blood.

She twisted away from them all and tore out of the townhouse and down Candlemaker Row, her flats slapping the cobblestones, throwing sounds off the stone walls of Ivy's Food and Photography Emporium, where she and Father had eaten steaming bowls of onion noodles in a room with changing walls of Japanese landscape photos. Sucking air, she passed the red glass windows of the perfumery, where they'd hashed out which scents brought forth which memories, leading to the theory about the vision-inducing gum.

She imagined his kind eyes squeezed shut in pain. Someone hitting him. Strangers dragging his slumped body out of the townhouse and into a waiting truck.

Father. Father. Father.

Outside the iron scrollwork of Greyfriars Cemetery, she dropped to her knees and put her hands to her chest, trying to force air into her lungs. Her throat convulsed, and the musky air of Father's homeland finally poured into her.

Then Neve, Myles, and even Thane, were there, helping her up.

"I'm fine. It's fine," she said.

But they wouldn't let go, their voices kind and close to her ears. Her hands automatically tucked themselves under her folded arms to avoid touching anything that might hold a memory.

CHAPTER 4
WITHOUT

Hot water morphed into clouds of steam in the bathroom attached to Aini and Neve's room. Aini opened the shower door and stepped inside. With the glass casing, she was a caterpillar in a cocoon. But instead of emerging with strong wings and a new life, she'd leave this escape only to find a home without a father. A lab without a leader. A life without the one person left alive who'd known and loved her since childhood. Mother had died two years ago. Grandmother Wayan had followed three months ago. All she had was her father.

And he was gone.

The blood under her fingernails didn't come off easily under the bristles of a scrub brush. It hung on, clinging there and in the creases between her fingers. She pictured Father's laughing eyes, his jig in the lab, and last night with their Robert Burns poetry. Her heart clenched and sputtered, every beat a jagged spike of pain. The images of Father blurred.

The Campbells were the law. What did you do when lawkeepers broke the law? She'd thought abiding by the rules would give Father a peaceful life, a life he deserved. Mother had broken something inside him when she ended their relationship. Aini wanted to fix it with steady days of predictability, just enough excitement to keep things fun, but not dangerous—not too much risk.

Three months. They'd had only three months of peace.

Before all this, Aini's mother had moved her around so much in the colonies. Her dancing troupe toured almost continually, and they'd slept in a different bed every night during those trips, waking to new faces, working to say the right things and entertain the crowd and the ones who'd hired them. It'd been exhausting. They'd never quite fit in anywhere. Not with other colonists. Not with people born and raised in Bali, like her grandmother. And then she'd visit Father and never fit in here either. But at least when she visited him, she slept in the same bed, woke to him every morning.

A sudden thought of a kingsman's fist smashing into Father's bearded chin attacked her mind. The awful sound that would come out of him. Rough. Ugly. Not a sound Father should ever, ever have to make. Tears stormed from her eyes and she fell against the hard shower wall, slumped to the tub floor, and disappeared into pain, hurt, and wild disbelief.

CHAPTER 5
THE BLUEFOOT

Once Aini settled into her room with Neve, the scant amount of blood was scrubbed from the office and bedroom, and the authorities were called, Thane raged out the front door. What a joke. The authorities. As if they weren't ordered about by the very ones who'd taken him—Thane's own clan, the Campbells.

The mist outside had morphed into a wet, evening fog that cloaked Thane's face and made his shirt and trousers cling to him. He pulled his glasses off and swiped a hand over his head, sluicing cold water from his hair. He wished he could clean the Campbell from his flesh as easily.

Because they shouldn't have taken Lewis.

He was a good man. Not a rebel. Just a man who didn't want to get caught up in vicious politics.

An empty beer bottle nearly tripped Thane. He kicked it, and the glass shattered against the opposite curb. A group of younger guys laughed and pointed.

Stalking down the slate-colored road, Thane passed the

graveyard's towering stone wall and the unseen spirits who called it home. His thoughts rushed through one side of his mind to the other, his heart tugging at each worry, every consideration. For most of his life, it'd been fine serving his clan and the king. It wasn't a pretty job, full of morally gray duties that felt wrong, but led to good ends—keeping the country safe from rebels and under the protective thumb of his family.

But lately? Lately his father, Nathair—head of the clan and Earl of Argyll—made being a Campbell less of a noble duty and more of a horror show. He'd publicly executed those sixth-sensers and rebels without so much as a trial. Claimed they'd attacked the kingsmen during arrest. A lie. The rebels had hung the banned Scottish flag—the blue Saltire Thane couldn't help but love—over the king's residence at Holyrood Palace, but that was it. This time, the rebels hadn't killed anyone or sacrificed themselves in a bombing like they'd done in the past. It'd been a peaceful protest and one Thane might even see himself doing were he someone else. They'd called for a repeal of the king's rough new tax on factory workers throughout the Empire.

The tax would see more people on the street, homeless, but what did Thane know of what the king needed? Surely there was a safe, political way to battle the new tax. Something that didn't involve breaking the king's laws and incurring the wrath of the Campbells.

And the two sixth-sensers with the rebels? Well, it didn't matter what they'd done or not done. The king ordered them arrested and questioned just for having their strange abilities to see visions or talk to ghosts or whatever the skill happened to be—there were as many different senses as there were Campbells at the king's court. Thane supposed the king hated the sixth-sensers for what they could do for enemies—intel and all that. But he called them abominations. That wasn't right. It wasn't the sensers' fault. They were born with the sixth sense. It wasn't as if they chose it. So why did the king insult them so? Was there more to the king's hatred of sixth-sensers? Probably. But the old man wasn't talking of it to anyone, including the Campbells as far as Thane knew. He only passed on his hate and Thane's father ate it up and spit it back onto the Scottish people. Why did the right side feel so much like the wrong side? There was no right side. Not truly. Thane rubbed his face roughly, his mind whirring like a broken mixer.

The road in front of Thane opened into a courtyard called the Grassmarket, where farmers used to sell animals and crops. The moon shrouded the square of age-nibbled buildings in white light. Thane felt he himself was a ghost, seeing through insubstantial eyes. Anger burned through him, but he couldn't do a thing about it. He had no power to influence his clan's actions. None. His quiet swearing disappeared, worthless, into the growing dark. He could at least make it known Lewis acted as a good subject of the king. He'd shout it at his older cousin Rodric, a glaikit ape who, no doubt, had a big, dumb hand in the abduction.

Thane ran fingers through his tangled hair as he left the better area of Edinburgh. The overripe stench of poverty hit his nose when he reached the broken windows and the sagging two and three-story smoke shops and low rent flats of Bread Street. A man with a patchy beard leaned out from one of the windows above. Paint flaked off the sill and drifted over Thane.

"Lovely coat, richie!" the man said, pointing at Thane's leather jacket. The old man cackled into the midnight street.

Thane threw him a finger and kept on, his mind whirring.

He'd risk a beating if he spoke up about Lewis. Taking a deep breath, he considered it. His mother would want him to be brave for something this important. She'd want him to follow his heart, no matter the trouble it might give.

A sad smile stretched his mouth as he remembered the science fair during his first year in secondary school. When Thane's father had said attending to clan business was more important than going to a silly first prize ribbon ceremony, his mother had threatened to cut her hair off. The clan gathering was set for the next day and Thane's father wouldn't tolerate being embarrassed by his wife in front of so many. After a lorry-load of swearing, his father had finally capitulated and they'd left for the ceremony together. It was the first and last time both of Thane's parents had attended a school function.

A shout broke through the memories, and a cold wind gusted past, tugging at Thane's hair. Two kingsmen—not Campbells, just ordinaries—held someone across the street, in front of an old hardware store. The man pulled out of their grip, ripping his red striped shirt.

"I'm not a sixth-senser," the man said. "I've told you. I'm no Ghost Talker!"

The first kingsman grabbed him again with a meaty paw. "Then who were you talking to just now, your face as pale as my arse?"

The second kingsman snorted a laugh, lifted his stick, and struck the potential sixth-senser in the knee. They threw more questions at the man and shoved him against the mossy brick of the old hardware store. The store's sign—a painted hammer—swung above them in the unnatural breeze.

So that cold wind was a spirit. The man was definitely a Ghost Talker, one of the four types of sixth-sensers currently known. They could speak with the dead and the dead told them secrets of the past supposedly. Thane wasn't sure why the king cared much about that sixth sense. What would the dead have to do with now? Maybe in murder cases or some such. Yeah. That made sense. The other three types of sixth-sensers did seem relevant to gathering valuable intel for certain.

Threaders saw brightly colored strings of light connecting people to people or people to objects when strong emotion was involved. That could really help an enemy of the king find spies like Thane. He swallowed. He hoped he'd never cross a Threader's path. He'd be found out and have to go back to round-up duty and all that blood and beating.

Another type of sixth-senser was a Seer. That type was merely a legend. Supposedly, a very powerful Seer would one day find the Coronation Stone and name an Heir to the Empire's throne. But no one had rounded up a Seer as far as Thane knew. Seers could touch a thing and see a memory. It didn't seem like a sense the king would care about, but Seers remained top of the list for round-ups despite them being as common as a magical unicorn. Maybe the king believed the stupid legend.

The sixth-sensers that made Thane most nervous were the Dreamers. These people dreamed about things that might happen in the future or about what part that person had to play in history as a whole. His own bizarre, recurring dream didn't show him anything as important as all that, but it still didn't seem normal. If anyone ever questioned him about dreams, he knew he'd stumble and say something that could be dangerous. Even though he knew he didn't have a sixth sense.

The second kingsman snorted again and hit the sixth-senser in that same knee. Thane winced and the man fell, yowling.

"The people won't put up with this forever," the sixth-senser said. "We won't! You have no proof against me!"

"Our own word is proof enough for our commander," the big kingsman growled, throwing the sixth-senser into a government car parked at the curb.

Glad that he didn't have round-up duty here in Edinburgh, Thane shoved his hands into his pockets and wound through two narrow, twisting streets before heading toward the back entrance into Bluefoot public house, a Campbell haunt open only to those in the clan. He was known only in here and only by those fairly high up. He'd never worked as a kingsman officially in this area so as to keep his identity a secret. He pushed what looked like a regular wall—a part of a shop that had been closed for years—and it swung open to reveal a dark alcove. It looked like a forgotten spot between two buildings. He kicked the left wall and it popped open, placing him in the back of the Bluefoot. If he'd come in through the front where another hidden entrance sat, he'd have to have spoken to the codekeeper to gain entrance and he didn't want to be seen right now. Or ever really. Only a camera watched this back way in and Bran kept an eye on that screen this time of day. Bran was always on Thane's side.

The sounds of a tambourine and a guitar filled his ears but rage about Lewis filled his chest, stronger and more visceral, taking hold of his mind and heart like a vicious hand as he wove through the back of the club.

In the main room, hammock chairs suspended on plastic links, hung from the ceiling like money bags. Instead of being filled with shining coin, they swayed and dragged toward the cigarette-ridden floor holding men with DRFs, Daily Racing Forms, in their hands. Every man's eyes were on the wall-sized TV screen opposite the copper-topped bar. The screen blinked out another row of numbers and stupid names—horse race stats from Newmarket and nearby Musselburgh—in a chalky white. The lists faded and stomping fillies appeared, ready at the gate on Goodwood's long, green track, far away in England's West Sussex.

The busty Cora greeted him with a sweet smile, a rag in one

hand and a glass of whisky in the other. "Good to see you, young man." She probably knew his name, but also knew it was wiser not to mention it.

"Can I get an ale?" He didn't usually drink, but tonight called for it.

Her lips pinched to hide a smile, but she nodded, always obedient to the Campbell name.

The other men eyed him for a moment and went back to their DRFs. Standing beside the hanging seats, the pub's regular clutch of low women laughed and chatted with the patrons. Some women drifted away to perform feats of flexibility on the scarves that dangled from metal bars crisscrossing the ceiling. One girl, upside down, her leg twisted in a scarf, reached for Thane and ruffled his hair like he was a wean—nothing more than a child. Scowling, he slipped around her and found Bran in the workout room.

Beside a well-worn heavy bag, Thane's bushy-haired pal ringed knuckles and palm with a fighter's wrap.

"Just the man I wanted to see," Bran said.

He was about Rodric's age but, alternately, had a functioning gray mass between his ears. Up near Inveraray, where Thane had grown up, local teens spent their free hours at a nature reserve. There, among pines and stolen cigarettes, Thane and Bran had forged a vague friendship, full of secrets but strong enough to get an orphaned Bran to relocate to Edinburgh when Thane had started at university down the way at St. Andrews.

"You look ready for a real fight, my friend," Bran said.

"Aye." A florescent light flickered as Thane paced the small room's red floor, his hands flexing in and out. "They've made a mistake, Bran. A bad one."

The doorway into the main room was empty, but Thane kept an eye on it just in case.

Bran's thick brown eyebrows rose. "You're posing as one *Thane Moray* in the house of that candy chemist?"

"I am. And Rodric and the rest were calling him, asking to get him to...juice up his creations for us."

"Sweets as weapons?"

Thane nodded. "That and more. Ointments, unguents, all sorts of chem work." He hung a hand on the chain linking the bag to the ceiling beams. "The chemist said *no* and they took him. Just like that." He snapped his fingers. "Ruined a good man's life."

"Maybe Nathair will release him."

A laugh jerked from Thane's throat. He took his jacket off and tossed it onto a shabby table near the door. "Right. All sweet and cozy like, I'm sure."

Bran shrugged. "Here's hoping."

Thane leaned his forehead into the heavy bag, inhaling old sweat and listening to his heart drive Campbell blood through his body.

"He has a daughter," Thane said quietly.

The speed bag secured to the wall thumped as Bran—wise Bran—let Thane talk.

"Most of the people I've spied on," Thane said, "they're as looney as Gran on Hogmanay."

Bran snorted a laugh.

"But this girl..." An image of Aini and Lewis working side-by-side in the lab whisked through Thane's mind. "She's so..."

He remembered the fear in her face when she saw the blood.

Heat blazed through his chest and he rammed an elbow into the heavy bag.

"It's terrible what they've done to her and her father." He gave the bag another hit. "And I don't know what I'm going to—"

Cora appeared at the door, ale in hand. "I didn't mean to interrupt..."

"No bother. Thank you." Thane took the drink and gulped it down. A line of cool liquid ran down his throat.

"And what's this?" a deep, sour voice said from the door. Cora was gone and she'd left Rodric in her place. "Has the wee doggie come out to play then?"

Thane's first memory of his older, second cousin consisted of nothing but Rodric's ducky laugh, the bottom of his boot, and pain. The oaf pulled his flat cap down over his eyes and squared his shoulders. Rodric was big enough he didn't need to act like a tough man. He couldn't help himself. Big, stupid bully.

Rodric sucked the last bit of his cigarette and threw it to the dark corner, where it glowed like a rat's eye.

"Can we not do this?" Thane said. "This whole 'Rodric is tough and older and wiser, and Thane's a wee prick, no matter he stands a foot taller than me now'?"

Rodric answered with a swing aimed at Thane's head. Thane dodged it, ducking and pushing the strike past his ear. His cousin grabbed his shirt and pulled, ripping it along the collar.

"Nathair's wrong, you know," Thane spat. "The candymaker is a good man."

"That lab rat needs to know his place." Rodric faked another shot at Thane, who didn't flinch. "Treasonous rat is what he is."

The ape threw a vicious punch into the heavy bag and Thane stepped back as the target swung wildly.

"He's not a traitor, Rodric. I'm telling you."

Rodric's gaze went up and down Thane, an ugly grin tearing at his mouth. It reminded Thane distinctly of his own father. "What's it to you anyway?"

Bran stepped forward, rubbing an uneven spot out of his

wraps. "Thane is only working to keep you from wasting your time, pal."

"You'll mind your own business." Rodric poked Bran in the chest with a sausage-like finger. "Pal."

Thane pushed Rodric back. "Lewis MacGregor is not guilty of treason. He's just a chemist who doesn't want to hurt anyone."

"Oh aye?" Rodric leaned into Thane's face. His breath smelled like cigarettes and hate. "Then why did Seanie find the man on an old Dionadair list just yesterday?"

Thane froze. Why would Lewis's name show up on a search for rebels?

"I see you didn't know about that, huh?" Rodric said.

"It's a mistake."

Rodric shrugged and picked at his teeth with his smallest finger. "Maybe. But what if he only refuses to weaponize his candies for us because he's already doing it for the Dionadair rebels?"

Dionadair meant *Protector* in Gaelic. But from what Thane had seen, the members didn't care about protecting anyone except their precious cause—to liberate Scotland from the English king. Sure, their latest flag stunt hadn't been violent and Thane didn't agree with how his father had handled their punishment, but still, the rebels were low folk and he didn't care for their type any more than he liked Rodric and his.

"You're wrong. I know it." Thane swallowed and set his empty glass on the table.

Rodric spread his arms wide. "Well, make sure you're not leaving any stone unturned, doggie. Sniff him out and prove the chemist's innocence. Maybe then Nathair'll let him be. Not without a bit of obedience training first, of course, but..."

"He can't force innocent subjects to do his bidding," Thane said. "It's wrong."

"Nathair—your own father—is the law. Don't forget it. The rebels are worse than ever and Nathair is sick of playing by rules no one else follows. It's only right we use whatever means we see fit." Rodric popped his knuckles and punched a palm.

Thane's stomach twisted. No. It wasn't right.

He clapped Bran on the shoulder. "I'll see you soon, pal." Picking up his jacket, he shouldered past Rodric and found the back door.

"Remember who you are, doggie," Rodric called out. "Don't forget who your master is. I'll be sure to tell him you've gone soft. He has some new ideas about how to train wee doggies. Best keep up your tinkering and hope you craft something worth a crap to make up for the report I'll be giving to the good chief."

Thane slammed the door. He wasn't giving him anything. Nathair and Rodric could come after him all they wanted. He would not stop defending Lewis, not even if it cost him a beating worse than the ones from training.

He pulled out his phone and rang his mother, but she didn't answer. She could've been sleeping. He pictured her in the big four poster bed, a science journal open beside her outstretched hand and her reading glasses still on her nose. She'd given him her love of science. Through hikes spent identifying trees by leaves and bark. During television episodes on planets and the mysteries of space. She always asked the best questions, ones that had him rifling through her collection of journals in their cavernous library and searching the world information cache online.

It was surprising that a woman so smart could be trapped into a marriage with his father, a man so obviously unfit for a loving relationship. It'd been her passion that trumped her good sense, her sharp mind. She must've fallen for his powerful presence, his standing in their hometown, his way with words.

Thane bowed his head. His own passions pushed him to do things he had better sense than to try. He wondered if his growing concern for Aini and Lewis would be his own undoing.

~

THE TOWNHOUSE DOOR CRACKED OPEN NOISILY, BUT THE front room was empty, the lights out. Thane started toward the bedroom, but moonlight from the window crashed across Lewis's office, tempting him. He took a slow breath, Rodric's words coming back. *Then why did Seanie find the man on an old Dionadair list yesterday?*

The office looked as it always did. Rodric and the rest hadn't searched it. Yet.

After hanging his jacket on the doorknob, Thane sat in Lewis's chair behind the wide, metal desk, smelling only printer ink and bleach, not blood.

Fine. He'd look around. Just to prove there was nothing to find.

He started in the drawers, then moved on to the safe. The combination was his fifth guess—the atomic numbers for the elements in sugar. Hydrogen. Carbon. Oxygen. 1. 6. 8. Inside the metal box, a stack of pounds sat near the deed to the townhouse, permission papers for developing recreational sweets decorated with the royal red wax seal, and a few other legal odds and ends. Nothing interesting.

Closing the safe up tight, Thane began searching more clever spots like behind the loose windowsill and the back of a filing cabinet. Nothing. For good measure, he grabbed a mono-grammed snochterdicter—a handkerchief embroidered with Lewis's initials—from the desk drawer and used the fine cloth to wipe the safe's lock clean of his fingerprints.

He was right. Lewis was no Dionadair.

Returning the cloth to its home, he slid the drawer back.

It caught on something.

Thane's pulse knocked on his throat. He crawled under the desk, clicking on the small torch he kept in his pocket. A picture was taped to the underside of the desk, just past the point where the drawer should stop. Some of the tape had come loose and gummed up the drawer's track. Gently peeling the photo from its spot, Thane imagined what it might be. A shot of a lady Lewis shouldn't have been thinking of? A picture of a special creation from the candy lab?

Thane unfolded himself from the small space and turned, leaning against the desk. He pulled his glasses out and slid them on, an ugly feeling uncurling in his wame. The picture showed Lewis MacGregor with a red-bearded man, toasting with what looked like dark whisky.

The two stood directly in front of the Saltire—the banned Scottish flag.

Thane swore and kicked the filing cabinet.

"Thane?"

He crushed the picture in his hand. Aini. Why was she always around? Spinning, he faced her. Suddenly, he forgot to breathe. Her hair fell over her shoulders in a sheet of black satin. The belt of her robe was tied in a neat bow beneath her chest.

"You...you should be in bed, lass."

Though it was nothing but silver and blue in the unlit room, he could still see the color rising in her cheeks. Her hands went to her hips.

"Don't order me around," she snapped. "Why are you in here in the dark anyway?"

Thane slipped the picture into his pocket—and with larger movements to draw Aini's attention—grabbed a pen. "You're right. Sorry. I just saw no reason to wake everyone by turning all the lights on. I thought maybe your father might've left some sort of clue as to where they were taking him, or something."

"Oh. I'm sorry. You're right." Her voice broke.

A fissure started somewhere deep inside Thane. He came around the desk and she let him draw her into his arms. Her hair smelled like sugar and that scent girls always had—like shampoo or lotion.

"I didn't mean to boss you." He pulled away a bit, his hands on her shoulders.

Her dark, wide eyes reflected the window's scant light. "I know. It's just..."

She stared at his necklace, two lines appearing between her slim eyebrows. Good thing he kept the Campbell seal turned toward his throat.

"They'll bring him back, right?" Tears welled in her eyes.

Anger against Lewis simmered under Thane's sternum. Lewis had done this to Aini, put her in this position. Her *and* Thane. The traitor. How could he not have realized the nature of the man? He'd been so wrong, so, so wrong. His teeth ground together.

"I don't know, hen."

He ran a hand over her forearm, and a feeling like electric shock danced up his fingers. Swallowing, he stepped back, giving her what he hoped was a noncommittal, friendly smile. His thoughts and emotions knocked around his body and brain like thrown rocks. He looked out the window. He felt so heavy, so tired of...everything.

The place his mother used to take him washed through his mind.

"You ever been to the Highlands?" he asked her quietly. "Green and gold grasses. Puddles of water so still... Mountains like great castles. A man could hear no sound but his own voice, if he wished it." He was daft. What was he even talking about? His thoughts slipped around like he'd had a boatload of whisky.

"I went there once." Aini's voice was light as star shine. It was surprising she didn't think him completely cracked. "With Father, on holiday."

He turned to see her shudder and wrap her arms around herself.

Thane's watch said it was near midnight. "It's late. Can we talk over everything tomorrow?" What he'd say, he had no clue. Smart as she was, she was blind as hell. Not that he could talk. He didn't have a clear view of anything.

Nodding, she started toward the door, then paused. "What happened to your shirt?" Her gaze slid over his bare shoulder.

"Caught it on the doorframe." His jaw muscles tensed painfully. Lying came far too easy these days.

She looked him over a bit. He tugged his ripped shirt up best he could as heat crept into his cheeks. Running a hand through his hair, he silently berated himself for blushing.

Brushing past her, he snatched his jacket from the doorknob. They traded an awkward, "Good night then," before he sped off to his room.

PACING HIS BEDROOM, THANE STEWED. LEWIS HAD PRETENDED such innocence. Acting as though he cared for the king's law. Saying *that* was the reason he wouldn't do as Thane's clan asked. Stopping at the wall, Thane clenched his fists. Lewis had probably been crafting weaponized sweets for the Dionadair. Thane rammed a fist into the wall, welcoming the pain that matched the hurt inside him. Was there no one he could trust in the world?

Myles's bed creaked. "Hey, Lord of the Tattoos, keep it down, okay? I need beauty sleep if I'm going to battle your handsome tail for the ladies."

"Aye. Sorry." Flexing his now bloodied hand, Thane lowered himself into his own bed.

He was too. Sorry he couldn't leave now and forget about Lewis and Aini and the lab. He had to stay and work on what Lewis refused to. Had to give his clan the terrible things he created. For his mother. And because it was his duty. Campbells who didn't do as ordered didn't enjoy long lives.

Thane fought the droop of his eyelids.

At the edge of his mind, his recurring dream lurked, waiting for him—the one of his fingerprint turning black as a corpse's. It was hours before exhaustion finally washed through Thane's boiling brain and drowned him in a troubled sleep.

CHAPTER 6
SECRET

Aini sat on a kitchen chair, fully dressed in tapered trousers and a green silk striped shirt, but she'd no idea how she'd ended up there. Coconut pancakes steamed on a plate in front of her. She folded and creased the napkin someone had thrown beside the fork. Then she aligned the fork with the napkin and plate, making it picture-perfect.

Myles padded barefoot across the room. He smiled kindly, his usual swagger replaced with concern. "You're supposed to eat it, sweetheart. Not organize it."

If anyone else had called her sweetheart, she'd have set them down for a good one, maybe two hour lecture, but Myles actually meant the word as an endearment. There wasn't any condescension in his tone.

"I made these pancakes, didn't I?" she whispered.

He paused, the coffee pot suspended over his blue mug. "You did." Taking a seat, he put his free hand on hers, a brotherly gesture.

She frowned as the black spot in her memory cleared.

Now she remembered wiggling the turner under their crisp edges to flip the pancakes. The cane syrup had come out too quickly when she poured it, and the liquid had pooled against the plate's lip.

"Hey. We're going to figure this out," Myles said. "After all, you're organizing again." Pointing to the folded napkin and aligned fork, he grinned encouragingly. "It's an Aini MacGregor sign of survival and fortitude."

A tentative smile crept over her lips.

Neve scurried into the kitchen, only one of her eyes ringed in brown liner. "I meant to get up before you." She knelt and patted Aini's leg. "Anything I can get you? Seems you already made your own breakfast."

Aini squeezed Neve's hand, closing her eyes and hoping the comfort of her friend's touch would drive out the buzzing under her skin. She took a deep breath, feeling like insects crawled under her flesh. "The Campbells have my father. Right? It couldn't be anyone else, right?" She needed to make a list of possibilities and potential actions to take. "Does anyone know where my phone is?"

Neve and Myles stood, their heads turning and their faces blank. Neve's mouth tucked up at one side. "You're usually the one who tells us where everything is."

Swallowing, Aini pushed away from the table to look in her bedroom as Thane walked in. He held her phone out to her.

Gratitude warmed her. "Thanks." Before she opened a fresh list on the screen, she met Thane's gaze. Red lines crossed the whites of his eyes, and his normally pink, full lips were pale. Swallowing, she put a hand on his sleeve. The rolled edge of the expensive colonial cotton was worn and soft. "Myles made coffee." She didn't know what else to say.

Thane rubbed his face roughly, his tattoos dark against his

fair skin. His hair was a beautiful disaster of gold and honey. She wondered if he'd slept last night.

His eyes flicked open, the irises gray as storms. "You...I... thank you." He pushed past, jerked the coffee pot up, and poured some into a mug, spilling a little over the edge.

Nodding, Aini went to the table and started a list. Her fingers shook and made it tough to type. "First thing." She looked at Myles and Neve. "Who took him and why exactly?"

The two sat side by side, Neve with her fingers laced and a pinched mouth, Myles biting his thumbnail.

"Idea One. The Campbells." With each word typed onto the screen, it became easier to breathe. "They took him because he refused to do what they wanted. He shouted at them over the phone, disregarding their status, and so they acted. Idea Two. A competitor abducted him. They want his recipes. Idea Three—"

"You know it's the Campbells, Aini. It's why the authorities were as useful as teets on a goose." Myles slowly peeled paint off his thumbnail, not meeting her eyes.

With a quick swipe, she deleted ideas two and three. She blinked away tears to see the screen. "Okay. Then what actions to take?"

Neve slid her untouched plate closer, glancing once at Thane, who drank his coffee in silence in the corner of the room. "If they see his behavior as treasonous, they'll question him at the Court of Empire Crimes."

Aini slammed her phone down. "That's ridiculous." Standing, she braced her hands on the table. "He's only obeying the king's laws. He's a loyal subject. More loyal than any other man in Scotland. The Campbells are out of control."

Thane muttered something sharp.

"What?"

"I said," he put his cup down too carefully on the counter and glared. "Maybe your father is not who you think he is."

"Excuse me?"

His eyes narrowed. He took a step. "You ever seen anything to tie him to the Dionadair?"

"The rebels?" Her brash colonial accent was leaking out. "Of course not," she said, careful to soften her consonants.

He looked at her mouth, then shook his head. "You'd never check up on your own father. Would you? It's against your precious *rules*. It wouldn't help you *fit in*."

He turned away, but she grabbed the sleeve of his wrinkled button-down. "Why are you saying this?" she asked.

"People lie, Aini." Bending at the waist, he put his face near hers. "They hide things. Especially from those they love."

Heat flared across her chest. "Don't be an...an ass." Blushing, she leaned closer, her nose almost touching his. "If you've got something to say, say it."

Straightening, he spoke quietly like he struggled to get a hold on himself. "Before this week, did you ever think your father would shout at a kingsman like he did on the phone?"

Aini looked down, her chest hurting.

He pulled something from his back pocket, his face sad and furious at the same time, and thrust it under her nose. "I didn't think he was a rebel either until I found this."

It was a picture. She took it, heart shaking.

It showed Lewis and another man having a drink together. No shock in that. But as her gaze dragged over Father's smile and into the background, she saw it. The banned flag.

Her hand went to her mouth. "The Saltire."

"Aye. It was taken at a club where Dionadair used to meet."

The floor seemed to move under Aini's shoes.

Leaning over her shoulders, Neve and Myles looked at the picture. Neve deflated and dropped into Aini's chair. Myles turned and raked hands through his bright hair.

But it didn't have to mean Father was a rebel. "It's just a picture. An old one. It doesn't mean—"

"Forget it." Thane cut her off and ripped the picture away, his bright gray eyes outlined by black lashes. "If you're determined to live in your pretend world of perfectly organized right and wrong and lists and rules and everyone being exactly who you think they are, nothing I'm going to say will snap you out of it."

Her legs jerked and trembled, threatening to crumble. Like it belonged to another person, her hand drew back, then slapped across Thane's cheek.

Neve gasped.

Thane's nostrils flared. He shut his eyes as his chest heaved. "Aini—"

Twisting, she shoved Myles out of her way and flew up the spiral stairs to the tower lab.

AT THE SHELVING ABOVE THE COUNTERTOP, SHE BEGAN alphabetizing the spices and dried herbs, taking simple pleasure in the clean, white labels and their dark green lettering. Agrimony. Allspice. Angelica. Anise. Arnica. Father didn't like them this way, but he hardly had to measure flavors out anymore so it didn't matter. Bay Leaf. Bergamot. Bilberry. And he wasn't here anyway, so it *really* didn't matter.

A hysterical laugh erupted from her throat, and she paused, a jar of cayenne gripped in her sweating hand.

Thane was right.

People did lie to those they loved. She had.

Her own father didn't know about her sixth sense. She'd been lying for a long time now.

She set the cayenne down and walked across the lab, stopping between Father's neatly arranged work area and Myles's desk, which overflowed with pastel chalk adverts and filthy electronics.

The jars of blue and green sugar sparkled on the far wall. Why were they over there? They really should be stored with the rest of the decorative sugars. She'd take them down. A project would clear her head. On tiptoe, she squinted at the antique bronze hardware that kept the blue sugar jar on the wall. It was a hinge. Hmm. Maybe if she could get to the screw hiding in the hinge's fold, she could undo it. Reaching high, she grabbed the container and pulled it forward. The glittering contents shifted with a hushing sound as the jar tipped toward her.

A jagged rectangle covered in the same uneven stone as the rest of the wall swung open.

A hidden door. Mind spinning, she walked inside.

Secrets and more secrets.

The bare bulb above didn't provide much light, but a layer of dust was visible on the tall filing cabinet and the trunk. The cabinet's tracks squeaked as she slid the first drawer out and peered inside. A brown envelope, worn at the edges and ready to burst, held a huge stack of papers.

She pursed her lips and breathed through her nose. Her world was pulling apart, thread by thread. Slipping a finger under the envelope's flap, she opened it. Drawings. Pictures. Cards. All from her. There was the unicorn she'd made for him in primary school. Her first school picture. Every Christmas card she'd ever bought for him. She hugged the package to her chest and looked up to keep the moisture from leaking out of her eyes. Tucking everything back into place, she returned the envelope and shut the drawer. The middle drawer held all her essay papers from upper school, all the way through last year, when she'd graduated early. In the bottom drawer, large rubber bands held together ticket stubs from her parents' honeymoon trip and anniversary cards from before the divorce.

So far, no terrible surprises.

She eyed the trunk on the dusty floor. Brass grommets stood like sentries along its lid. She pushed on the lobster claw latch. Rust flaked from the metal, but it wouldn't budge. With a fist, she hit the clasp. Pinching the little lever, the latch slid out of the brass loop with a grating sound. She threw the lid open, and the scent of aged paper curled into her nose. The mildewed trunk held an invitation to the king's thirtieth birthday party. Someone—*Father?*—had scrawled the word *Remember* in black over the front. Next to the invitation was a picture of Aini as a child with chubby cheeks and an armful of half-wilted flowers. She remembered picking them out of Grandmother's garden in the colonies. Aini had sorted the bouquet into colors and presented them to Father for Easter. Next, carefully moving a first edition of Father's favorite novel, she uncovered a tuxedo jacket, maybe the one he'd worn at his wedding. She lifted it and something fell from its folds, thudding to the hidden room's oak plank floor.

It was a tiny square of linen sewn like a pocket. Something weighty hid inside. The lightbulb above flickered, highlighting the tiny bumps and ridges in the rough fabric. Stitched words, red as blood, ran across the front.

For the Seer.

A chill spilled down Aini's back.

She'd done everything possible to hide her ability for two years. Feigning a stomachache when she touched a coin that someone had kept for a while before dying. Wearing gloves the moment the weather was anything less than hot. Telling Father the secondhand jewelry stores he liked to peruse weren't her sort of thing.

But this trunk had been shut for a long time, judging from the dust layer. And the yellow and brown of age had crept into the fabric. She lifted the small pouch's flap and peered inside. It was a gold brooch, similar to the decorative pin Granny MacGregor had worn on her cardigan. But hers had the MacGregor family crest. This one was different.

She studied this brooch as best she could without touching it, sweat dampening her palms and the back of her neck. Inside the brooch's circle, a golden otter bared jagged teeth. An inscription decorated its edges, but the words were tiny. She squinted.

If she took it out of its wrapping and ran a finger over it, she'd break her number one rule. But her father had some sort of rebellious past, and she had to know if he had any more secrets, and how far this went. She tilted the linen pouch and the brooch slipped into her palm, cool and heavy.

The world dropped away. A vision took hold.

Face partially covered in shadow, a man shoved the brooch into Father's hands. Fear rose from him, green and black, and he shook his head. Both men turned, something surprising them. The other man ran off. Father still held the brooch. Behind him, a tattered blue flag with a diagonal, white cross hung on the wall. The Saltire.

The memory disappeared—she'd never see it again—and a new one bled into its place as Aini curled her fingers tightly around the pin, lost in the vision.

A handsome young man with a wide mouth gripped the brooch. Wearing old-fashioned clothes, he shut his eyes and envisioned a large room with rough brick and stone walls.

Was this man leaving an emotional imprint on the brooch on purpose? Impossible.

Water dripped from the ceiling. There was a large knife—a dirk— with a hilt black as coal. He thought of a number. Eighty-five.

Seer, *his mind said.* Find the knife, first in the *clah-na-cinneamhain* trail.

An oddly shaped rock came into view. Very large. Sloping upward toward the back, hollowed in the middle like a seat. Circles. Swirls.

Make certain the time is right, *his thoughts shouted.*

His dark eyes grew larger and larger, shining, wild, closer, closer. Seer! See me! Find the knife!

The vision disintegrated, and Aini sucked the air of Father's hidden room as the brick and cement walls bubbled into view. The brooch fell from her fingers and thunked to the floor.

She still wasn't used to her sixth sense, though the process was fairly straightforward. The first time she touched an object with strong sentimental value to someone, a moment of imprinted emotion played out in her head like a movie. At least it only occurred the first time her skin made contact.

She'd seen Mother in a pearly veil when she'd touched Father's watch. That had been a nice one. Unfortunately, they weren't all so pleasant. When she'd touched the chain Myles wore around his wrist, she'd seen a vision of Myles's mother turn her back on him before his trip here to be an apprentice.

And this vision, the first one in the brooch, it showed Father with a stranger, standing in front of the banned flag. She looked at the ceiling, her fingers going cold.

Father, what did you do?

She squeezed the brooch and pressed a hand against her forehead. This could ruin everything. It was one thing if the Campbells took him because he'd refused their plan; it was quite another if they found out he was a traitor. She breathed out slowly, trying not to panic.

The second vision in the brooch had been so strange. The man had seemed to speak through the memory. He'd told her to "find the knife."

Crouching, she gathered the brooch. The light glanced off the tiny words around the border. It was a clan motto. Most were in Latin or French. "*De bonnaire...*"

"Graceful," a deep voice said.

Thane walked into the lab, his face pale except for the red mark of Aini's fingers on his cheek. Then he froze. His gaze roamed the hidden room.

She cupped the brooch, then hid it in her pocket. "Is that what the French means? Graceful?"

"Aye." He looked at her, his stare unrelenting.

Standing, she pulled her shirt back into place and wiped the sweat from her forehead. "I didn't know you spoke French."

"You could fill the North Sea with what you don't know about me," he mumbled, running a hand through his hair and looking generally miserable.

Aini wasn't sure how she felt about that. She shut the trunk and dusted her hands together. Thane's gaze burned a hole in her back.

"Aini. Listen. I'm sorry. It's not your fault your—"

She held up a finger, and he paused as she shoved the hidden room's door closed. "You said the picture you found was taken at a club. A rebel club?" She faced him.

His gaze fixed on the jar of blue sugar as it slid back into place with a mechanical clunk. "I did."

"I'm going to that club tonight," Aini said. "What's it called? Where is it? Is it still open?"

"You can't go there. It's not safe."

"I have to know how serious this all is."

"Bad sorts go in there. You can't just walk in there with not a thought to—"

She started down the stairs. The smell of coffee and the cool air of the stairwell cleaned the rest of the vision away. A quick thought of her dark room and bed beckoned, but she couldn't hide away.

"Aini." Thane came up behind her as the stairs opened into the kitchen.

Neve and Myles's heads lifted, their faces drawn.

"Aini. Please. Listen. The Origin is not a Dionadair meeting place anymore."

"The Origin? Perfect. Now I know where to go." Snatching her phone, she searched for the location.

Neve stood and frowned at Thane. "And how do you know so much about the Dionadair?"

"The club is on George IV Bridge," Aini said.

Thane raised an eyebrow at Neve. "*You* know enough to call me on it."

Red splotches rose on Neve's neck. "I hear urban legends and...things...when I lead tours. I have one this weekend..." She chewed her lip and blinked under his stare.

Aini glared at Thane. "Leave her alone."

Neve knew more about Scotland than all of them.

Aini's phone said The Origin opened at ten o'clock. "So who's with me for clubbing tonight?"

Myles snorted and gave a weak version of his normal grin. "I could be persuaded to gyrate under obnoxious lighting while flocked by women. Only if it'll help you out."

Eyes wide, Neve looked from Thane to Myles. "Will someone please tell me what's happening?"

Aini tucked her phone into her waistband and took Neve's

hands, swallowing with the effort not to scream or cry or lose it completely. "That picture Thane found shows Father in a rebel club called The Origin."

Neve started shaking her head slowly back and forth.

Aini squeezed her fingers. "I'm going there to see if I can learn anything."

"This isn't a good idea," Neve said. "I've heard that place is rough."

It was probably true. If it used to be a rebel hang out, chances were the people there liked risking treason to have a little wild fun. Stupid. But Aini couldn't sit around here doing nothing. It was one night. One trip to find out what exactly Father had done in his past and how bad it was. One risk that could give her what she needed.

She met Neve's gaze. "I need answers."

"The Dionadair rebels won't be there with name tags on. You'll never find one, even if they are there and know something of your father's past."

"I have to try."

Plus, Aini had the brooch. A stranger, most likely a rebel, had given to Father. If she wore it in plain sight in the club, maybe the Dionadair would recognize it and tell her more. Information was power, and she needed every bit she could find to untangle this nightmare.

She started out of the kitchen, the brooch warm in her pocket.

She wished she could tell them why a rebel might know to approach her, but she couldn't explain about what she'd seen, about how she knew the brooch had belonged to a rebel. The king and Nathair Campbell called people with talents similar to hers "abominations." And those who covered for sixth-sensers were taken for questioning, and were either sentenced to death for treason or simply never returned to their families, lost in the Campbells' famed prison cells under Edinburgh.

Thane stood in her way. In the dark hallway, his glasses hid his eyes and Aini felt oddly frightened of him. The feeling only lasted a moment, and she felt stupid about it immediately after. She knew him well enough to know he was a little unruly, but nothing to be afraid of.

"This is a waste of time," Thane said quietly. "The kingsmen raided the place countless times. Aside from some rebel wannabes and a few black market operators, the kingsmen have found nothing. Not in years."

"Then it shouldn't be too dangerous to go. Excuse me." She shoved past him to her bedroom door.

When she grabbed the doorknob, he covered her hand with his. His long fingers were smooth. Small calluses on his palm pressed into her knuckles and part of a tattoo—$CaCo_3$—marked his thumb.

"Just because it's not a Dionadair nest doesn't mean it'll be a sweet, little place." His thumb twitched, brushing across the bone in her wrist. They were both breathing like they'd run down the hallway. He pulled his hand away and rubbed his face. "Look, I don't want you to get hurt."

"Just because you're twenty-whatever and I'm seventeen doesn't mean I need you protecting me." She jerked the knob and threw the door open.

A black sweater and a pair of blue leggings lay on Neve's bed. She went to her armoire and surveyed her own wardrobe.

Thane's boots knocked on the floor behind her. "It's not about age."

She picked out a black and blue striped dress she'd never worn and held it up. "This should work, right?"

He put fisted hands against his eyes, shoving his glasses into his messy hair, and leaned his head back. Making that Scottish sound of annoyance in his throat, he stalked out the door.

But it didn't matter what he thought. Aini had to do this.

The dress fit perfectly. She dropped the brooch into her bag, not wanting anyone to ask her about it before they were at the club. The less they knew, the better.

CHAPTER 7
THE ORIGIN

Turns out, Aini's dress wasn't going to work. She fought her impatience and tried to be thankful for Myles. He'd picked up some clothes at the thrift shop. Richest guy ever to go into a secondhand store. With his plantation-owning mother, he could've *bought* the thrift shop.

Myles put a hand over his heart, his fresh hair dye bright as spring grass and his sleeveless suit jacket blue as the sky. "One must demonstrate one's lusty beauty before time snatches it away." He kissed his wiry bicep.

Chewing a nail, Aini rolled her eyes. "Maybe in Mylesland." A fleck of gold mascara dropped under her lash.

Myles sighed and fell backward on Aini's bed, arms and legs splayed, knocking bolsters and circular pillows all over. "What a gorgeous idea—Mylesland." Aini hoped he planned on putting those pillows back the right way. "It would be filled with honey and paint and pictures of me."

He and Neve had both been trying to be cheery all afternoon. They'd pushed hope and positive thinking as the group had draped a golden length of taffy over the pulling machine's metal arms. By the end of the six-on-the-dot greens and lean protein dinner Aini served everyone, they'd managed to calm her down, taking her from crushing panic to manageable anxiety.

Now, sitting at the vanity near Aini, Neve made a little groaning sound. Leaving the mess he'd made of Aini's bed, Myles pushed the corners of Neve's mouth up. He stepped back and her feigned smile fell.

"I look a proper idiot," Neve said.

Myles shook his head. "No. You look...delicious."

"He's right," Aini said. "You are beautiful."

Aini had braided Neve's hair into an intricate mess on top of her head. Her outfit consisted of a flowy top with straps and a short skirt. She did not look one bit like a mouse tonight.

"I'm not going to be able to dance in these." Neve pointed to her stacked boots.

Aini smiled down at her own matte gold heels with matching feathers that fluffed out at the ankles. Practical was best, but sometimes lovely things were good too. This dress was another world entirely with its agonizingly short, puffy layers of white colonial cotton and fake gold threading. It was pretty seriously inappropriate.

"Are you sure I can't wear the other dress?" Aini said. "This one is—"

The sight of Thane erased her ability to make words.

His suit jacket had sleeves, but lacked a shirt underneath. His flat stomach was totally on display right there. Right. There. And his dress pants hung way too low on his hipbones. He stood, looking at Aini with those gray eyes framed doubly by black lashes and glasses. His gaze warmed her forehead, nose, the delicate skin over her chest, all the way down to her ridiculously shod feet. His tattooed fingers twitched at his sides.

Aini swallowed, her heart running triple speed. Blinking, she focused instead on Myles and Neve. "I should change," she said. "I'm practically naked."

Turning away, Thane muttered something and shoved his hands in his hair.

Neve bit her lip and gave Aini a trembling smile.

Myles grabbed Neve up and pushed her purse into her arms. "You're fine, Aini. Now it's time to go, people."

Thane made a strangled noise from the door, kicked his heel backward against the frame, then walked into the hallway. Myles trailed him.

Thane spoke to him, voice rolling around the corridor outside the door. "I'm putting a shirt on. This is nonsense."

Aini stopped Neve, laying a hand on her back. "Is this...am I...am I doing the right thing?"

"As if I know. But we're with you. No matter what."

Aini hugged her tight. "Thanks. Thank you so, so much."

She wasn't half the woman Neve was. Working two jobs, Neve supported a sick mother and so many little brothers that Aini could never remember the count.

With a shaky smile, Neve turned and Aini followed her to the front door, worry and guilt hovering like dark ghosts.

The rain pelted them like bullets as they climbed into a taxi Myles had set up.

It was time to find some rebels.

RAIN CLAPPED AGAINST THE CLEAR TARP SHIELDING PEOPLE waiting to get into The Origin. At the front, the bouncer held out a hand for Aini's Subject Identification Card. The pale stone facade of the club towered over them with arching stained glass windows. A body-shaking bass line, cigarette smoke, and the musky scent of incense leaked from its insides.

"Not you. Too young," he said, handing the card back.

Heat rose to Aini's cheeks. She pointed to Myles, who stood beside Neve and Thane at the club's door. "My friend said most places let in fifteen and up. I'm seventeen."

The baldheaded man shook his head and gestured for the next person to come forward. A girl elbowed Aini in the back. Aini turned to say something but ended up staring at the girl's forehead. A tattooed third eye peered back. Aini shook her head.

"Go home, you wee thing," the girl said nastily. "You heard the man."

The boy next in line wore a tight leather shirt that was ripped down one side. "Aye," he said. "Go on." Tiny chains dangled from his lips and ears, and swirls of black paint covered his bare shoulder.

"I am not going home." Aini glared at them. "Nor is this any of your business."

Myles came over and flashed a handful of pounds. He tucked them into the bouncer's shirt pocket. "Let the little lady in, pretty please?"

"Thanks for the tip, pal, but no." The bouncer trained his eyes straight ahead, arms crossed.

Thane said something in Neve's ear as she peered into the club. Red lights colored their faces. Then he waved Myles over and they both looked at Aini. After their tête-à-tête, during which Aini was pushed out of line by the eye tattoo girl, Myles trotted to the middle of the street.

"Check this out!" he called to the bouncer.

Suddenly, he was upside down in a handstand.

Thane walked over as the bouncer looked at Myles and snorted.

Thane took a loud breath, and with one look over the distracted crowd, he snatched something small from his boot and put his arm around the bouncer's big shiny head. He laughed too loudly and swept a finger across the bouncer's upper lip before the man could pull away. The bouncer slumped forward on his stool and Thane eased him to the ground.

"Drank a bit too much, did you?" Thane's voice was too high and his smile didn't reach his eyes. He patted the man's back genially. "I'll get the manager. We're tight." Crossing his fingers and holding them up for the crowd, he leaned toward Aini. "Get inside now." His breath warmed her ear. "I'll meet you."

A broad-faced woman halfway under the tarp shouted, "Don't mind if you get tight with me, blondie!" Several other women howled, and the men laughed.

"What did you do?" Aini demanded. "Did you use something from the lab?"

"Aye. Now go." He jerked his chin toward Neve and Myles, who stared, eyes wide.

"What if the manager comes out? The people saw you and me."

"Aini," Thane hissed through his teeth. "Quit worrying about all the wrong things, will you? Now, go on."

He clapped the bouncer on the back again and scowled at the increasing flow of creatively inappropriate remarks about his backside coming from the line.

Aini rubbed her temples. Thane had used Father's chemicals and herbs on that man. He was trying to help, but that was not okay. Sighing, she stomped across the red and green glass mosaic floor, took Neve's arm, and entered The Origin. Myles hung back, waiting on Thane.

Inside the club, a dance floor, a bar area the size of Aini's bedroom, and two balconies with railings made of what looked like bones greeted them. Red electric lights blended with what had to be a thousand candles, giving the room a sickly pall.

Neve looked over her shoulder. "What's happened to the bouncer? Did Thane hit him?"

Aini's single dress strap dropped off and she tugged it into place. "No. He gave him something. Wiped something under his nose." Her stomach rolled. They were falling further and further from her comfort zone. She had to get some information and get out of here before they all ended up in jail.

Neve bumped into a five foot candle, and Aini caught the thing before it hit the elaborately painted stone floor. "And the stuff knocked the man out?" Neve asked.

Aini nodded.

Artistic vines curled underfoot from the door to the bar. A painted mouth surrounded the dance area like the people were tiny offerings about to be devoured. Over them, an automobile-sized skull with long, stringy hair hung from plastic links.

Shaking her head, Neve followed Aini closer to the dancing crowd. "Did he use stuff from our lab?" she asked. "You'll give him trouble for it, aye?"

"Count on it," Aini said.

A violin and the beat of percussion instruments punched against Aini's eardrums. She inhaled a deep breath of patchouli-scented air. This place was like some outer circle of Hell.

"Okay. The plan is to mingle and keep our eyes open." She lowered her voice. "If you see anything that says *Dionadair* to you, please tell me. I want to talk to anyone who looks like they might be involved."

"I know one thing to look for." Neve wrung her hands. She peered over the mob of sweaty dancers. "I've heard if one rebel meets another, they cross thumbs like this." She held her hands out, low enough so no one would notice, and laid one thumb over the other, creating an X. "It's for St. Andrew's cross. The one on the banned flag."

Coming from behind, Myles raised his arms and jumped into the crowd. "Oooaaaah!"

Some girls, wearing shirts about as appropriate as Aini's excuse for a dress, fell away from him, tripping over one another. Two raised their noses until they noticed his cute face. Then they closed ranks around him.

Neve shook her head. "If you can't beat them..."

Moving onto the dance floor, she wiggled her hips to a rhythm that had nothing in common with the music. But even as Myles shook his shoulders at her, their eyes moved from side to side, scanning the room. They weren't just goofing off. They were looking for signs of rebels. Aini gave them an encouraging smile even though she felt like vomiting or screaming or perhaps some horrid combination of both.

Thane walked up, his false smile from outside gone and only a frown to take its place.

Anger flared through Aini's chest and she crossed her arms. "Want to tell me what you did out there?" Deep scuffs marred the toes of his thrift shop kingsmen boots. "Have you been taking chemicals from the lab?"

He bent to scratch his ankle. The long line of his back and shoulders stretched the jacket's fabric. Small curls gathered at his neck. She wished very, very hard that she didn't like the look of him so much. "It was only an altered cherry drop."

Aini clenched the layers of her dress. "That. Is. Illegal."

Thane threw his head back and sighed. "You're a crabbit, wee thing."

He had no idea why she cared so much about the laws and the rules. If he only knew what she was and what would happen if anyone found out, maybe he'd understand and quit taking unnecessary risks. Not that being here wasn't a risk, but this could be done without drugging people. She almost wished she could tell him about her sixth sense. But no. Everyone viewed sixth-sensers as abominations. Freaks. She'd lose him. And Myles and Neve. Then she'd be alone and Father would be worse off than he already was.

"I'm going to the bar."

"Wait." Thane tried to grab her, but she pushed through the crowd toward the bar.

The banned flag wasn't behind the green and brown liquor bottles anymore, but she could tell it used to be. The countertop was copper like the one in the picture and in the vision imprinted on the brooch. Five hooks marked the mirror above the row of liquor bottles. It was definitely where Father had toasted with that rebel and where he'd received the brooch.

The barkeep, wearing a simple shirt, skirt, and apron, handed the person next to Aini a beer. The froth overflowed onto the keep's finger, and she licked it off.

"What do you want, then?" the woman asked.

A tattoo showed under her short sleeves. It was a woman with a flowing skirt filled with designs. Very specific designs. Aini gasped. It was a cleverly concealed Saltire. Thane elbowed her and she closed her gaping mouth.

"Cranberry juice, please," she said.

The keep nodded and jerked her chin at Thane.

Ignoring a blue-eyed girl to his right who grinned like Thane had invented rainbows, he said, "Ben Nevis Ale."

Drinks in hand, they put their backs against the counter. The juice in Aini's glass quaked in her shaking hand. Thane's sleeve brushed her bare arm with each of his breaths. His eyes trained on the dance floor, he moved a feather's width away. Cold air from the overhead vents rushed down, and she shivered. She was on emotion overload. Worry for Father. Shock at the gall of the keep. Anger and—she hated admitting it to herself—lust toward Thane. She was a total, ridiculous mess.

Muttering something under his breath, Thane faced her. He set his ale on the bar. "I truly am sorry for snapping at you before."

She rolled her dress hem between her fingers. She'd hit him, but that was before she'd seen the vision, before she knew Thane was right about suspecting Father's dark past. But she couldn't tell him about the vision.

"I know you're sorry," she said, not looking up. "It's not okay. The snapping, I mean. But I get it. I do."

A shaky smile pulled at one side of his full lips. A dimple was there and gone in a heartbeat. "I think we should dance," he said.

Her heart snapped like a rubber band, and she slid her juice next to his empty glass before she could spill it. Remembering that Thane was *not a good choice* was going to be that much more difficult in a dancing, bodies-touching-occasionally situation. "Why?"

"You can't hide if you want them to see you," he said.

She narrowed her eyes. He didn't believe there were any of *them* here anymore—any rebels, he meant. He'd said it himself at the townhouse. But whatever his real reason for wanting to dance, it did work toward her goal. She did need to be seen to get this horror show on the road. The sooner she learned something, the sooner they could leave this awful place and return to the order and familiarity of home. She only needed a clue as to what Father was involved in and how to manage rescuing him.

While he paid the keep, Aini pulled the brooch out of her dress pocket—the only practical thing about this get-up. The gold blinked in the sporadic light as she pinned it on and led Thane to the dance floor.

CHAPTER 8
DANCE AS IT ALL GOES DOWN

With bodies bumping against her, Aini moved her hips and hands with the beat, not making eye contact with Thane. Heat crept into her face. Her nerves wouldn't stop jumping. She stopped for a second, eyeing the beautiful Edinburgh girls with their stylish, messy up-dos and confident dancing. Closing her eyes, she fell into the music.

From the time she could walk, she'd spent hours and hours next to her mother, dancing to her Balinese music. She smiled. She'd forgotten how much she loved letting go, falling, allowing the sound, the beat, to wrap around her and set her adrift in pure feeling.

Thane's body brushed hers, and she opened her eyes to the black lapel of his jacket, the dark gray of his shirt, and the candle and rain scent of him. The drums pounded around them, seeming to push them together. He stared, and a slow-burning fire spread down Aini's back and legs.

"You look very bonnie." His mouth was very, very close to

her temple. Delightful chills stretched across her scalp and over her neck.

She forced her gaze to the balcony where a few figures stood utterly still in the middle of more dancing. Could they be the owners of the club? Maybe they knew something about the man who'd given Father the brooch.

The music's baseline slowed, and the violin shared time with the sounds of an entire orchestra. Thane looked at her lips. His nostrils flared once, a small movement, and suddenly she was breathing too fast.

Thane lifted her arms. She jumped at the touch, but let him put her hands on his shoulders.

"Just to blend in..." he murmured.

She nodded. His eyes strayed to the balcony. His muscles were tight under his clothes. His light, wool jacket was a strange combination of rough and smooth under her skin. His hipbone glanced against her side.

"Where did you learn to dance?" he asked.

The odd people at the balcony faded into the crowd. A guy in blue face paint fell against Aini, and Thane grabbed his shirt and pushed him away. Thane's arm circled more tightly around her. He was like a big, handsome wall, and considering the raucous group of dancers surrounding them, it wasn't a bad thing to have the shelter his body provided.

"My mother traveled with a Balinese dance troupe. She always had music on, was always practicing."

Two men darkened a side door on the first floor. More bouncers. Were they looking this way?

Thane's hands spanned her lower back, his thumbs pressing lightly into her ribs.

She took one of his hands and turned it over, studying it as they moved slowly with the music. "When did you get your tattoos?"

His chest moved more quickly as she traced a chemical structure that covered the back of his hand and reached along his thumb and first finger. There was a hexagon, a pentagon, and the combinations HO, NH, and NH2.

"Is this what I think it is?" she asked.

Thane's Adam's apple drew up and dropped again. She drew a finger across his palm and he cleared his throat.

"Aye. Probably. The chemical structure of serotonin."

She grinned. "As in, the chemical for happiness?"

Lifting one shoulder, he put his hand on her back. The music's tempo sped up, crushing them with colorful, minor key melodies and a spine-bruising baseline. Incense soaked the air.

She imagined what the gold stubble on his cheek would feel like under her hand. "I like your tattoos. And I think, after this song, we should find a new place to...hang out." Maybe the balcony.

"You do? I would've thought a rule-follower like yourself would hate my unconventional tattoos."

He leaned close and tipped his head closer, though his gaze followed first one stranger and then another.

"There's nothing inherently rebellious about tattoos," she said. "It's merely not a cultural norm as of now."

Please let someone notice the brooch, she wished silently.

He laughed, and his eyebrow reached above the line of his glasses. "You do surprise me, Aini MacGregor."

The words felt like praise and she couldn't fight a smile.

His mouth, with its peaked upper lip, was only a breath away. One side drew up into a cocky sort of grin.

Then his eyes locked onto the brooch.

He jerked back a step, and before he could say anything, the chain at his neck brushed her finger. The club and Thane peeled away, and the colors of a vision became pictures.

A garden. Leafy trees. Blue blossoms like a carpet. A pebble path. A blond-haired boy stood near a tall woman. The woman pulled the boy to her, and he grinned, saying something. Mother, *his mind echoed. Blue-green happiness and golden contentedness swirled through the boy's mind.*

A man tore into the garden, breaking a branch from a sapling near the path.

He handed a silver necklace to the boy, who took it with wide and innocent eyes. The man tried to put the chain on the boy. The boy shook his head of shaggy hair. His mother held out an arm, stopping the man's hands from circling the boy's neck. The man's mouth opened in a shout. Emotions like a storm of color spun around the boy's head. He looked up through black lashes at the scarred man. The boy's eyes weren't wide and sweet anymore. They were sharp, cold.

The vision embedded in Thane's necklace shimmered away. The boy—grown now—looked into Aini's face.

"Aini? Are you all right?"

No, no she wasn't. "Yes. Sorry. Yes."

"Let's get you some water." Leading her off the dance floor, he pointed at her shoulder. "Did you know that's a Bethune brooch?"

"Is it?" She hadn't searched for what clan claimed the motto *Graceful*. She should've. Thane shouldn't have been more informed than her. "It was in Father's trunk. In that room."

At the bar, Aini sipped a glass of water, the cool liquid clearing her head.

Thane downed his ale and paid the barkeep. "Do you know about the Bethunes?"

"I just thought if it belonged to Father and certain people recognized it..."

"The last time kingsmen raided this place with any real

75

success," Thane said quietly, "they found a few of that clan. Seemed to be running the Dionadair here in Edinburgh."

Aini set the glass down and liquid splashed over the side. "What happened to them?"

Thane's eyes went cold as the waters of the Firth of Forth in January. "You really need to ask?"

"Right."

Someone touched her arm. It was a guy with the beginnings of a beard. He would've done better to wait another year before sporting that look. A pudgy man in thick, steel-toed boots stood by him. The liquid in Aini's stomach iced. They were the men from the balcony—the ones who'd been watching. Suddenly she wasn't so confident about her plan.

"Come with me," the first one said, his eyes bright, confident.

Thane made a derisive noise in his throat. "And who exactly are you?"

Neve and Myles appeared, their faces flushed.

Aini put herself between them and the strangers. "First tell me what this is about."

The second man's gaze slipped to the brooch. "You know what."

Aini cleared her throat and tried to stop her heart from beating too quickly. Thane touched her arm, and she gave the men a shaky smile.

"Give us a minute, please," she said.

They stepped back with a nod.

"Please don't do this," Thane said into her ear. "If they're not rebels, they're a waste of your time. If they are...these people don't care about anything but their cause. They're dangerous."

Myles butted in. "I don't know your plan here, but be careful, sweetheart. These people have knives in their fancy boots."

Discreetly, he pointed to the stranger's feet. Something silver showed at the second man's ankle. "If you do go with these losers, I'm going with you. We all are."

Thane nodded.

Myles's mouth fell open. "Wow. You actually agreed with me."

"But you're not going," Thane said to Aini.

"It's Aini's decision," Neve said. "Not yours."

Thane nodded tightly, but Aini could tell it was killing him to let her put herself in danger.

"That one guy looks my age," Aini said. "He can't be that dangerous."

"Shows how little you know," Thane said as he looked over her head at them.

"Number One, you wait here," Aini said. "Two, watch where he takes me. Three, if I don't come back in fifteen minutes—"

"No." Thane said, shaking his head and jabbing a finger. "That's definitely not what we're doing."

Aini may've growled. "This may come as a surprise to you, Thane Moray—I know how geniuses are used to getting their way—but I don't actually need your permission."

"I can't stand here and wonder if you're all right and—"

Aini didn't stick around for the rest of that statement. She started toward the strangers. "Let's go, gentlemen."

Thane slammed a fist on the bar top, rattling bottles and glasses. The keep said something to him that the music covered, and Aini heard Myles and Neve working to calm him down.

The men led Aini to the back of the club and up a wide staircase that led to a large balcony level with its own bar. Black bottles and bone cups made rows against its lighted back wall. Long red booths and sleek tables crowded the area. Past the seating, a hall led to the right, going toward what she could only guess was another interior part of the building. They didn't go far enough for her to find out. Instead, the two strangers stopped at what appeared to be a blank wall. The younger of the two pushed on the chaotically designed green and black wallpaper, and a door swung away from his hand.

"She'll want to see your brooch straightaway," the bearded man said, gesturing toward the hidden room. Then he walked off down the hallway.

"Of course." Aini headed through the doorway. Her pulse raced and she wiped sweating palms on her dress.

Before the man shut the entrance, leaving Aini on her own, she caught a flash of movement. A glimpse of green hair. One wide brown eye. A tattooed hand.

She sniffed to cover a nervous laugh. Myles, Neve, and Thane had hidden behind one of the red booths out on the balcony.

Inside the hidden room, red velvet-like paper covered the walls. Wrapped in a gold and black striped dress and leggings, a dark-haired young woman sat at a round table cluttered with electronics, and oddly, jewelry. A box near her elbow held a nest of shining things—a blue enameled ring, a silver brooch made in the shape of antlers, and several gold brooches. A beefy guy with pock-marked skin stood next to her, chewing on a drink stirrer. He had hair dark as midnight too, but freckles dotted his nose.

They were familiar somehow.

The woman's wide mouth puckered, and she looked Aini up and down. "I'm Vera. This is my brother, Dodie. Now where did you get that brooch?" She scooted forward on her chair, her hands clasped on the table.

Aini coughed, her throat dry. "It was...I found it. In an old trunk."

Vera's eyebrow lifted.

Aini stared the beautiful woman down.

Smiling a smile that would look perfectly at home on a boa about to squeeze someone to death, Vera pushed away from the table, pulled her dress down a little, and sauntered over. Aini silently named her perfume *Too Many Roses*.

Vera bent and squinted at the brooch. "*De bonnaire.*" Her eyes met Aini's.

Aini stepped back.

"A Bethune brooch," Vera said. "I'll give you fifty pounds for it."

"I don't want to sell it. I just wanted to know...have you seen it before?"

Turning away, Vera waved a hand in the air. Her nails were short and chipped. Aini chewed the inside of her cheek. Odd for a woman like her to have messy nails. Aini wondered what she did when she wasn't lounging in a club, buying up black market jewelry.

"There are so many like that," Vera said. "I'm really just paying you for the gold in it."

And yet, here she was, meeting Aini in a private room in a club where rebels used to meet.

"I'll go then." Aini shrugged and made for the door, running her damp palms down her sides again.

Vera's voice went higher, tighter. "Eighty pounds. Last offer."

"I want to know its provenance. Not its worth on the black market."

Vera's eyes widened, but Aini didn't wait for an answer. The walls were closing in, and that big man—Dodie?—had pulled something out of his waistband. A knife? A gun?

"Take it from her," Vera said.

Dodie rushed her. His thick fingers ripped the brooch from her dress, tearing the outer layer of white and gold fabric. Not thinking, just doing, she grabbed for the brooch, but Vera pushed her toward the door.

"Out with you, richie. I've no use for those who live well on English money."

Before they opened the door, Aini jerked hard and shoved Dodie. He fell, and the brooch flew from his hand. She leaped for it. Vera shrieked and came at her, ragged nails like claws. Diving for the brooch, Vera raked Aini's arm. Heat and needles seared Aini's skin. The door swung open behind her and strong hands wrenched her from the room.

"It's us, hen," Thane said into her ear.

Recovered, Dodie charged.

Myles shouted a warning and Neve took Aini's arm. Thane spun and smashed a boot into Dodie's stomach as Vera shot from the room. The two men who'd first led Aini through the club came running from the back hallway. Before Vera could get to them, Myles, Neve, and Aini hurtled down the stairs in a series of teeth-clattering leaps.

"Emergency!" Myles shouted into the crowd.

Aini looked over her shoulder. Still on the balcony, Thane had the bearded man in some sort of headlock. The chubby man waved a knife at Thane. He kicked the man's hand and the knife jumped into the air.

Downstairs, a cluster of girls wearing feathers in their hair separated Vera from Aini, Myles, and Neve. Vera's pretty face contorted as she made eye contact with Aini, but she didn't call out.

"This girl's going to upchuck!" Myles shouted. "Unless you want groceries tossed all over your fab attire, I suggest you move it!"

A girl in a mini skirt and three men with mohawks pushed

people aside as they fought their way through the red lights, candles, sweaty dancers, and skull-numbing music.

"What about Thane?" Neve shouted above the drums and trumpeting horns.

"He's a big boy." Aini helped Myles push the door open. Guilt nudged her, but she figured a man who drugged bouncers could probably take care of himself.

Outside, a mist that was nearly rain filled the air and weighed down Aini's elaborate and quickly dying hair style.

"Let's go, girls!" Myles tried to grab Neve's hand, but she didn't notice.

They tore into the street, dodging a car full of people singing along to the radio. A truck veered around them and blared its horn. The pavement glistened in the damp, slick under Aini's stupid, fancy shoes. At a dip in the road, her ankle rolled, sending a shot of heat up her leg.

"Hold on," she called out.

But Myles and Neve bolted past a pizza place with bright green walls, then a coffee house. They were headed for Candlemaker Row, for home. They couldn't lead these maniacs to the townhouse.

She tugged off her extravagant shoes and held them as she ran. "Stop! Wait!" The weak glow of the street lights teased her, not fully illuminating the wide road of George IV Bridge. It met with Candlemaker and the entrance to the graveyard. "We can't lead them to the townhouse," Aini said, panting.

Myles slicked water from his face. "We'll lose them in Greyfriars Cemetery."

Neve whimpered.

"The spirits can't hurt you." Aini tugged Neve, trailing Myles.

"I'm Scottish. We don't like to tangle with ghosts." Neve pushed the ends of her dripping braids out of her face.

Aini's stomach twisted. She was Scottish too. One half. She loved being Indonesian as well, but the color of her skin tended to make people around here forget her veins could hold blood from any number of countries.

Greyfriars' towering iron gate creaked as they hurried in. The rectangular windows at the top of the guard house doors were dark—it was after midnight—and the only sounds were the drips of rain on the trees that hulked over the old burial ground. At least, Aini hoped that was rain and not footsteps. Thankfully, the surrounding buildings' buttery light illuminated the grave-yard well enough to navigate the city of wet tombstones.

"We can cut through the back, right, Neve?"

Aini clutched the brooch like a talisman, the memory of the vision running through her head.

The man handing Father the brooch.

The stranger from the past and the carved stone.

The knife.

The stranger's thoughts, the directions he'd purposely imprinted that almost seemed directed at her, a Seer.

Myles started up the paved walkway past the western façade of the towering church with its arched windows and bone-colored walls.

"If the gate to the Heriot School is open," Neve said, "we can go through their grounds and come around the block the back way."

A chill swept past. A barely audible shushing sound rolled over Aini. Neve snagged her arm, both of them shaking. The walkway was too narrow for all three of them to continue side by side. Aini handed Neve off to Myles and stepped into the grass. Mud squelched between Aini's bare toes. The scent of wet earth and ancient soot, clinging to gravestones like permanent shadows, rose into the air.

Neve began singing nervously. *"Macbeth's Seer rises nigh."* Her timid voice strained over three minor key notes. *"A stone reflected in his light eye, and he bumped the man upon the chair, ripped him up by the hair."*

"What are you singing?" Aini asked. "You sound like Myles."

"Say thank you to the lady, Neve," Myles said shakily.

"It's something my mum used to cant in the kitchen."

Aini's foot splashed into a particularly disgusting patch of black mud and Neve's eyes widened.

"Did you know that you're walking on 40,000 bodies?" Neve whispered. "When it rains like this, sometimes bones pierce the ground and come up under you."

Aini shuddered and edged around another cold spot. "Neve. Please. Save it for your tours."

Footfalls sounded behind them. Aini turned as Vera and Dodie rounded the pub at the cemetery's entrance and stopped.

Aini squeezed Neve's arm.

Myles swore.

Vera smiled.

CHAPTER 9
AN ANCIENT FEUD

On the club's upper floor, Thane held the bearded man in a makeshift bear hug and kicked the knife out of the other man's hand. The hairy lad wiggled out of the hold and caught Thane with an elbow. Salty blood ran into Thane's mouth as he slipped his head left to dodge another strike. He drove well-worn knuckles into that fool's beard, then spun to face the man's larger associate, who howled and held his kicked, most likely broken, fingers.

"You Dionadair?" Thane knew his smile probably looked a good bit like his father's. His stomach rolled, but he straightened his shoulders. Sometimes cruelty was called for.

The big man spat, the warm blood hitting Thane's jacket and hand.

Keeping the knife within his peripheral vision, Thane glanced at the dark splotch on his jacket. "You'll need better aim than that to down me."

The man launched himself at Thane.

Arms raised, Thane dove and blocked the man's knife arm.

Thane's hand slid to the man's wrist, where he kept the knife low and away from his body as he kneed the idiot in the balls. Clutching his groin, the man fell. Thane kicked him in the stomach and picked up the knife.

Racing down the stairs and licking salty blood from his lip, Thane broke through the club's crowd and rushed into the street. He prayed silently that his naïve lab partners wouldn't head home. Shouting once in frustration, he headed toward the townhouse. He'd tucked his newly attained knife into his boot and the edge bit into his skin a little as he coursed into the mist.

His blood shot through his veins, hot and raging. There *had* been Dionadair at the club still. Four of them, at least. Just the name *Dionadair* molded his hands into fists.

The rebels had long been Campbell enemies. In 1819, Thane's ancestor, wild-eyed antiquarian Donan Campbell, and the man's assistant—Angus Bethune, founder of the Dionadair —uprooted the Coronation Stone somewhere north. The old stories claimed the stone would roar under the hand of Scotland's rightful Heir. What *roar* meant exactly, the stories didn't say.

Thane's ancestor, Donan Campbell, had insisted on bringing the potentially politically damaging stone back to the reigning king of the time. But Angus Bethune hid the artifact. Angus claimed the stone must be used when Scotland was ready for its true Heir.

Whatever that meant.

Donan Campbell had knifed Angus Bethune in the back for his treason. And since that day so long ago, the Campbells had continued the search for treasonous Dionadair.

And two of those vicious rebels were closing in on Aini, Myles, and Neve right now.

Numb with the adrenaline, Thane wished he could run faster.

He was almost to Candlemaker Row when the memory of Aini's mouth, nearly touching his own, burned across his mind.

As they'd danced, everyone else was gray near her bright color. She surprised him at every turn. The violent defense of her father when she'd slapped Thane. Her determination in going to The Origin even after everyone tried to stop her. The courage in her walk as she left her friends and followed strangers in an effort to get answers.

A thrill snaked through him, but he stomped it down, subdued it. If he became involved with Aini, he wouldn't be able to stomach lying about his name, concealing his part in all of this. If he told her the truth...would she understand that he really had no choice, that this was his clan and he couldn't escape? No. She wouldn't listen long enough. And he wouldn't blame her. Not when they'd taken her father. It didn't matter if Lewis was working for the Dionadair, for the rebels. She'd see Thane's involvement as a betrayal, because that's what it was.

Shaking his head to clear it, he rounded the curve in the road. A shout from Greyfriars Cemetery stopped him. He went cold all over. Aini's voice echoed through the fog.

Entering the graveyard, Thane rushed past leaning obelisks and domed, cracked tombstones. A flash of movement shoved his heart against his ribs. He jumped over a mud puddle near the kirk, the grand church's pale walls nearly invisible in the soupy weather.

The two Dionadair operatives loomed over Aini. They weren't waving any weapons around, but they could've tucked them up sleeves or into waistbands. Neve trembled at Aini's side and Myles took a step forward.

If Thane moved in, the Dionadair would attack. Better to wait and see how this played out. He concealed himself behind a massive oak.

Myles's brow knotted. His shoulders were all up around his ears and he bounced on the balls of his feet, ready to spring. "What's so important about a piece of jewelry that you'd waste one of us to get it?"

"My sister wants that brooch, and she'll have it." The huge man's pock-marked face twisted into a grin as he pushed his sleeves up.

Aini's slender fingers clenched the brooch, her knuckles white. Thane put a fist over his heart. She was thinking of her father, and for some reason, she'd latched onto this piece of old jewelry as a key to finding out what was going on with him. Thane shook his head, his chest aching for her. To be so lost, and yet so smart...

Facing the man, she said, "I'll give you the brooch if you tell me why you want it so badly. You wouldn't rough up your own countryman, would you?" She took a shuddering breath. Drops from the trees ran down her face and into her mouth. "You're better than a Campbell, aren't you?"

Thane fell against the tree, the strength gone from his bones. His surprise only proved how she blinded his judgment. Of course she hated Campbells. These days, she'd be crazy not to.

The Dionadair woman's voice cut through the mist. "Shut your gob, girl. You're not even Scottish. You're colonial. And rich as a sheik. Dark as one. You're the furthest thing from Scottish." Her voice grew shrill. "Now hand it over."

Squeezing the oak's trunk until his fingers throbbed with the effort, Thane gritted his teeth. Racist rebel. Ignorant fool. Aini was a Scot through and through. Her pride. Defiance. The courage she'd shown. Her loyalty to her father. Thane fisted a hand and pounded the trunk. The stupid rebel woman's ignorant comment would prick at Aini's soul, he just knew it. The girl did everything she could to fit in here—following every one of the king's directives with regard to the lab work, dressing like the other Edinburgh girls in stripes and leggings, working to shed her colonial accent.

Aini raised her chin, courage shining like stars in her black eyes. "I won't."

A proud grin spread over Thane's mouth and his eyes shuttered briefly.

"Dodie," the woman said, her lips barely moving.

Thane's fingertips tingled. Dodie was going to attack.

Leaving the oak, Thane ran at the man, hoping Myles would go for the woman. But Myles struck out at Dodie, his small fist connecting with the man's stomach. Dodie didn't fall. He just smiled and cracked the back of his hand across Myles's jaw. The colonial dropped like a sack of tatties.

Neve shrieked and called out for help.

Vera leaped at Aini, but Thane was there in a breath, grabbing the woman's hair and pulling her back. He threw the rebel to the wet grass as she shouted.

Aini paled and looked to him. "What can I do?"

He would've laughed at her business-like tone if this weren't the situation it was. "Keep her there," he said.

In one fluid motion, he pulled the knife from his boot, came up behind Dodie, and put the blade to the man's throat. The wet air dragged Thane's hair into his eyes.

Myles lay moaning near a dead man's slab.

Neve ran to Aini and the girls held the rebel woman, each latched tightly to an arm.

Dodie struggled against Thane's hold. The cutting rank of fear and sweat rose from the larger man. Thane couldn't kill him. He'd never killed anyone. Not with his hands. His gut torqued, bringing a sour taste to the back of his throat. He wasn't innocent. He'd doomed plenty with the weapon of information.

Vera yanked her arms free. "Now what, tough man?"

At least she didn't realize Thane was a Campbell. If she said anything and exposed him...

The vial of sleep-inducing gel in Thane's pocket pressed against his side. Aini swallowed and clenched her jaw. Neve's eyes were round as the moon. There wasn't enough left of the gel to knock both these Dionadair rebels out. Could he bring them in? What would Aini and Neve say if he suggested it?

Dodie struggled against Thane's grip, so he tightened his hold. "I'm trying to decide whether to kill you or not. Suggest you behave your sweet, wee self."

The man made a strangled noise as the knife bit a little deeper into his skin. Hot blood trickled over Thane's fingers.

"We'll go our separate ways," Thane said to Vera. "You lost today. We keep the brooch. You keep this man with throat intact."

The woman stared, seething. Studying Thane, she pushed a strand of hair out of her face and pursed her blood-red lips. "Agreed."

Myles lay very still, his chest moving slowly up and down. He'd had a rough knockout, but Thane could tell he was awake.

"Aini, take my place here please." Thane gave Dodie a knee to the kidney for good measure. "I'll help our friend."

Aini moved toward Thane, and he handed the knife off, his fingers brushing hers. Aini's small hands were like ice, but she managed to keep the blade at Dodie's throat as Thane walked over to Vera. The woman stared up at him, anger pouring out of her. This one would have to be dealt with. He grabbed her by the hair. Aini and Neve gasped. Did they think she deserved better treatment? Because Thane didn't. It was really for the woman's own good anyway. If he held her any other way—the wrist, the shoulders—there was a good chance she'd strike out at him and he might have to hit her. He didn't want to do that. Not really.

"Neve, get the vial from my pocket," he said.

Neve twisted her hands together. "The what?" Her voice trembled like a poor recording of herself.

"The vial."

Aini made a noise. Dodie's eyes swung to look at Thane and the lout gritted his teeth.

Thane clicked his tongue. "You'll mind the lady's blade unless you long for a good kick in the teeth."

Neve took three tiny steps and reached a hand in to find the gel. "Got it."

As Vera moved around under the clenched bunch of her hair, Thane pushed her to her knees. "Now open it. Don't touch it, Neve. Drag the opening over Vera's wrists."

"What are you doing?" Vera tried to turn and look up at him.

His fingers curled and she yelped, now staring straight ahead and kneeling as still as a virgin at her prayers. Thane nodded, and Neve moved to follow his directions. People could say what they liked about positive reinforcement—money and lands—but pain did the job in a grimly satisfactory and rather timely manner. Thane took a breath of the wet, night air and wondered what sane people did on their Charlesday evenings.

As Neve stepped away from Vera and capped the vial, Thane locked gazes with Aini. "Now, release him," he said, gesturing at Dodie. "Keep the knife."

Thane freed Vera's hair and she crumpled at his feet. The gel, once again, had done its work.

Dodie stumbled toward her, a hand at his bleeding throat. Red trickled thinly through his fingers. It wasn't a big enough cut to do anything. Just enough to make him think twice about doing any more fighting tonight.

"What did you do to my sister?" Dodie demanded.

Thane hurried the girls out of the cemetery, and left the Dionadair behind like ghosts—one silent, one shouting—among the tombstones.

Myles mumbled something.

Neve put a hand to the colonial's forehead as Thane carried him.

"We need a taxi. Now." Thane waved a car over and they worked Myles inside.

They gave the driver the address for the townhouse, and the curly headed man twisted in his seat. "Don't you think he should be going to the hospital?"

Thane put two fingers under Myles's jaw, feeling for his pulse. "Just do your job, man."

Raising his hands, the driver shook his head. "Fine. It's your friend. Not mine."

"He just had a hit on the head, right?" Aini looked from Myles to Thane to Neve. Her eyes were wet with tears and it made Thane want to punch things.

"Aye." He thumbed a clod of mud from Myles's eyelid. It was just a hit on the head. Not serious. At least, he hoped not.

As they bumped down Candlemaker Row, Aini and Neve's gazes never left Myles's face. Aini kept her hands firmly on his stomach to steady him. Neve cradled his shoes like they were treasures.

Thane looked at the water-stained ceiling of the car. *Your friend,* the driver had said. Aside from Bran, who felt more like family, Thane had never thought of someone like that. He hadn't had the opportunity.

He leaned toward Myles. "You better not go all dafty on us, friend."

CHAPTER 10
A QUESTION

"Should I get smelling salts from the first aid kit?" Aini asked, watching Thane carry Myles through the front door of the townhouse. "You should lay him in his bed."

"Where did you think I would lay the man down?" Thane rolled his eyes. He mumbled at a sleeping Myles. "The numpty. Why'd he think he could take on a man that size?"

As they hurried through the entryway, Aini was glad to see Thane moving carefully, his gaze on corners and furniture that might trip him.

Myles had sat up once during the ride home, given everyone an okay sign, and then promptly fell asleep. Aini didn't know much about concussions, but she didn't think sleep was a good thing at the moment.

Holding the boys' bedroom door open, Neve chewed her lip. "And you don't think we should've taken him to a doctor?"

"Nah," Thane said. "It's a knockout. That's all. A rough one.

If we can rouse him again, there's no more to do than let him rest. If we can't wake him..."

Aini rushed into the kitchen. "I'm getting the salts. Just in case."

A yellow nightlight glowed over the stove, illuminating the room. She slipped past the round kitchen table and headed up the dark stairs to the lab, praying silently that the salts were in the first aid kit. The last one to use the kit was Myles. But of course, the first aid kit wasn't where it was supposed to be—by the stove, in the top cabinet.

Aini dashed to Myles's massive desk and began rummaging. She tossed a stapler and two chewed pencils into the first drawer, where a scattering of charcoals hid. She stacked four small blank canvases at the corner of the desk and peered under a tattered portfolio. No first aid kit. Only a calendar of women in bathing suits. After shuffling through some drawings, she turned her attention to the other side. Lifting the edge of a large sheet of green and pink painted butcher paper, she slid the bottom drawer open and finally found the emergency supplies.

"Myles!" Neve's voice came from the kitchen.

Aini looked up, the kit in her hands and her heart pounding.

Myles appeared at the open lab door. He leaned a forearm against the frame and heaved a breath. "Don't wrinkle that butcher paper."

Aini pinched her nose with two fingers. "You come back from unconsciousness to keep me from wrinkling your latest advert idea? When your desk rivals a rat's nest for the Most Horrifying Mess award?"

On the paper, the cotton candy colors and emerald hues blended to form representations of the visions their chewing gum induced.

One of Myles's eyes was nearly swollen shut and the side of

his face was puffy. "The advert is enthralling, right?"

A wry laugh crept out of her. "It is pretty fantastic."

She helped him into a chair as Neve and Thane burst into the room.

"Daft colonial." Thane shook his head of golden hair.

Neve kneeled at Myles's feet. "Why did you go flying out of bed like a dog had bitten you?" She turned to Aini. "He sat up right after we laid him down. We were about to call for you."

Smiling, Aini waved her off.

Myles pointed a finger, then winced and bowed his head. "I knew Aini would be looking for the first aid kit." He cocked his head at Thane and Neve. "And what would our Miss MacGregor do if she had more than a second at my creatively arranged work station?"

Thane and Neve spoke in unison. "Organize it."

Aini raised an eyebrow. "*Someone* should."

Taking a copper pot from the cabinet, she ran a finger over a ding in the side. Her body felt heavy with what had happened. "Those people could've killed us."

She set the pot on the stove and began heating sugar and cornstarch over medium just to keep her hands busy.

Neve hummed two notes, the sounds she made when thinking about new candy flavor combinations. She walked over, eyed the pot, then slid the large cutting board from the lab table's lower shelf.

"Golden taffy, aye?" she said to Aini, her voice as artificially bright as Myles's hair.

Picking up a folded cloth from the counter, Thane cleaned some water from the edge of the sink.

Tears rose, hot and sudden, and Aini dragged a hand over her eyes to smear them away. "I'm sorry I put you all in this position."

Myles coughed. "We knew what we were getting into."

"I didn't," she admitted.

Neve blinked. "Me either."

Thane stared, the cleaning cloth thrown over his shoulder and his eyes weary. Aini wondered if he'd lost his glasses in the graveyard.

"Where did you learn how to fight like that?" she asked him, adding the butter and salt.

"Not everyone had a sweet childhood like your own."

"I just...thank you. For—"

"What did the rebels say to you in that wee room of theirs?" he asked.

Neve gave Aini the container of orange flavoring and the jar of golden dye. "Aye. Tell us. Did you learn anything about Mr. MacGregor's past?"

Aini measured, then remeasured the flavor and stirred it in. After all they'd risked tonight, they deserved to know everything. But if she told them about being a sixth-senser—specifically, a Seer—they'd immediately have knowledge they were required by law to report. If they were caught hiding her, they'd be taken for questioning and possibly be in an even worse situation than Father probably was right now.

The cutting scent of citrus bit into her thoughts.

Neve donned some hefty oven mitts and removed the pot from the heat. She frowned and added the gold.

Myles laid his head on the back of the chair. "Aini, you need to tell us exactly what's going on."

Once she told them, everything would change. It would be a jump off a ledge, the lighting of a match, pushing the first domino. Aini moved her mouth, but the words wouldn't come. Neve asked her something, but all Aini could hear was her own heart knocking. She had to tell them. She couldn't tell them.

CHAPTER 11
CONFESSION

"**D**oes it have anything to do with that brooch you're wearing?" Neve poured the taffy onto the cutting board.

Aini swallowed. "I found it in Father's trunk. In the hidden room behind that wall." She pointed to it, certain Thane had told them about it, but Neve and Myles's eyes widened.

"Hidden room?" Neve said. "Does everyone in Edinburgh have a hidden room?"

"Only rebels." Thane's hands fisted at his sides. "Sorry. Ignore me." His fingers went to the chain at his neck, the one that held the vision of him as a child.

Aini suddenly felt crushed under the weight of his judgment against her family.

But he was right.

Father had been involved. Somehow. She didn't know how deeply, but he'd been tied into the underground world of rebels at some point.

Looking at her clothing and touching her updo, Aini gritted

her teeth. She'd tried to fit into Edinburgh society. Talking like the upper class, well-respected Scots and Englishmen. Following every rule that she could. And now Father's past could erase all her efforts to give him the peaceful, successful life he deserved. The life she'd thought he deserved. *No. He still deserves happiness.* Surely his mistakes didn't go so deep.

Her shoulders and back tight, she removed the brooch and passed it around. "The brooch has the Bethune clan motto. Thane tells me some Dionadair rebels are Bethunes."

"Aye." Neve handed the piece of jewelry to Myles. "The ones sentenced to death when we were still in grammar school."

"Yes." Aini pressed the flat spoon into the mixture, inhaling the comforting scent of sugar and oranges. "When I...when I found the brooch and touched it..."

Myles snorted, looking at the pin. "An otter. Real tough." He rolled his eyes and gave the brooch to Thane, who looked at the piece like it would explode in his hands.

"Shut your gob, Myles," Neve chided.

As Aini laid the turner next to the mass of sticky sweetness, Thane slid the brooch down the silver lab table. It scratched across the surface and Aini caught it neatly. The metal was warm from his fingers. She cleared her throat, touching the tiny, rough lines that made up the rebel clan's motto. Her stomach burned under her ribs.

Myles slowly opened his swollen eye, obviously in pain. Neve was pale as milk as she looked at Aini with the kindest eyes. The taffy was going cold, forgotten. A purple and green bruise colored Thane's knuckles.

"I'm a Seer." The words fell from her mouth like they had a life of their own.

Neve's head jerked up. "What?" she whispered like someone might hear.

"I have a sixth sense." Sweat rose along Aini's back, and she grabbed the turner and folded the taffy, once, twice, three times, her arm muscles tensing. "For two years, I've been able to see emotional imprints, memories, on sentimental items when I first touch them."

Neve's mouth dropped open. Myles blinked, frozen, and Thane's face was unreadable.

"I touched your bracelet, Myles," Aini said. "I saw your mother. Curly hair. Not the nicest person."

His lips opened and shut and opened again.

"Thane, I..." She licked her lips quickly. Her mouth was dry as sand. "I accidentally touched your necklace and a vision of you played out in my head. You were little. Your parents were there. I couldn't see them clearly, but..."

"Can you even believe it?" Neve said quietly. Then she clapped her hands once and laughed. "That's amazing!"

"You're...you're not scared? Of me? Of disappearing into prison for knowing me?"

"I'm scared of prison. But not you. Course not you. Aini...it's brilliant."

Aini smiled shyly, but when she looked at Thane, her grin faded. His face was a sketch in harsh lines and tired eyes. She rolled her mother's ring around her finger.

"And I saw a vision when I first touched the brooch too. It was in The Origin. Near where the picture was taken, the picture Thane found in Father's office. A man gave the brooch to him. Father didn't want it."

Thane narrowed his eyes. "How do you know?"

"I can...see some emotions in visions. Father was scared. Unhappy. Worried. Another vision followed. In the second one, a man in strange, old-fashioned clothes said something. It was like he knew he left an emotional imprint and wanted to talk to the Seer who would experience the vision. So weird. It was different from the other visions I've seen." Aini shivered. The man's eyes had been so bright, so passionate. "He said something about a rock or a trail or something." Her mind went foggy with fatigue, and she rubbed her eyes. She needed sleep, but obviously that wasn't happening anytime soon.

Neve's head went slowly back and forth. "I knew there was something special about you."

A strangled laugh bubbled out of Aini. "You don't think I'm an abomination?"

"I know you." Neve played with the braid hanging over her shoulder. "You wouldn't use your...ability to take advantage of people."

It's what many people thought about sixth-sensers—that they'd use their extra sense to one-up everyone else.

"I hope I don't get you all into trouble." Aini blinked back tears.

"Bit late for that," Thane said, softening his words with a shaky smile. "And the king's law is wrong." Venom leaked into his voice. "He should not call your kind what he does. It's not your choice to have this ability." Crossing his corded arms, he popped a knuckle and mumbled something under his breath.

"I've only known one other Seer," Myles said. "An old woman who worked for my mother. You're a truckload better looking than her. Guess you don't have to be a hag or a lying cheat to be," he wiggled his fingers, "in touch."

A sad smile drifted over Aini's mouth. He was a friend. She hadn't had many in her life of traveling with her mother and the dancing troupe. She memorized how he looked right at this moment, with his sly grin and green hair and wide eyes, and tucked the image into her heart.

Neve sighed at him. "Myles. Really." She checked his puffy

jaw and eye with her fingers. Aini guessed growing up with younger brothers almost qualified Neve as a nurse.

"My life's an open book. Read at will, Aini," Myles continued. "I'll warn you, it's not for the faint of heart."

The lab's overhead lights suddenly felt too bright. Aini slid her mother's ring from her first knuckle to the next. Neve helped Myles to the stairs.

"This man needs his bed," Neve said.

Myles put a hand over his heart. "Oh what I could do with that phrase if I wasn't three shades shy of full function."

Neve gave him a look he completely deserved. "Aini, I'll wait up to talk to you. In our room. If you want."

They disappeared into the dark, and Thane turned the oven's temperature up. He scooped the cold taffy lump onto a baking sheet.

"We should get some rest." Aini swallowed. "You don't have to do that."

He pulled his glasses out of his pocket. So he hadn't lost them. He'd prepared to jump into the fray at the cemetery, removing his glasses before fighting.

His eyes were very gray as he looked at her over the black frames. "I know what it's like to need normality. To make taffy when you should probably be thinking over what you've been through."

"You've made taffy when your world was coming apart?" She let out a half sob, half laugh.

"Not taffy, no. But I—I understand."

The oven door closed with its usual squeak. Aini sat on a stool and hugged herself. She felt empty. Confused. Lost.

After eyeing the taffy through the oven's window, Thane leaned back on the table beside her. His left hand was tucked under an arm, his right picked at a thread on his belt loop.

"A Seer, aye?"

"Yep."

"Pretty rare."

"Uh huh."

The corner of his mouth pulled toward a dimple. "So the rule-follower is really one of the King's Most Wanted." He took her hand—his was hot—squeezed it quickly, and then pulled away. "I'm sorry. I shouldn't joke."

"It's okay. It is kind of ironic."

"Kind of?" He nudged Aini with his shoulder. That grin of his would've melted her if she hadn't been so miserable. But his powerful smile faded fast. "Hey, hey, I'm sorry. I'll shut my gob."

And then she was crying and he was holding her against his chest and she didn't even remember putting her arms around his waist. He felt so strong, his muscles taut and coiled with potential.

"I've always held myself back from my ability," she said. "To protect everyone. So I wouldn't see into their personal thoughts, their memories. It's an invasion. I know it is. I never once stayed at a friend's house. Not that I have any to speak of...I was afraid I'd see something I didn't want to. You can't unsee those most important memories. I have to pull back when someone goes to hug me or put an arm around me. Everyone thinks I'm cold, but...I hide what I am so if I'm taken for questioning," her throat clenched painfully, "no one but me will be hurt. But Father, he was always in danger from me. Just for being my father."

Her skin felt too sensitive, raw and hurting. Her chest ached with her father's absence. She wanted more than anything to hear his voice and the people at the club had tried to take her only clue—the brooch—instead of helping to figure all this out and it was too much, too much, too much.

She choked back a rasping sob. "The rebels...they're just so... I don't know how Father could've helped them. They're awful. You saw them! I don't know what to do."

Thane made a soft hushing sound over her head. "Easy now, hen. One thing at a time. You love lists, so let's make one."

Sniffing, she nodded and broke away. They stood side by side, leaning on the lab table and a little on one another. One of her arms was still behind him, her hand on the edge of the cutting board. The scent of sugar and rain filled the air.

"Information Item One," she said, and he laughed sadly, the vibration humming through the place where their bodies touched. "Those were Dionadair rebels. Two. They want the brooch. Three. Father has some connection to the club or what used to be there or both. We know because of the picture and my vision."

As she pulled her hand from behind Thane, her forearm dragged over the waistline of his trousers, rucking up his shirt a little. A sliver of his skin touched the inside of her wrist. He sucked a quick breath and looked down, his eyes serious. She swallowed, feeling very warm. How would it feel to run a whole palm against his bare back? Her mouth went dry. Thane twisted and leaned in, his gaze so heavy on her lips that she could almost feel the pressure and the heat of it. She imagined his breath tickling her chin and—

The oven beeped.

She jumped to get the taffy, hearing his deep inhale behind her. With oven mitts, she removed the candy from its warm hideout and set it on the table. Her heart wouldn't stop drumming. Her lips wouldn't stop feeling that imagined kiss. They both touched the taffy to test its temperature and the mix stung her fingers. The pain faded quickly. She wished these inconvenient feelings would disappear just as easily.

"Perfect temp." She looked to him.

"What?" He glanced at her, and then at the candy. "Oh. Yes. Right."

Together, they lifted the sticky stuff and draped it over the taffy puller machine. Thane switched the puller on. It began humming, drowning the sound of the oven's fan and the small cooler's buzz and clank.

"Thank you." She rubbed her eyes with the back of her hand. "For listening. For helping me tonight."

A length of taffy drooped away from the machine's silvery arms. They reached for it and their hands collided in the warm candy. They lifted the draping, golden strand, then stood there, facing one another. Aini had ended up with two delicate strands of taffy on her fingertips. She ate one and gave him the other.

He grinned and took it between finger and thumb.

The space between them begged to be filled. Aini's fingers twitched and longed to reach out and touch the bruise below his eye, his proud chin. She wanted to feel the strength of this genius who could somehow fight too.

She took a shaky breath. "I'm sorry for all the problems I've caused."

Lines appeared between Thane's eyebrows, partially blocked by his glasses. He bit his lip and shook his head. His mouth opened, shut. Then he said, "Do not say that. Aini, I—"

"I should've listened to you about the club. About the danger. If I had, Myles wouldn't be injured."

She was breathing quickly. Thane too, his tee shifting as his broad chest moved.

"And all you did," she said, "was what you thought was best in a situation I should never have dragged you into. You were amazing. The way you fought. Your quick thinking."

She wanted to kiss him. A terrible idea. But here he was, by her side, with his patience and his eyes going all soft and after what he'd suffered for her tonight and all he'd risked...

It was like a magnet sat in each of them. The pull grew stronger with every breath.

Making a noise in the back of his throat, Thane closed the short distance and cupped her chin in his long, taffy-sticky fingers. Heat bloomed over Aini's cheeks as sparks ignited under her skin and spread down her throat. The scent of summer, embodied in fruit and syrup, soaked the air around them. His body pressed against hers and she was melting like chocolate.

Her heart boomed in her ears. "I should've listened to you."

"No, hen," Thane whispered, eyes half-lidded.

Gently, she pulled his hand away from her chin. "It was wrong. I am sorry."

Thane's eyes matched the sky's light through the window. The sun was rising. "Aini, you're so...good. I've never met someone so true to themselves. And you're insanely brave, you wee fool." A lightness rose inside her at the praise. Then a raw, vulnerable look crossed Thane's features, the same look she'd seen flashes of ever since they'd taken Father. "You make me feel like some daft poet," he said, smiling.

"Robert Burns wasn't daft." She grinned and raised an eyebrow.

"Not like him. A poet without any proper words...only the emotions to make me wish I had them. *Where're you bide in the world so wide, we wish you a nook on the sunny side, With a muckle of love and little of care...*"

It was absolutely lovely, and she felt so much like he was a part of her life here now, that he understood her and what she was going through. She was so lucky to have him here. He was going to help her solve this and save Father. It was all going to be okay.

"What's it from?" she asked.

He looked down, his cheeks going a little pink. "It's a wedding blessing. The only pretty thing I know." His black lashes brushed his glasses. "Aini—"

She couldn't stand it anymore. Rising onto her toes, her lips stopped his words.

He kissed her back—a hard, pushing embrace—and a burn worked its way from his velvet lips, to her mouth, down deep into her heart. Each time he pressed into the kiss, a pulse of heat flared from her chest, all the way to her taffy-covered fingertips. Goosebumps trailed down her legs. Moving backward, she bumped into the table and tasted the taffy again in her mouth and his. She pulled back.

The Cone5, the ingredient that caused the enhanced color vision in the taffy, took effect. A halo of blue-purple shone around the edges of Thane's hair. A teal-pink hue showed in the lines of the tattoos on his hands and in his glasses' frames. Aini put a hand to her head. It felt light as feathers and all her worries dissipated.

Thane's gaze flew over her face and hair and dress. "The colors...it's...I didn't think you could get any more bonnie, but this is—"

He eased against her, his calloused hands on her cheeks, then sticking in her hair. His flat stomach was hot through their clothing and Aini curled her fingers into the soap-scented fabric of his shirt. He tilted his head to the right, and their noses brushed awkwardly before he corrected, grinned against her mouth, and brushed his lips over hers. Aini's pulse beat hard and fast in her throat. She pulled him closer, loving the feel of his breath, his teeth, the quick slip of his warm tongue over her top lip.

Neve hurtled into the lab. She'd changed into pajamas, and

because of the taffy, her purple top glowed in three shades Aini didn't have names for.

"The people from the club," she said, blushing and looking from Aini to Thane and back again. "They're at the door."

Aini jerked away, head spinning. "They're here? The Dionadair? How do they know where I live?"

Neve bunched her pajama top in her small, white hands. "Suppose they asked around about an Indonesian girl. Not a lot of those in Edinburgh. They've brought another man. Never seen him."

The effects of the small amount of taffy began to disappear. Corpse-gray light dragged through the window and gathered in the corners of the lab. Aini shivered.

Thane had gone all still and quiet, his arms hanging loosely at his sides.

Going to the sink, Aini grabbed a towel and ran it under water. "Should we...should we go talk to them?" She cleaned her fingers and handed the towel to him.

A muscle in his jaw moved as he rubbed the taffy off. "I'll go."

Following Neve, Aini started down the stairs. Thane trailed her.

"No," Aini said. "This is my problem. You all stay inside and I'll talk to them on the front stairs."

"We're here in whatever way you want us to be," Neve said, stumbling over her words.

The light of early morning slid into the kitchen and along the hallway where it blended with the shadows. Aini's mind was a buzzing whirlwind. She couldn't contain the dangers she'd brought on herself. Telling Thane, Neve, and Myles about her sixth sense. She'd kissed Thane. He'd kissed back. They'd almost been killed by people who were now at her front door. And she was about to chat with them like it was normal as tea on a Henrysday afternoon.

Staring ahead, Thane set a hand briefly on her back. Neve took Aini's fingers in hers and gave them a squeeze. The boys' bedroom door was closed; Aini guessed Myles was resting. Soft music trickled from within as firm knocks at the front door echoed through the entryway. She nodded at Thane and Neve, and took a breath.

"It's all right," a crisp male voice said through the door. "We come to apologize."

Thane laughed once, low and heavy with sarcasm. "Right."

Unlocking the three bolts, Aini put a hand on the cool, bronze doorknob. Her heart clanked like a kicked tin can.

Thane's phone hummed from his pocket. He took it out and mumbled something fierce.

Aini opened the door to Vera, Dodie, and a man in round glasses and a trim red beard. He wore a pair of striped trousers and a bow tie.

A slick of cold sweat covered Aini's back and upper lip. "What do you want? I'm not giving you anything."

The red-head held out a hand. "I'm Owen."

"You'll not touch her," Thane spat.

"I can speak for myself, thanks," she snapped.

Owen held his hands wide. "No worries." His owl-like stare locked on Aini. "Vera and Dodie are my siblings. They made a mistake. They saw the Bethune brooch and...acted rashly. Our apologies."

Aini kept a few feet of space between them. "We don't want your apologies. I want to know what you know about this brooch and what my father might have to do with its history."

Owen smoothed his beard. "Yes. Of course."

Vera's arrogance had fled her features. She watched Aini with rounded eyes, her hands clenched at her sides. "We think—"

Owen put a hand on her arm. "We believe our father and yours were close friends, associates." Pushing his glasses higher on his small nose, Owen traded a look with Dodie. The big man still looked murderous, but that could've just been the way his face was made. Clearing his throat, Owen said, "We believe you may be...someone important."

Thane snorted. "That's specific."

Neve stood behind Aini, her warmth a comfort against the cool dawn air.

Aini wasn't about to play stupid games with these people. They might've thought of themselves as representatives for the Scottish people, some sort of vigilantes, but she'd felt that woman's nails and heard the crack of that man's hand on her friend's jaw. They would've done worse if Thane hadn't intervened. These rebels were the picture of danger, standing in the flesh on her front steps. They—or those like them—were the reason Father was suffering questioning somewhere. The Dionadair had probably coerced him into doing something long ago. And now, instead of the Campbells simply leaving Father alone when he refused to help them, they had something to use against him.

She crossed her arms. "Explain."

Vera stepped forward, and Owen rubbed his hands together. "If you are who we think you might be, find the knife," Vera said.

"The what?"

"There is a legendary knife. And if you are who we think you are, you'll be led to it."

"Why would I care about some knife?"

Vera sneered. "Because the future of Scotland relies on it. As well as your father's well-being."

"What do you know about my father? Tell me."

Owen rubbed his chin. "When you prove you are the one to find the knife, we will tell you everything." He laid a hand on his stomach and gave a little bow. The three turned as one, walked quickly down the stairs, and disappeared into the lightening day.

Aini stood there, watching them go. "What? No! Tell me now!" She ran at them, but three sets of hands held her back. She turned to see all three apprentices. "What was that? What are they talking about? We have to go after them!"

"You should think first," Neve said, her face drawn with lines of worry and fear. They went back inside and shut the door. Neve locked it. "Have you ever heard your father talk about a knife? Is there one around here?"

Thane's forehead wrinkled and he took his glasses off, shaking his head. "They want a knife now? What in God's name..."

Numb and lost, Aini walked through the entryway, passing Father's glass-walled office. Their reflection looked eerily similar to a vision.

Aini froze.

The doors of her mind flew open.

"I did, Neve," she said. "In the brooch's vision. I saw a knife."

Thane frowned, and Neve cocked her head. "How would they know you saw a vision?" she asked.

"Maybe that's why they want the brooch so badly," Aini said. "They're aware of its embedded vision and want to know if I saw it."

Thane's boots knocked along the floor as he began pacing.

Thinking, Aini chewed the inside of her lip and leaned against the couch that framed the living room.

"Why would this particular knife matter to rebels?" Neve asked, her eyes red with fatigue.

Pausing, Thane shoved his glasses into his messy hair. Five dabs of taffy marked his collar. Aini flushed. Her fingerprints. He glanced from her to the prints. Looking down, he swallowed and continued pacing the wide, wooden floorboards.

She coughed. "I don't know. It doesn't make sense. Even if they somehow knew the brooch held a vision, how would they know what the vision showed? And why would they care?"

"Maybe if we go to sleep, our brains will figure it out for us," Neve said.

She was right. No matter what they decided, their bodies needed sleep before they could do anything.

Neve said good night and went to bed, promising first to check on Myles. Switching all the house lights off, Aini followed in her wake, Thane behind her. Her feet were concrete blocks. She blinked, clearing her fatigue-dry eyes.

At the door to the girls' bedroom, Thane put a hand out to stop her, his glasses on top of his head and tangled in his hair. The stubble on his sharp jaw had grown. In the hallway light, the tiny hairs glowed gold like the taffy they'd sampled. Aini didn't need recreational candy to see the beauty in him. It was all there in his high cheekbones, bow-shaped lips, and those sea-storm eyes that, when they focused on her, smoothed a warmth over her heart, down her stomach, and below her navel.

"Aini, I should not have—"

She put a hand on his chest and his heart beat against her fingertips. Like her dress was made of lead, she felt so heavy, tired. "I know. The timing...but don't think I," she cleared her throat, "that I didn't want..."

His lips quirked to one side and his eyes grew sad. "Go on to bed. I won't bother you anymore tonight." He looked toward the dawn streaming through the front windows. "Oh. Today."

She laughed sadly. "I'll set my alarm and get you up if you want me to."

"Sounds good," he said, but his tone sounded anything but good.

With a quick goodnight, she went into the bedroom.

Sleep didn't want to take her away though. She rolled her mother's wedding ring around her finger. Neve snored lightly across the room, the tiny, square skylight laying sun over her ever-present, painfully messy mound of pillows and blankets.

Aini picked up the brooch and thumbed the Latin words of the motto. How was she going to puzzle all this out? Would her life ever go back to normal? She turned over, carefully folding the end of her sheet over the duvet's edge. *Normal.* What a beautiful word. She longed for her organized days of lists and rules that she could follow.

But she was a living, breathing joke. She'd been breaking the rules all along, being what she was, doing what she did. She was a fake, an illegal sixth-senser posing as a loyal subject who did as the law demanded. Pressing her face into the pillow, every bone in her body ached, longing, moaning for the simple life she'd somehow lost.

CHAPTER 12
GUILT AND OATMEAL

The lab air cooled Thane's face. Good thing too because his brain was on fire. Aini was a sixth-senser. A Seer, of all things! And right here, under his nose. Rodric would've had a grand time with that knowledge. Thane pressed his fists against his pounding head. She'd hid her ability so well. This proved what Thane had believed though. That sixth-sensers had no choice at all in being born with their talents, so to speak. Aini didn't deserve punishment. The poor lass had enough of that in her life now.

He took a deep breath, smelling heated metal, oranges, and sugar. The scent produced an image of Aini's face. A pleasant shiver ran from Thane's chest and down.

That kiss.

It shouldn't have happened. His stomach clenched with the thought of her lips under his. He shoved the feelings to a far removed corner of his mind as he gathered ingredients from the mini ice box and turned on the stove. If he didn't turn in a new recipe for weaponized candy to Rodric soon, his cousin would pay him a visit.

The traditional Scottish sweet called tablet normally consisted of nothing more than cane sugar, sweet condensed milk, unsalted butter, and a bit of fresh milk. But Lewis's special formula negated the effects of certain other recreational sweets.

And that gave Thane an idea.

First, he could amp up the color-vision Cone5 taffy recipe— the stuff he and Aini had sampled during the kiss—and make a gas version so it'd be easily dispersible. When released, anyone in the area would see far too much ultraviolet, too much of every color in the spectrum. They'd be temporarily blinded by color. Unless they had also eaten the juiced up negating tablet Thane was about to create. It'd be perfect for undercover Campbell operatives.

Two recipes. Surely it was enough to get him off the black list with Rodric. And it wouldn't be as bad as giving them the paralyzing stuff he'd crafted.

Yes. Two recipes should be fine for now.

If Thane turned it in.

As he stirred the pot of ingredients over medium-high heat, steam clouded his glasses. After twenty minutes, the mix's color took on a golden brown hue. Removing the tablet from the heat, he stirred it vigorously, then poured it into a buttered baking tray. Before it could cool, he sprinkled Lewis's canceling powder over the top. It was a combination of powdered sugar, a mild steroid, and a hormone that blocked the vision enhancement chemical in the taffy.

With the tablet complete, he attempted to focus on a formula to turn the taffy's essence into a gas.

He swallowed, his heart as heavy as his eyelids. Aini had confessed her greatest secret. She was a Seer. And a good one, it seemed. What exactly had she seen on Thane's necklace? His tongue tasted bitter. Served him right if she saw some painful secret, a clue to his true identity, in that vision of his childhood.

Rubbing his face harshly, he scratched out his formula, then started again.

His phone buzzed from the pocket of his pants. It was Rodric. He should report Aini right now. He should report this recipe. He hit the ignore button on the phone. For once, just once, he didn't care about *should*. As if it'd heard his thoughts and had a mind of its own, his long-ago broken rib pinched his side. Rodric had cracked that bone, and here Thane was, basically asking for a repeat performance.

After finishing up in the lab, Thane hurried down the stairs to the kitchen. Weak light drifted from the front of the townhouse and lay in tattered strips along the wooden planks of the floor. Suddenly longing for comfort food, Thane switched the light on over the stove and started a pot of oatmeal cooking. His skin felt too tight. Too warm. Itchy. Like he wanted to crawl out of himself and be someone else.

His phone buzzed again. He tossed it on the countertop and kept stirring.

"If you whisk that oatmeal any harder, you're going to dig a hole to Russia." Myles raised his eyebrows as he ambled in. "Or whatever's on the other side of the planet from here."

The colonial started some coffee, then pulled out a chair and sat backwards in it. His face looked like Thane felt. Bruised. Knocked off kilter. An ill fit for the bones beneath it.

"How d'you feel man?" Thane poured the oatmeal into two bowls and threw some blueberries on top. "Your head aching?"

Myles accepted the bowl and added a boatload of honey. "I'm all right. Not too bad. You know your phone's going off."

Neve and Aini walked in. Neve was all in black, and Aini

wore a short, blue dress that hugged her waist. Her eyes were big and haunted, circles ringing them. She'd not slept enough. And no wonder. Aini flipped the kitchen's overhead light on and her gaze went from his face to his bare feet. Her eyelashes were black and thick and pure sexy. His heart clunked hard, just the once, under his breastbone. She blinked, and her apple cheeks darkened a shade.

Myles nudged Thane's wrist with a finger. "Probably shouldn't stare. They don't like that."

Thane swallowed and looked into his oatmeal, his face hot. "Shut your gob, colonial."

Snickering, Myles bid the girls a good morning. Neve poured out some orange juice while Aini eyed the stairs to the lab.

"Neve, I'm going to need your help," she said.

Neve sat beside Myles. "Aye. Course. To find that knife?"

The coffee maker let out a low screech and a puff of steam, its familiar finale. Aini handed a mug to everyone and took the chair between Thane and Myles. She braced her shaking hands on the cup, and Thane's heart cinched in his chest.

"So in the vision on the brooch, I saw a lot of things. One being the knife I believe those Dionadair mentioned."

"Could you tell where the knife was?" Myles slurped his coffee.

"It was in a brick and stone room. And the place was dark." Aini stared into her mug like she could see the vision again. "Water dripped from the ceiling. If the knife is close enough that the rebels think I can just go and get it, it must be here in Edinburgh somewhere. The only place I can think that would look like the location is the underground vaults."

Thane reached a long arm out and grabbed his phone, pocketed it. "A good place to hide something."

Neve hugged herself. "I hate that place. I used to run a tour there. It's full of spirits. And not the nice kind."

Myles laughed. "You Scots are adorable. Believing in ghosts and all that."

Thane and Neve glared at him.

"We'll see how cute you think I am," Thane said, "when I make your right eye match the left."

Myles made an *Oooo* sound and pretended to shake in fear. Thane took a drink, raising his middle finger over the side of the cup so only Myles would notice it.

"The man in the vision mentioned a number." Goosebumps raised the fine hairs on Aini's arms. "Eighty-five."

"Yes," Neve said. "The vaults under Cowgate Road are numbered for sure. I don't know about the others. But those are."

She pushed away from the table, left the kitchen, and returned with the patched satchel she usually brought on her tours.

"Look at this." She took a map from the bag and spread it between the coffee mugs. Steam rose from the drinks as she smoothed out the paper's folds with a palm. "Eighty-five should be about here." Her finger hovered over a spot north of the townhouse. "This is the vault you're looking for. This section was abandoned around 1835. But you can't go in, Aini. They walled plague victims up in certain spots down there. The spirits—"

Aini slammed her fist on the table and everyone froze.

"I'm sorry," she said, her voice shaking. "But I have to go in, Neve. You know I do."

Neve nodded, and Myles patted Aini's back.

Thane stood and took a better look at the map. Running a hand over the black lines and scrawled names, he remembered red tape and an announcement about the vaults.

"Neve's right that you can't go down in the vaults," Thane said. "But not because of ghosts."

Aini frowned. "Why not?"

"The Dionadair used them to move around the city and orchestrate hanging the banned flag on Holyrood Palace in the spring. The king has closed them up now. You can't get in."

Myles frowned. "How do you know all this?"

Aini's eyes went all fiery and angry. "I have to know what Father did or didn't do. A padlock isn't going to stop me."

"Oh no?" Thane cocked his head. "A past in breaking and entering is it then?"

"No. I...I'm claustrophobic." She swiped her palms on her dress. "Father taught me how to pick locks in case I was stuck somewhere."

She was always surprising Thane and now was no different.

Myles's eyes widened.

"So I'll be fine," Aini said. "I can get in and get out. No problem." She swallowed, not convincing at all in her cavalier attitude.

She was going to get herself killed. Thane stood up, went to the sink, and pressed his hands into the countertop.

Aini gathered Neve's map, smoothing and smashing it until the thing submitted to her demanding folds. "I'm leaving. Thane, will you go with me? Neve can stay here and keep an eye on Myles."

"What about the kingsmen guarding the vaults?" Myles asked. "I'm guessing there'll be at least one of them at the entrance. Probably need to worry more about them than ghosts. Ghosts don't have swords. Oh. Wait." He tapped his head. "I have a great idea."

Thane snorted.

Myles cleared his throat like he was about to sing. "Get a

dog," he proclaimed.

"A dog?" Aini put her head in her hands.

"Listen." Myles held up a finger. "Toss a row of sausages at the first kingsman you see. Thane will be wearing one of Neve's dresses and—"

"I prefer blue." Thane shrugged. "Sets off my eyes."

"You're taking this seriously?" Aini asked.

"None of it's happening anyway. You'd never get away with it. No one would," Thane said, his voice rougher than he meant it to be. But he had to stall her. "I may as well have fun with the colonial's imagining."

Myles pumped a fist in the air. "Even our Thane can't deny my fantastic forethought. He can go after the dog while you head for the vaults."

Sighing, Neve grabbed the sugar bowl. "Why does Thane need a blue dress?"

"Don't encourage them," Aini said.

"I told you, Neve," Thane said. "Sets off my eyes." He fluttered his lashes.

"Stop," Aini said. "We need to—"

The colonial clucked his tongue at Neve. "Never underestimate the power of your attire." He shook a finger at her.

Neve dropped a spoonful of sugar into her drink. "I learned all about that when we went to The Origin," she whispered at Myles.

The cocky gomeral's face reddened. "Oh. Yes. You, that outfit..."

Thane smiled, glad he wasn't the only one feeling exposed on matters of the heart.

Aini lifted her shoulder bag off the chair and her ebony hair swung across her back. "I'm going to the vault." Thane's chest tightened as she made for the kitchen doorway. "No matter how many ghosts or kingsmen trouble me," she said, still not facing him. She ducked her head to draw the bag's strap over her shoulder. "Or how much Thane scowls. And yes, Thane, I can feel your dissatisfaction burning into the back of my head."

He couldn't let her do this. She'd be caught. No way she'd hold up under questioning. Brave, she was. Tough? That was yet to be determined. She'd done well enough with Vera and Dodie, but...

He stepped forward. "I'll fetch the knife. You don't need to go."

"Of course I'm going."

"We'd have to go in right off High Street. Right, Neve?" Thane asked. "That's the only door even remotely accessible."

Neve nodded.

"There'll be loads of kingsmen in that area," Thane said to Aini. "And you know it."

"Look. You were right about the club. You're probably right now. But I'm going anyway. I have to. The Dionadair promised information. I'm going."

He shook his head. "Too dangerous."

Myles laughed. "Sorry, my lord Highlander. I don't think this one," he jabbed a thumb at her, "is going to swear fealty to you anytime soon." The colonial grinned and began mumbling something about the merits of female domination and leather.

Thane shot him a look, and Myles clapped a hand over his mouth.

Aini had her planning face on. "We'll find a spot to watch the vault entrance for an hour. See if any kingsmen are specifically assigned there."

"Yeah. Look for patterns of their movement, all spy-like," Myles said.

Thane felt sick. "Patterns? In an hour?"

"We don't have all the time in the world. The Dionadair might change their minds," Aini said. "And Father is suffering. I can't sit and observe them for days like we probably should."

Neve cleared her throat. "Why don't you go around lunch? Maybe they take a break patrolling or might at least be distracted by the crowds heading in and out of the eateries."

Aini nodded. "Good idea. And Myles is right."

"I am?" He made a fist again. "I am."

"We need a distraction," she said. "We could...report something to the kingsmen's office. Over the phone. Maybe they'd send their closest men to investigate, leaving the vault door unguarded."

Neve picked up Aini's phone from the table and handed it to her.

Aini set the device down. "Not from my phone. Not from any of ours. If the Campbells in the office recognize one of our numbers, they'll know I'm not following their directions to keep quiet about Father's abduction. They might...hurt him. Or worse. We have to find another phone to use."

"And what are you going to pretend to know about and report?" Thane asked.

This was getting messy. If Aini created some sort of ruckus, there'd be kingsmen everywhere. Some Campbells would recognize Thane. Some wouldn't. The English kingsmen who worked here in Edinburgh wouldn't. They weren't welcome at the Bluefoot or any other secret Campbell haunts.

"I wouldn't mention rebels," he said. "Keep it something small and simple, so they don't call in more kingsmen. It must be something the men in the area can deal with."

Aini twisted her gold ring around her finger, her gaze distant. "How about a mysterious package at Deacon Brodies Tavern?"

Myles made a face. "Like a bomb threat?"

"Yes. I mean, aye." Aini's cheeks went pink.

Neve smiled. "Just be yourself, Aini. Quit trying to be what you think you should. No need to fash yourself over your language."

"Fash?" Myles asked.

Thane tossed his coffee into the kitchen sink and rinsed the mug. "It means stress, or trouble."

"Thane. I wish you'd get over it and help me," Aini said sharply.

She could've saved her breath. "You know I will," he said.

"Then what? You don't like the plan? If you have any ideas, I'm open to them."

"It's not that." He wanted to tell her everything. But how could he? He was the enemy. It would ruin everything. It would blow his mission. And he had his mother to think about. If Aini could just be stalled until he figured a way out of all of this... "I think we should wait," he said.

"For what?"

"You need to think this through. It's no little thing to call something in, to make a report."

"I know that. I'll keep it anonymous. None of this is little." She tucked the map inside her shoulder bag. Her hands were still shaking and it tore at Thane's heart. "It is terrible and big and horrifying. But oh well." She practically shouted that last bit, then lowered her voice to add, "There's an old phone booth behind the hostel on Cockburn Street. Father used it once. We'll go straight out after I make the report and watch the vault door for kingsmen."

Neve and Myles wished them good luck, and Thane followed Aini outside, into the summer sun. He took a minute to close his eyes and pray for a better outcome than the one he currently had raging through his brain.

CHAPTER 13
THE VAULTS

Sea birds squawked overhead as Aini and Thane headed toward High Street. Three men in suits—Londoners, according to the accent—strolled into a pub, their ties bright pink, blue, and white. A handful of university students took sadly scant sandwiches from a narrow shop and called out to a friend across the street. Tourists in sunglasses meandered around, snapping pictures and bumping into one another. A few studied the king's latest news release on the public board. If everything went as planned, Aini would have the knife from the vision embedded in the brooch in less than an hour.

She tucked her hand into the crook of Thane's arm, hoping he was okay with that. Honestly, she wanted him here beside her being all stern and big. She knew the dangers they faced. Having a backup that could throw a punch and kept a knife wasn't a bad idea. She had to shake her head at herself. Two days ago she never would've thought something like that.

The rolled edge of Thane's worn button-down was smooth under her fingers, but his muscles beneath tensed. He shut his eyes briefly like her touch caused him pain. She stole a peek at his profile, with its peaked lips and strong chin. He wore a hoodie partly pulled up over his rumpled hair. He glanced back, then away, a reluctant grin tweaking one corner of his mouth. She smiled nervously, her insides fluttering.

The crowd thickened. A group of school-age kids bumped past, their parents mumbling apologies as they wove through, trying to catch them up. Urged into an orderly line by some kingsmen, a bus load of elderly tourists spoke French to one another.

Thane tugged his hood down, and Aini slipped on a funky, black hat she'd borrowed from Myles. If any Campbells had been watching, maybe now they'd lose them.

To the left, a kingsman scrubbed at some silver graffiti. Two thumbs crossed. The Dionadair's sign. Seemed Nathair Campbell, the king's vicious head of security, was having trouble stamping out the growing flame of rebellion.

A memory of the men and women accused of treason and shot down by Campbell's men in the middle of the Grassmarket courtyard splashed across Aini's mind. A sharp chill raked over her. Their wide eyes. The pooling blood. A rush of quiet like a wave washing over the gathered Edinburgh natives. No tourists had been there that day. Had Nathair Campbell made sure of that?

She blinked the memory away as they worked their way through tables of knick-knacks and tourists, and came out on High Street. A street performer in red gloves juggled knives on the pavement. Next to the man, the sun glinted off the shiny brass toe of the Hume statue. Her heart contracted, recalling the superstition Father had taught her about touching the toe for wisdom. An ache filled Aini.

Four kingsmen sauntered down the pavement opposite them,

eyeing the juggler. Street performers were permitted to have weapons for show as long as they weren't sharpened. The shortest kingsman held a hand out toward the performer. The juggler stopped tossing the knives and handed one, hilt first, to the kingsman.

Her hands sweating, she tightened her grip on Thane.

The kingsman said something to the performer and handed the dull weapon back.

"Here's Cockburn Street." Thane touched her hand.

She swallowed and headed toward the red phone booth. *Please let this work.*

Thane stood outside as she slid the door open. Lifting the receiver to her ear, she pressed the gold Crime Report button below the zero. The line rang and suddenly she wasn't so sure she could even talk.

A click. "CR line. What's your situation?" a gruff male voice said.

She tried to talk, but her tongue stuck to the roof of her mouth. *Go away, nerves.* "I...there's..."

"Are you an American colonial?"

"Yes. No. Why?"

Thane peered in, scowling.

"Only English and Scottish subjects may use this line," the voice said and it sounded like he was going to hang up.

"Wait! I'm a Scottish citizen."

"All right then. What is the problem?"

"I saw something strange in a tavern on High Street. A box. It was hidden...under a table in the back. It was black and there were wires going from it into the wall."

"When and what tavern?"

"Five minutes ago. Deacon Brodies."

"We'll check it out. Your Subject Identification Number,

please."

"I don't have my card with me."

"You don't...you must! Young lady, I fear—"

Aini hung up. Her heart clawed at her throat.

Thane popped in. "Did you do it?"

"Yeah, but he wanted my SI number."

"You didn't give it to them, did you?"

She shook her head. "I hung up."

Thane shrugged one shoulder. "Guess we'll have to wait and see if it works."

THE DOOR LEADING TO THE VAULTS HAD BEEN PAINTED BLACK and a strip of plastic tape fluttered from the lintel. One kingsman hung around the entrance and a padlock the size of Thane's fist hung from the door handle.

Around the corner, staying somewhat cloaked in a group of university students waiting for food at a place that only served baked potatoes, Aini pulled her pick set from her dress pocket. Her hands were steady, but sweat slicked her palms.

Thane's eyebrows went high. "You weren't bluffing about the lock-picking then, were you?"

The kingsman who paced back and forth in front of the vault door wasn't a Campbell. He wore no tartan, just black military pants. His eyes were half-closed as he watched his own boots. At least he wasn't a horrible Campbell.

"He's never going to leave, is he?" she whispered.

The walkie talkie on the man's belt made a scratching noise. He turned it off.

"Why isn't he answering that thing?" she asked. "I bet they're trying to call him now."

Another kingsman, this one in a blue and green Campbell

kilt, stalked down the road and met with the one they watched. She swallowed the growing lump in her throat, wanting more than anything to run at that man and demand to know where Father was and why they insisted on making life in Scotland so much more difficult than it needed to be.

Thane turned away and leaned against the restaurant's brick wall. A sheet including all the king's updated rules fluttered beside him, the words written in a jagged style. "Fantastic," he muttered, scanning the street.

The guard at the door talked as the Campbell threw a hand toward High Street.

"We should go." Thane squinted at the flow of people in the wide avenue.

"Not yet."

"We can't spend all day here, waiting for someone to spot you. Things will only get worse."

"I think they're leaving," Aini said.

Both men faced High now, the one all in black speaking into his walkie.

"They're not," Thane said.

"Five minutes."

"Aini."

"Thane."

The Campbell started back toward them, toward High and the crowd. With one look at the door to the underground vaults, the other kingsman followed him.

"Yes." Aini turned her face to the menu taped to the window and pretended to study the differences between prices for English and Scottish customers. The king was so cruel, so petty.

"They're gone. Let's go," he said.

The buildings shadowed them as they approached the taped-off door. There weren't any crowds here to hide them and they couldn't be sure when the kingsmen would be back.

At the padlock, Aini's tongue moved around in her mouth as she angled the pick up and left. The pick caught the mechanism inside the hunk of metal, but it slipped out of place. She grumbled. It'd been a while. A long while.

Thane leaned against the moss-covered wall near the door and crossed his arms like it was an average Williamsday afternoon, and they weren't trespassing into territory owned by the king. He really was good at pretending a casual attitude. Aini envied his self-control. Her nerves always had her in their grip; he seemed able to rein them in, to subdue them.

The pick finally dislodged the mechanism and the hook popped from its hole.

"Yes!" Aini shouted, then clapped a hand over her own mouth, watching for the kingsmen.

"Come on," Thane grumbled.

They scuttled through the door and shut it quietly and quickly. They had to hurry.

The crumbling steps dove into the darkness, and the air stilled, quiet as the dead.

"We probably have twenty minutes? What do you think?" A chill drew nails down Aini's neck as their steps echoed off the walls.

At the bottom, black tunnels stretched left and right into the bowels of the city. The odor of mildew and muck assaulted her nose. Raising a flashlight, she tried to remember Neve's directions.

"I'd say that's a good guess." Thane's voice seemed to surround her in the dark.

The ground sloped downward and Aini put a hand on the wall. "You know, Father told me about this place." The bricks were moist. Ugh. She pulled her hand back. "He said he got lost down here as a kid when Granny MacGregor brought him to the library." He'd told her about the hatch opening that hid beneath the tiles on the main floor, said all the kids in Edinburgh told stories about it. "He received the whipping of a lifetime when she finally found him." More tunnels loomed around every corner. Aini really hoped Neve's directions were right. "It's like a labyrinth." The walls felt too close and getting closer.

"Will you tell me again what the knife looked like?" Thane's voice rumbled behind her.

She knew what he was doing. He was distracting her from the walls, the stale air, her fear. She forgave him a little for trying to lord over her back at the townhouse.

"The hilt was made of very dark wood," she said as the image flickered through her mind.

"Bog oak."

A drip from the ceiling landed on Aini's cold nose, and she wiped it away. How many layers of ancient stone and dirt and filth were between her and the sky? A tremor bit into her and she gripped the flashlight more tightly. Were bodies really buried behind these walls?

"Bog oak. Yes," she said. "That's what Neve guessed." A rock caught the toe of her flat, and she pitched forward.

Thane caught her under the arm. Although he released her immediately, his fingers left a subtle warmth behind. "Should've worn smarter shoes," he said, not unkindly.

"Black flats work in all situations."

"Did that rock not get the memo about the flats?"

She glared at him over her shoulder and shined the light in his face.

He raised his eyebrows over his glasses. "Sorry. Go on about the knife."

She gave him an eye-narrowing before turning back around. "It was big. Big as your forearm."

"So the man in your...vision said eighty-five, you're certain, aye?"

A rat scurried somewhere not far enough away.

"The man in the vision didn't really *say* it," Aini said. "He thought it. He imprinted the idea, the number, on the brooch. That was the first time I'd ever seen a vision where the person knew they were leaving emotions and thoughts."

She kicked yet another rock across the floor. It clattered until it met with something in the dark and went quiet. Another chill wrapped arms around her.

"Hmm. The man knew he was doing it?" Thane asked.

She nodded. "It scared me."

"So does this wee tunnel, but you're here."

Some of her fear melted at his praise. "Into the dark, to be free of the dark."

"Aye. I'd take physical dark over informational dark any day."

As the tunnel opened up a little, she noticed Thane looking at her, his eyebrows drawn together, knuckle absently rubbing across his bottom lip. Like she was a chemistry formula he couldn't solve.

The flashlight flickered. She smacked the end of it until it brightened.

Before she could focus on anything, the scent of whisky flew into the air. A figure came around the corner and hit her.

A man. A fist. Pain.

Circles of red and gray floated in front of her eyes, and her heart beat wildly.

Thane shouted and moved away. Then she realized she was sitting on the floor, holding herself up on her elbows. She hadn't blacked out, but everything had just happened too quickly for her to keep up. She blinked. Blinked again. And there was Thane's face, his hair falling into his eyes. Pain pounded like drums in her skull. The flashlight sat beside her, illuminating Thane in its blue-white light.

"Aini, please. Say something. I'm going to murder that..."

He put his warm hands on either side of her face and Aini's fuzzy brain didn't stop her sigh of pleasure in time. A smile spread across Thane's face. She shut her eyes, cheeks burning.

"Wh...what happened?"

The warmth of his hands disappeared. "A man tried to take your purse."

"He hit me." A knot throbbed on her head, above her ear. She cracked her eyes open and sat up, Thane's hand on her back. "Where is he now?"

Her small bag still hung securely over her shoulder. Thane's gaze flicked to it, then to the nearest corridor that hung open and black like a ghost's groaning mouth. Blood ran down his knuckles.

"Are you hurt?" Her hand flew to the splatter of red coloring his shirt.

"I'm fine. It's him that's hurt." The muscles at the back of his jaw flexed. "He's gone now." He helped her stand. "Do you feel well enough to go on?"

Her knit dress was twisted around her middle, so she tugged it back into place and adjusted her leggings. "I have to." Pain banged against her eyes with each word.

He nodded and handed over the flashlight just as it blinked, faded, and went dark. Immediately his hands were on hers, trailing their way to the light.

"I'll check the batteries," he said as she released the tool to him.

Musty air brushed past. She coughed and squeezed her hands

into fists, longing for the sight of the open sky and the feel of clean air.

A quiet crack sounded above them.

Aini stepped back, catching up on Thane's foot. "Are you hearing this too?" she whispered.

The sound of metal on metal told her he was unscrewing the base of the flashlight. "Aye." He didn't sound scared, only wary. Like he was keeping an eye on a large dog he didn't know.

In front of them, something thudded against the wall.

The hairs on the back of Aini's neck rose. "What was that?" It could've been the mugger returning.

"I'm not sure, but it's not the man who attacked you. I promise you that."

"How do you know?" She couldn't keep the panic out of her voice.

"It's all right, hen," he said softly. "These noises—it's just a wandering spirit. Not an angry one."

The air blew past again, cold and old. "I think Neve was right about the ghosts not wanting us down here."

A click and another metal scrape later, a blue-white glow flooded from the end of the flashlight and spilled light over Thane's sharp nose and deep eyes behind his glasses. He handed her the flashlight and they started down the corridor again, her head aching like something was trying to crawl out of her left temple. She needed to go home and ice her head, but she'd probably never get the chance to find this knife again. Without it, Owen and the others wouldn't tell her what they knew about Father.

To their right, six brick alcoves sat in two levels. Black numbers marked each arch. Seventy-eight, seventy-nine.

"Look." Thane pointed at a spot past her.

She shone the light in that direction. Another arched area was labeled with numbers.

And there was eighty-five.

Excitement zipped through her. She took the light and propped it between two rocks on the floor. The entire room bloomed into view. Pits and cracks in the stone walls had been repaired with rough cement. Other spots were brown and black as if touched by fire. Vault eighty-five consisted of two bricked, arched spaces for storage. The bottom one was big enough to walk into, the top was the size of a small fireplace.

The outer wall of the alcove was rough under her fingers, but there weren't any loose stones. Nothing seemed out of the ordinary, not that she really knew what to look for.

Copying her movements, Thane ran his large hands up and down the bricks on the other side of the vaulted space. Bits of brick and little plumes of dust fell in the wake of his fingers.

A sneeze blew out of Aini. On tiptoe, she reached into the smaller compartment above her head. Dirt, little more than dust, coated her fingertips as she searched the edge of the wall that divided this vault from the next. Half way to the back, the corner of a stone lay a finger's length higher than its neighbors. She inhaled, her heart speeding up. With one hand over the lip to pull herself higher, she tried to slip her fingers over the back corner of the stone. Her arm just wasn't long enough. She dropped back, her toes trembling from the effort of rising up.

"Thane, can you help me?" A muscle in her neck and back twitched. She'd stretched too far. "I found something."

Looking up through his black lashes, he linked his fingers to make a step. "I'll give you a boost."

"You sure?"

"You weigh about as much as a bowl of porridge. Think I can handle it." He frowned and jerked his head at his hands.

Headache worsening, Aini put her shoe in his makeshift step and pushed up. To his credit, Thane didn't grunt as he lifted her high enough to bend over the rough edge of the upper alcove. He put hands around her ankles, holding her steady as she extended an arm. She prayed he wasn't staring at her backside.

She squinted into the near dark. Instead of being surrounded by aged mortar, the stone in question was framed by black space. Leaning all the way on her stomach, with the vault's edge biting into her, she grabbed the stone and wiggled it. With a grating sound, it came free.

"There's a hollow here." Her teeth clacked together. The walls crowded in on her and stole her air.

"All right. Slow that breathing, lass."

She nodded, drawing the chilly air in, and reached into the hollow the brick had concealed and blocked up. The space cooled her fingers immediately. Stone scraped the back of her hand, but there wasn't anything there. Just a hole. And she'd been so sure. Her lungs tight, she put her other hand on the bricks near her head.

"It's not here."

"Come now," Thane said softly. "Why don't you get down? You've—"

As she started to pull her hand out of the hollow, something slightly pointed on the space's wall dragged across her pinkie finger. "Wait!"

She pinched the object and tugged hard. It broke from its hiding place with a scraping sound, and she flew backward, landing in a heap on top of Thane. Their fall knocked the flashlight off its rock supports and illumination swiped across the room like a lighthouse beam, halting at the back corner and leaving them in near darkness.

Her back to Thane's stomach, she sat up holding the item

she'd pulled from the vault, but couldn't get her feet under her. Thane grabbed her arms and tried to help, mumbling something in rough Gaelic. As they untangled, every line and curve of his body pressed into hers.

Finally, she stood, the object in hand.

Thane grabbed the light. "Is that..."

A leather sheath. Black hilt. Despite her aching head and the walls being too close and the air too musty, a light of hope warmed her.

This was the knife from the vision.

Every three inches or so, bronze scalloped fittings wrapped around the knife's case. The bog oak hilt had been carved into the shape of twisting ropes that came together at a bronze tip.

"This is definitely the one I saw, the one that man embedded into the vision."

But she hadn't seen any visions when she touched it. She frowned.

"Maybe you have to touch the blade itself?" Thane suggested. He was so good at reading her body language. He seemed to know her worries and how to potentially solve them before she said a word.

"Good thought. Let's go. I don't want to have a vision here, with that man around and this awful place's walls closing in on me."

A shower of glistening drops fell from the ceiling near the door they'd come through.

"Ugh." She shook it off and Thane smiled a little.

AT THE DOOR, THANE TURNED THE KNOB. A SLICE OF SUN blinded them.

"I'll go first," Aini said.

Thane looked like he wanted to argue, but he stepped aside.

Heart cracking like fireworks, Aini peered out. Crowds filled the main road beyond this one. A kingsman hurried down that main road, but his eyes weren't on the door to the vaults. He was headed away toward the sound of a man screaming. Someone was being arrested. Her stomach turned.

She nudged Thane with an elbow. "I think it's safe for us. Come on."

Outside, Aini ran a hand over the back of her sweat-damp neck and sighed heavily. It was beautiful to be out of that dark, close place. Taking another good look around for kingsmen, she gripped the knife and studied its ornate hilt.

"How are we going to get this thing home?" she whispered. The crowd's rumble reacted to another of the arrested man's shrieks for his family. A sudden thought had her leaning against Thane's solid form. "What if they're taking him for the fake bomb report I made?"

"No. This happens constantly. What are the chances?"

"I don't know. It could've been my fault."

"I doubt it. Now, will you let me take the knife? I can fit it in my waistband easier than you." His eyes were wide and sincere.

If he were caught, he'd be tried, convicted, and imprisoned. Or shot like a traitor.

"Fine."

With a curt nod, he took the knife from her, his eyes scanning the street, and hid the weapon behind him, beneath his untucked button-down. The hilt bulged a little, but she prayed it wouldn't draw any attention.

CHAPTER 14
A TANGLE OF LIES

T hane's nerves jumped and buzzed as they continued down the side street, taking a less populated and winding way back to the townhouse.

That evil creature Rodric.

He couldn't believe his cousin had attacked Aini in the vaults. There was no way it was on orders—outright attacking the people Thane was meant to spy on? Not very undercover. The ape. Anger lashed through Thane. He must've been following them. Rodric's stupid warning from earlier rang through Thane's memory. *Don't forget who your master is. I'll be sure to tell him you've gone soft.* Thane knew very well who *him* was and that Rodric had overheard the bit about Lewis's daughter, about Aini. Rodric was playing with Thane. His cousin was such a sick waste of space.

Grime lined the doorways and windows of the leaning buildings. One lonely tree drooped in its squared off piece of dirt in the pavement. A tattoo parlor boasted a sign in the shape of a fire breathing dragon with wings and slitted eyes. The road curved past an abandoned hostel.

A kingsman appeared around the corner.

"Just keep on," he whispered.

The man said something into his walkie and tucked it back into his belt, glancing once at them as they passed.

"You there," he said.

Thane and Aini froze.

Thane turned and made easy eye contact with the man. "Aye?"

The man's jacket was jet black against the ash-colored buildings as his beady-eyed gaze flicked over Thane's middle. The man rubbed a hand over the back of his tidy brown head of hair. It seemed like he didn't really want to be where he was. Thane knew the feeling too well.

"What do you have there, Scot? Show me what's under that shirt," the man said. His accent said he was from somewhere in northern England. Lancashire maybe.

If the kingsman did take Thane in, his identity would come out; he'd be released, quietly and for some well-crafted, false reason. He had only to show the man the back of his necklace, which bore the Campbell crest. It'd be difficult, to say the least, explaining his release to Aini without exposing his cover.

"I don't know what you mean." Thane gave a simple smile to the kingsman.

The kingsman frowned. "You have something there. Perhaps a souvenir or..." He gave Thane a mean grin, looking ready for a fight now.

Thane took the knife from his waistband, and Aini stepped forward.

The kingsman's eyes scoured the ancient-looking blade in its black sheath. "So we *do* have something to discuss."

"It belongs to her family," Thane said. "We were only having it appraised." He offered the knife for closer inspection.

Fingers lighting on his gun, the kingsman leaned closer.

Thane eased Aini behind him.

"I'm sorry," the man said to Aini. Now his glaikit smile was real—the complete opposite to the wolf's smirk he'd given Thane. "I'll have to take this." The kingsman nodded at the knife. "I won't report you because I can tell you're not a rebel. Too pretty and smart, eh?" He grinned and gave her a thorough once over.

Thane's stomach clenched. The kingsman could not be allowed to take the knife. Well, it was too bad, but violence couldn't be avoided here.

Thane whistled. "Eh, lover boy." He threw a fist into the idiot's face.

Aini's hands went to her mouth.

With a groan, the kingsman fell to his hands and knees.

"Come on." Thane tucked the knife away and grabbed Aini's slender fingers.

They ran down one street and then another. He was mad for heading this way. He should've fled north. The windows in most of the buildings here sported jagged breaks or nailed down boards. And there, up ahead, was the Bluefoot.

The kingsman would be here in a heartbeat. There was nothing for it. Thane would have to take Aini in through the back door and hope the lot inside would keep to their drinks and not mind him. And pray Aini wouldn't ask too many questions.

"Are we lost?" she asked, grimacing at the filth in the street and the swear words sprayed on the buildings.

He laughed bitterly. "No, hen. I've been to the worst of... never mind." He dragged her into the small space between the buildings, then through the hidden back door of the pub.

"What is this?" Aini's eyes grew as she studied the swinging section of the wall that made up the passage into the Bluefoot.

Smoke and the smell of fried fish choked the air. Two men leaned against the bar top, talking to the keep and drinking pints. Their black kingsman jackets hung over a nearby chair and their Campbell kilts were bright against the dark wood of the bar. Another man laughed with a woman near the stairs.

"I don't like this," Aini hissed. "Those are Campbells!"

God above, this was a mess. Thane pulled her to the back, past the stairs, under the balcony, and into the workout room. The flickering light shuddered off the heavy bag and red flooring.

"Do you come here a lot? Why is the door hidden? You need to stop shoving me around and tell me what is going on."

She was going to get them caught with her blathering. He didn't want anyone seeing her here. Except Bran. "Just come on. It's better if you don't know anything about this place."

"We're well past what's better for me, don't you think? How is hiding in a place where there are Campbells smarter than running?"

"The man will have called reinforcements. We wouldn't have made it another two minutes." He had to lie. There was nothing for it. He had to add another layer of deceit to this or she wasn't going to give in. He knew that determined look on her face. The girl was like a pit bull. "My friend Bran...he...he has connections with the Campbells."

"What? Is he horrible? Why are you friends with him?"

"The Campbells aren't all horrible. They've been helping Scotland...well, until recently."

"Until they decided to start competing with the king for the title of Worst Ever?"

He had to calm her down, steer this conversation. "Bran

wishes he didn't have to...work with them. But he tangled with the Campbells when he was very young—just out of secondary school. You can't just tell the most powerful clan in Scotland to leave off when you choose."

Aini's shoulders dropped and she let out a breath, staring at the heavy bag. "I suppose you're right about that." She bit her lip, her fear probably coming back as her anger receded.

"I can hide the knife under the floorboard in my room. With the brooch," Aini whispered. "If we can just get there. That way, if they come to question us—"

Thane shushed her and suddenly Cora was there, frowning. She gave Aini a tentative smile. "May I help you somehow?" Cora asked.

"Aye. There's a..." He peered toward the stairs where the man and woman joked. If they heard him worry about a kingsman, their ears would surely perk up and he'd be in an even more awkward situation. He lowered his voice. "There's a kingsman after us." Pinching his lips, he looked from Cora to Aini, willing Cora to understand what was going on.

Cora's mouth opened, but she shut it again, her brow tangling.

Thane glared at her.

Her face smoothed slightly and she said, "Well, all right then." She pushed them toward the stairs. "Up here."

Aini stared at the scarves flowing from the ceiling. "Thane—"

He put a hand over her mouth. "Stay quiet. Please." He had to keep this as simple as possible.

She nodded, trust and mistrust warring in those big, cat-like eyes of hers.

Cora led them up the creaking stairs to the row of closed

doors that faced the open area of the balcony. The rest of the pub spread out below them like a circus after hours.

The couple at the bottom of the stairs went quiet, and Thane looked over his shoulder to give them a glare. The man mumbled something, and the woman laughed.

Thane had never been upstairs. He knew full well what sometimes went on here.

Cora stopped them at the last door. "Go inside. You'll want to see Bran as usual, I'm guessing. And we'll keep the man away from here if that's what you need."

"Thank you, Cora."

"No bother," she said quickly, not meeting his eyes.

Thane opened the door for Aini. "I'm sorry to take you to a place like this." Heat flooded his face. "I just know Bran can help."

Arms crossed over her chest, Aini took three steps to the bed at the back wall. It was covered in a dingy, calico print duvet.

A knock made them both jump. "Have fun in there!" a man's unfamiliar voice said.

Aini's cheeks matched the red in the calico print. Thane was fairly certain his own did too.

He swallowed and rapped a fist against the door. "Be gone with you."

A laugh echoed from outside, then faded along with the sound of footsteps.

Thane rubbed his face.

Another knock drummed against the door. *What now?* Thane cracked it open to see Bran's warm eyes and bushy eyebrows.

"Do you need me, friend?" Bran's gaze stayed on Thane's face. Most men, knowing what these rooms were for, would've peeked right over Thane's shoulder. But Bran was not most men.

Thane nodded. "I have a...friend here."

He stepped aside and opened the door fully. Aini gave Bran a wave. Bran smiled at her.

"We have a weapon," Thane said. "And a kingsman followed us. He's seen the thing and won't leave us alone now that he has."

"There's news," Bran whispered. "Nathair has ordered every kingsman in Scotland to pledge allegiance solely to the Campbells. It's being done quietly. On paper though. And I strongly doubt the king knows of this."

Thane gripped the side of the door. Edging out of the room, he kept an eye on the pub's first floor, watching the front entrance. "It's madness."

"Aye. It is that," Bran said.

As Bran opened his mouth to say something more, the front door of the pub banged open, knocking the codekeeper off his stool. The kingsman raged in, blood dripping from his nose.

"Anyone seen a big, fair fellow about twenty or so?" he shouted across the pub. "I don't care that this is an illegal gambling den. I need to find the man."

Thane made a fist and pressed it against his mouth. "What can I do, Bran?" He flicked a glance at Aini.

Bran's gaze followed the line of Thane's eyes and clicked his tongue. "Hmm. Wait for a count of ten, then go out the window."

"The window?" Aini leaned to look out the glass.

"The roof's not a far jump," Bran said. "You'll be fine. The building next door has a fire ladder down the back side."

Before Thane could argue, Bran pushed him back and shut the door in his face, his deep voice booming over the pub's TV.

"Saw the very man," Bran shouted. "Ran right past to the next bus stop. Just down to the corner."

Heart thudding, Thane jerked the tight window open. "...eight, nine...go, Aini."

She rolled her eyes and huffed, but climbed out. Thane followed, and they stood on a slim ledge outside the window, staring at the neighboring low roof.

Aini dusted old paint off her hands. "Well," she said shakily. "No use waiting around. The roof isn't coming any closer."

Thane reached an arm out as she leaped over the four foot space, her hair flying behind her like a cloak. His heart jumped too. Right into his brain. His hands went to his knees as she landed safely in a crouch.

She scowled at him over her shoulder, then stood.

First bending his knees, Thane exploded off the ledge and ended up a good foot beyond where she'd landed. The roof's black top pulled heat from the sun and shimmered in the air around them.

Aini put a hand up to block the light. Her features worked into a frown. "Did you do a lot of roof-jumping in your childhood too? Along with the punching and kicking? And befriending Campbell lackeys?"

She was too smart for her own good.

"Aye."

He didn't wait for her to ask more, but hurried to the rusty handles of a ladder. He went first, averting his eyes as she, still in that short dress with leggings that clung to every curve, made her way down after him. The knife's sheathed tip dug into his right buttock as he climbed. He paused to adjust it.

At the bottom, they took off for the townhouse, him leading the way and hoping against all that the kingsman would be put off their trail and that none in the pub would remember Aini's face. As if they wouldn't. Half Indonesian and more bonnie than any girl he'd seen, they'd remember. But there was nothing to be done for it.

As they ran, the sun burning their heads, Thane wondered

where this all would lead, what the endgame would be. Once they gave the Dionadair the knife, then what? Would the rebels tell Aini what they knew of Lewis? What was their motivation behind the telling?

He didn't like it. Not a bit. This was a dangerous game Aini was playing and Thane wished she'd just go back to the lab and stay there. If Rodric heard about the knife, if he found out Thane had it within his reach and didn't turn it in to the clan, he'd be insane about it. Nathair would want to at least *see* this artifact the rebels were going on about. Even if it wasn't really what they thought it was.

As if she knew his thoughts, Aini glanced at him. "Thanks for all the help," she said, her words breathy from running. They made it to the townhouse and she unlocked the door and went inside. "I am sorry—"

"New rule," he said. She gave him a scathing look. She liked to be the one doing the bossing. "No more apologizing," he said.

Taking a deep breath, she nodded. "Agreed. May I have the knife, please?"

He pulled the weapon from his back and held it out to her, a knight to his queen.

"Are you going to tell me more about Bran and that pub?" she asked archly.

Thane looked at the floor.

"They knew you there."

Aini raised an eyebrow.

"Bran deals cards there sometimes. For extra money. I gamble with him. He's a good man and I don't want to end our friendship just because he has a less than perfect...situation."

"I like him."

"He's a good guy."

She held the knife closer. "And so are you."

They stood quiet, the compliment burning down Thane's walls.

"I'm going to examine the knife. See if there's a vision in it."

"Of course. Yes. I'll be...around if you need anything."

With a serious look on her face, she disappeared into her room.

He'd told her more than he should've, but she needed something to chew on or she wouldn't have let it drop.

Heading for the kitchen, where it sounded like Myles and Neve were arguing jokingly, Thane raked fingers through his hair. His eyes filled with heat, moisture. He'd not cried in an age, but now, he wanted to. Seeing Aini in the Campbell pub. Her innocence, her goodness, against that place filled with people who were daily being drawn further away from doing right... His clan seemed driven now by a madman, by Nathair. A prickling ran over Thane like one thousand knives scratching his flesh. Willing the wetness in his eyes back to where it'd come from, Thane put his mask-like, blank expression on and went to the kitchen to wait on Aini.

CHAPTER 15
A CASTLE ON THE SEA

S itting on the bed, Aini set the knife on her lap and took a deep breath. Her head still ached and her jaw was sore, but she couldn't think about resting. Not even if she'd wanted to.

Thane spent time at a secret Campbell gambling den. He had a friend tied up with the Campbells. She rubbed her temples. Things were going from bad to worse.

The ancient weapon gave off an odd smell. Metal, certainly, but also mildew and some kind of herb. Sage, maybe. Cloves? It was so strange, a scent that stirred an irresistible need to inhale it again, to try and pin it down. A deep, quiet fear laced the curiosity, like the knife had been touched by something not normal, something not of this world.

Lifting the age-old weapon, she wrapped one hand firmly around the cool, black hilt and slid the steel from its ornate bronze and leather sheath. She lay the casing beside her and held the vicious-looking thing vertically. The light coming from her lamp flashed off its slanting angles. It weighed her arm down, heavier than it'd seemed earlier. Shadows danced in the corner of her room, echoing the movement of the light on the steel. The ceiling fan whisked air over her head.

The other apprentices knocked around down the hall. Myles's colonial banjo music carried through the house like sprites bouncing off the stone walls and wooden floors.

Thane's voice punched through the noise. "Turn that down!" His *ow* came out as *oo*.

Aini pressed her fingers against the flat side of the knife.

With a shiver, the vision dropped over her.

Seer! *The wide-mouthed man in the old style clothes, the same from the first vision, spoke.* Waymark Wall! *His face dissolved.*

Sandstone walls rose from a green lawn. Castle ruins. The structure was weather worn, the edges soft. Holes marred the once solid construction. A marking was set in one wall. A spiral. The curling line spun until it morphed into a sea bird, then a flock. The birds squawked. Waves rushed and roared, gray and sea-green, in the background. A piece of land hunched like an animal's back in the field of ocean. Then that odd, black stone appeared again—the one from the brooch's vision—its surface carved with swirls too. It stood chest-high, hollowed like a seat.

The images flickered, and the real world washed them away.

Aini's wood-paneled room appeared again. The rose carvings on her bed posts. The light on the metal. The ceiling fan pushed a piece of tickling hair over her face as she sheathed the blade. Her legs shook as she crossed the room to the vanity and jotted down what she'd seen on a slip of white paper.

Castle ruins.

A spiral carved into a wall.

The ocean.

The black stone marked like the wall, with spirals.

Pulling the stool out from the vanity, she sat, her head splintering.

The information from the vision explained nothing. Nothing.

A picture of Father sat on her vanity. She traced his face with a trembling finger. Her mother had taken the photo the day she'd presented her *wayang* show, a Balinese shadow puppet performance. Seated on a stool with one leg crossed over the other, Father looked on as she held her cutout puppet in front of a white sheet. A traditional coconut husk lamp lit the cloth from behind. Mother had helped her make it. Father's eyes were cinched up, partnering with his smile, as he focused on Aini, a nine-year-old at the time.

Keeping hold of the knife, Aini lifted the picture and carried it to bed. She curled into a ball around the wooden picture frame, and with one hand gripping the antique knife, let exhaustion take her under.

～

"WAKE UP, SWEETHEART." MYLES'S VOICE FLOATED ABOVE her head.

His face and Neve's slowly came into focus. Myles's eyes were bright and Neve's were pinched with worry.

"I'm glad you had some rest," Neve said.

Thane snored lightly in the rocking chair by Aini's bed. His glasses were askew and one of his long legs stretched over her duvet, his dirty boot marking the fabric. She frowned, but a glow filled her chest. His mouth turned down, and a flicker of sadness, or maybe frustration, wrinkled his brow as he dreamed. Soft light draped over his exposed throat and the proud lines of his collarbone. The scent of candles and chemicals wafted from his clothing.

"How long has he been there?" she asked Neve and Myles.

"A while," Myles said. "I know you don't feel well, but...did you see anything with the knife?"

An island. The sea. A castle.

The vision flooded back and she sat up. "Should I wait for him to wake up?"

Myles's trainers squeaked on the floor wax as he walked to where Thane slept. He shook Thane's arm roughly. "It's almost midnight, man. We need your brains and bulk on this mission."

Thane blinked, pushing his glasses into place. His eyes found Aini and he heaved a sigh. He pulled his leg off the bed and stood to check his phone. He groaned.

"Bad news?" She pointed to the phone.

"No. I just didn't sleep so well."

"A bad dream?"

"Not so much bad as it is confusing," he said. "Same one I always have."

He didn't seem to want to share. Letting it drop, she placed the picture of her father back on the vanity.

"The knife did hold a vision." Her note crinkled in her hand. The whole day and night felt like one big dream. "I saw castle ruins, birds, and that strange stone again. The ruins sat on the coast somewhere. A spiral marked one of the walls. Does any of that sound familiar, Neve? You know Scotland's landmarks."

Neve crossed her legs, making the bed squeak. "There are a few ruins that sit at the sea. I'll have to think. Something about that marking is tickling the back of my head."

"A spiral?" Thane asked.

Aini nodded. "Ring any bells for you?"

He looked away. "For a second, it reminded me of something. But...no."

She found a dark ruby ribbon Father bought for her years ago, maybe at Christmas, and tied it into her hair.

"Are we going to The Origin to show the rebels the knife?" Neve asked.

"I guess," Aini said. "But should I bring the knife *and* the brooch?"

With paint-stained fingers, Myles drummed a beat on his thighs. "I say hide the goods. That way, you'll have something to bargain with."

"I have to show them the knife. If I'm going to get any information out of them, I have to do that at least. But I can hide the brooch."

Thane pocketed his phone. "You're sure I can't talk you out of this?" His voice was cold as the dull morning after a great party.

"You know I have to do this," she said, quiet and sure.

"Aye."

It almost sounded like he'd given up. She tried very hard not to let his lack of faith crush her determination to find a way out of this mess, a path back to a life with her father.

Myles marched into the hallway, Neve following him. Thane stayed behind, an unreadable look on his face and his hands in his hair. He'd put on a thin and wide-necked, ivory sweater, and for once, his trousers weren't well on their way to totally unusable.

Remembering how she'd tripped in the vaults, Aini tied on a pair of flat boots. "Myles," she called out to him, "being knocked unconscious is not something to ignore. I wish you'd stay home."

"No chance. Besides, I heard you were hit too. A mugger, right?"

"Yes."

"You need all of us," Myles said. "End of discussion."

"You sound like me," Aini mumbled.

"I know. So bossy and sensible. Neve," he said, his voice

echoing down the hallway outside her door. "Say something I can turn into a dirty joke. I'm not feeling like myself."

Shaking her head, Aini dislodged the loose floorboard near the foot of her bed. Thane's gaze burned the back of her head, but he stayed quiet. Aini's childhood diary sat inside the hidden spot beneath the floor, dusty and full of forgotten, naive poetry. She took the brooch from the vanity and nestled it beside her diary. The board back in place, she stood and dusted her hands.

Fighting panic, she took a slouchy sweater from the armoire and slipped it on. Thane lifted the bog oak knife from the bed, sheathed it neatly, and handed it to Aini. Like Thane had done before, she tucked the weapon into the waistband of her leggings. Her dress slid easily over it, and the sweater covered its odd shape pretty well. Her mind wrapped around a new list of things to do. None of them were simple.

Number One: manage not to panic and get to the club without anyone seeing the weapon.

Number Two: show the rebels the artifact.

Number Three: keep eyes on the exit and listen to what they had to say.

Number Four: use the information to develop a plan to help Father. Even if he had done something unthinkable, he was still her father.

"Are you coming, Thane?" she asked, walking into the hallway and working the words so they didn't show how much she wanted him to say *yes*.

Without a word, he came up behind her, his warmth a solid comfort at her back. He held up a finger for her to wait, then ran through the kitchen. His boots pounded up the lab stairs. A minute later, he returned with a flat bag sort of thing with a strap and buckle. He lifted his shirt and secured the bag to his side, buckling the strap over the distractingly nice lines of his bare stomach.

"What's that?" Aini asked as they trailed Neve and Myles outside.

Talking in whispers, Myles and Neve passed under the skinny maple at the base of the townhouse's front stairs.

Thane smoothed his hair—a valiant, yet fruitless move—and regarded the rising moon before opening his mouth.

Aini raised an eyebrow like a weapon. "Save it. I know what you're going to say. The less I know the better. You know I'm not okay with that answer."

Thane shook his head and chuckled.

But she actually trusted him. The fact didn't sit easy on her shoulders. He was a rule-breaker, her opposite in so many ways, but his crooked path put him by her side. He cared for her, for her father, for Myles and Neve. He'd proved it. When he broke rules, it was for a good reason.

Thane clenched and unclenched his fists. His boots splashed through a shallow puddle left by the street cleaning machines. Aini sidestepped the murky water. The moon's blue light oozed off everything—the flat pavement, a tall street lamp missing its bulb, the massive wall that surrounded Greyfriars Cemetery. The quiet between them grew, the weight of it pressing on Aini's chest. It was so obvious he wanted to say something, but was afraid to do it.

"Thane, just tell me."

His eyes widened. "I said, the less you know—"

"I'm not talking about whatever you have in your little bag there. I'm talking about the other thing you need to spill."

He swallowed and stared at the pavement. "There's nothing."

"Whatever it is, I'll understand. You've been amazing about all my secrets."

"It's not that easy. I...I want..." He shoved his hands in his pockets.

"When you're ready, I'm here," she said. "And I'm not telling anyone. Not about the gambling or the Campbells or Bran. Don't worry."

Speeding up, he mumbled something like "...probably shouldn't be..."

Aini pulled on his sleeve. "Come on. It can't be that big of a deal. Not after all this."

Wincing, he said, "Ha. Right. Well, when we finish this mad quest you're on. Maybe...maybe I can tell you."

He probably had a gambling debt. Or public fighting on his record. Both. She didn't like it, but it didn't mean she couldn't trust him in important ways, ways that mattered.

They caught up to Myles and Neve. Myles had linked arms with Neve, but she detached from him and slowed to walk beside Aini.

"What will we do if you have trouble getting into the club again?" Neve asked. "Will they be looking for you?"

Aini shrugged. "They told me to bring the knife. I bet they'll find me."

Darkness swamped the street. The stillness crept along Aini's scalp. The nearby grocery's windows were black, the fruit and cereal left alone in the night. A car drove by, its engine whining about the hour.

"It's not open," Thane said as they neared the club.

No music drummed from the interior of the former cathedral and no light spilled from the stained glass window above their heads.

"It's WAN." She'd forgotten this was Weekly Address Night, when everyone gathered around the TV to listen to the latest mandates from the king. There was a new one, something about marriage between English and Scottish citizens. Ridiculous.

She led the group to the door.

Thane touched the place where his hidden bag hung around his body, and curiosity nudged Aini. She tied her questions up inside her and ignored their struggle for freedom.

Myles noticed Thane adjusting the bag though. "What do you have there, big man?"

Eyeing the club's gothic, arched door, Thane said, "Our escape plan."

"Um..." Myles ran a hand over the geometric designs on his bright blue shirt. "Care to explain?"

"Later, pal. Let's get this over with."

Myles began singing another Mint song. "*Be brave, bind boring burdens blue...*"

"That one truly makes no sense," Thane said. "Blue? Really?"

Myles crossed his arms. "You know nothing about poetry."

Aini put a hand on the door knob. "Should I knock or..."

Rolling his eyes, Myles kicked the door open and Neve squeaked in surprise.

"Subtle," Aini said.

Myles grinned with all his teeth.

Thane pursed his lips and nodded. "Well done, colonial."

The inside of the club smelled like old cigarettes and sour beer. It wasn't nearly as sexy without all the fancy lights and wild music.

"Hello?" Aini called out into the darkness, walking quickly toward the stairs that led to the room where she'd met Vera and Dodie.

A man burst from the corner and threw a sack over Thane's head.

CHAPTER 16
ATTACK

Aini's heart jolted. She started toward Thane. Myles and Neve shouted, and rough hands grabbed Aini from behind. Thane called her name and almost managed to toss his attacker over his shoulder, even with the sack over his head. People came out of every shadow, every corner. They snatched Neve and Myles, covering their heads with burlap like they had Thane. Aini caught one frightening flash of her friends, faceless, before she too was blinded. Myles's muffled and creative swearing echoed in the empty club as they dragged them back toward the door.

The night air hit Aini's forearms and an engine rumbled nearby, its smell of petrol and oil strong. Hands pushed Aini into a vehicle of some sort and onto a cold seat. The antique knife poked her back and began to slide out of her waistband.

Someone who smelled strangely like horse and sea air began to tie her hands with scratchy twine. Her pulse rammed against her wrists, neck, and temples like her blood wanted out, and the knife, pressing painfully into her spine, didn't make things any better.

"Sorry for the treatment." The man's voice was gravelly and calm. "But we know you and yours are fighters. We need you to come along nicely, then we'll have a good talk at the end of this."

He pushed her farther down the seat.

"Easy," she snapped, kicking out in his general direction. Something hard blocked her foot, most likely a gear shift or console.

"Aini?" Neve was suddenly beside her.

"I'm here," Aini answered, hating the fear in her own voice.

The vehicle's door slammed. Another opened. There was grunting, and the car or truck or whatever they were in moved around with all the activity. The radio blared guitars, a measured drumbeat, and a woman's soaring voice. She guessed their abductor was coming around to the driver's side.

"This is one heck of a welcoming party," Myles said from behind, making Aini jump.

"You're here too?" she asked, her hands like ice.

"Myles." Thane's voice, coming from beside Myles, eased her heart a little. "Stay quiet. Don't give them anything to use against you."

"What are you, some hostage situation expert?" Myles said. "You'd think being every girl's wish on a four leaf clover would be enough."

"Shut it, colonial. Save your nonsense for later. He'll be back in here in a breath."

The door of the vehicle they'd been tossed into creaked open. The seat eased toward the driver's side, and the same man said, "Comfortable? Good. Now keep still and everything'll be all right. Just taking a wee trip."

Aini's eyes strained to see in the dark of the black-dyed

burlap bag. "Are you Dionadair?" The blood rushed away from her face. A memory of gunshots exploded through her mind.

Neve made a little noise and bumped her shoulder.

The man laughed. "You're a brave one, aren't you? That's good."

"Why?" Aini wiggled her hands to loosen the ties' hold on her wrists.

"Keep quiet." Thane's voice was low and strained like he was in pain. "Please."

"You might want to listen to your friend," the man said.

The vehicle lurched and turned. Aini leaned into Neve. Sweat covered Aini's palms and back. She bounced an impatient foot on the floor as the axles croaked. The sounds of traffic faded, giving way to the hush of speed on an open motorway. She curved her thumbs toward her pinkies to make her hands as skinny as possible and tried to ease them out of the twine.

"Behave," the driver said quietly as the truck sloped downward like they were taking a roadway junction off the motorway.

Aini froze, the memory of gunfire popping through her mind.

WHAT FELT LIKE YEARS LATER, THE VEHICLE RUMBLED TO a stop.

"All right, beauties," the man said, clicking the locks.

His movement shifted Aini on the seat. His accent was light like Neve's, and his voice was annoyingly cheerful considering he'd just kidnapped them. The twine bit into Aini's wrists as the man cut her free.

"You may take your hoods off now," he said.

Aini's vision took a second to clear as she removed the bag and adjusted the knife so it wasn't jabbing her as badly. They'd parked in a grassy area, spotted with boulders and surrounded by fields. A road ran between the nearest field and the next. Their kidnapper, a short man with a large forehead, cut Neve's ties and climbed out of the truck.

As he took the sacks off Thane and Myles, he leaned across the back seat and said, "Don't get any ideas about fighting or running." His pocketknife made quick work of their ties. "There are a good number of people in that barn who do both those things better than any of you."

Thane's face was full of murder as he slid out of the truck, Myles next to him. Thane's eyes narrowed at the fields, the fences, and the sloping ground surrounding a huge barn.

Aini scooted across the seat and out of the truck behind Neve.

Under the dusky light of the half moon, a three-story, stone barn huddled like a grave marker against a rolling hill. Windows glinted every few feet along the walls and a set of double doors sat at the base. The roof, made of wood shingles, slanted up into the star-sprinkled sky.

"Oh, nearly forgot. I need your mobile phones," the man said.

Thane pulled his out of a back pocket, pushed a side button Aini was fairly sure didn't exist on her phone, and threw the device against a rock at his feet.

Her mouth dropped open. "What did you do that for?"

The driver raised his eyebrows and mumbled something.

"We're not going for a picnic with these people, Aini," Thane hissed.

She handed her phone over, still intact. "I realize that, but what if we get away? Don't we need to be able to contact people?"

"The risks outweigh the benefits." Thane watched the kidnapper pick up the broken phone.

The man marched toward the massive barn, his arms pumping at his sides.

Behind Myles and Neve, Aini walked close to Thane. "Do you have any idea where we are?" The darkness in the barn's windows made her walk even closer.

"We traveled mostly east. A bit north." Thane looked right and left over moonlit fields of waving winter barley almost ripe and ready to harvest for whisky. "We're nowhere near a town of any size, I'd say. Farms for miles."

He glanced at the man leading them, then jerked her to a stop. "I have to talk to you."

"What?" she asked. "Now? I thought you wanted to wait to talk after we'd met with...them."

"Aye. But that was before they brought us way out here. I don't know, I'm not sure..." His eyebrows furrowed, and his knuckle rubbed over his lip.

"What's wrong?" Her heart tapped an impatient rhythm on her ribcage. "Other than the obvious."

The driver waved. "You two." He and the others had reached the double doors and a woman in a short dress and tall combat boots held the entrance open wide.

Thane growled in frustration.

"Now." Their kidnapper pulled a gun from his belt. "I'd like to keep this pleasant, as I've been ordered, but I'll do what I must."

He corralled them into the barn.

In air scented with musty straw, mud, and machinery oil, electric lanterns shone from the hand-hewn beams crossing the impossibly high ceiling. Thick climbing ropes, knotted in places, reached down to the wide planks of the barn's wooden floor. At the far left side, four circular, black and green targets hung on the wall, flanked by row upon row of guns and knives in every shape and size. Guns had been illegal, for anyone besides kingsmen, since the last uprising over twenty years ago. Of course, some rural people still used them for hunting, hiding them away when anyone came around. Father had told her all about it. Maybe these were for hunting? She squinted, eyeing their black shapes.

They were for hunting all right. But not for deer or birds.

On the right of the barn, colored hand and foot holds dotted the wall. Near the door, a black cage of barbed wire surrounded a raised, rubber mat floor. Three jumbled pairs of boxing gloves lay scattered within the cage, dried blood marring the surfaces.

Neve rubbed a hand over her arm like she was cold. "What is this place?"

"Dangerous," Myles said. He chewed the inside of his cheek.

A set of metal stairs led up the side of the barn to a landing where a table with tubing, jars, and scales sat. A lab.

Below and beyond the small landing, a crowd of men and women sat on benches and stools and chairs around long wooden tables. There had to be over three hundred people dressed in everything from ragged trousers and T-shirts to suits and ties. Every face turned. Young. Old. In between. Aini recognized three people immediately.

Red hair, round glasses—Owen, who'd come to the townhouse with an apology. Barrel chest, bulging eyes—Dodie. Black hair piled high, combat boots, dress, and a curvy figure—Vera. All three had the same wide mouth. The room tilted. They reminded Aini of the man in the visions from the brooch and the knife.

Snarling, Myles jolted toward Dodie.

Thane's hand landed on the back of Myles's shirt, stopping him. "Whoa, colonial."

Myles whirled his arms around but didn't break Thane's hold. Thane said something in his ear, and Myles stilled, grimacing. Thane released him, and Myles straightened his shirt, his eyes throwing knives.

Dodie stood, his mouth parting to speak, but Owen rose and pushed him back into his seat.

"We're very sorry, friend," Owen said to Myles, no trace of sarcasm in his voice.

Aini's heart pounded in her ears. Every pair of eyes searched her face. She lifted the bog oak knife and held it out. "Is this the weapon you wanted to see?"

The room held its breath. Owen stepped forward and touched the hilt. His brown-orange irises developed a feverish sheen.

"Why is this so important?" she asked. *Somebody say something.* "Whose knife is it?"

"Your father knows," he whispered.

"What do you mean?" Her voice started tight and small but grew to a shout. "What can you tell me about my father?" She hadn't meant to walk away from Neve, Myles, and Thane, but suddenly she wasn't ten feet from Owen, Vera, and Dodie.

The crowd stayed utterly still, hands on knees, eyes blinking quietly, arms crossed, fingers linked.

A grin flashed over Owen's mouth. "He is a good man, your father." He spoke loud enough that all could hear.

The knife's cool sheath pressed into Aini's hands. "How do you know him? Even if he knew one of you once, he's not a...traitor like you."

"Aini," Neve hissed from behind.

The gathering murmured. Vera put a hand on her generous hip and snorted.

"Vera had to remind me who he was," Owen said. "She's our historian here. Lewis MacGregor used to work for the cause, for the Dionadair."

It was as if someone had poured a bucket of ice water down Aini's back. Her body quaked in the aftermath. This was exactly what she'd been afraid of. That Father truly did have a dangerous past. That this whole thing wasn't simply a mistake and easily solvable. Her own dear, sweet, genius father was a traitor to the crown. And being that, he was also an enemy to the most powerful clan in Scotland, the increasingly vicious Campbells.

"Your father and mine were good friends," Owen said.

Neve was whispering feverishly to Myles, who looked like he'd downed a sour cup of milk.

Aini swallowed, her throat on fire. "Who is your father?"

Owen, Vera, and Dodie traded a look, all downcast eyes and burdened shoulders. The people on the benches and sitting in the chairs around the tables set their mouths and straightened their own shoulders, protecting their leaders like a seawall shields a bay.

Owen quickly licked his lips. "Our father was a Bethune, as are we."

"The line of the first Dionadair!" a man called out. Another beside him patted his back and smiled grimly.

Owen gave his supporter a nod. "Yes, thank you." He looked at Aini. "And together, your father and mine had developed an invisible tracking powder."

Aini's hands shook as she gathered the knife closer, holding it, squeezing it, wishing it had some inherent power to help her out of this situation. She breathed once, slow and determined, through her nose. The air here smelled foreign. More metallic. Electric. And also like deeply churned earth.

"The powder worked well," Owen said. "But one of the ingredients had a traceable source in Isle of Man. The Campbells knew my father had contacts there. They came for him soon thereafter."

Vera trembled like a ghost had walked through her. "They sentenced our father to death."

"No." Aini's lips were cold and she touched them briefly, her fingers shaking. "My father is a sweets scientist. Not some wild insurgent. He can barely handle the tax men. He doesn't have it in him to rebel."

Owen raised his eyebrows. "From the stories, Lewis was a different man before he lost his closest friend, my father. The last of his rebellious streak was subdued when your mother left him."

She couldn't breathe. Her mother. That's why she'd divorced him. Because she found out he was a traitor. Her collar choked her. She tugged at it with icy fingers. "So, the Campbells do have my father."

"Yes. We're not certain what Nathair has planned for Lewis, what with the statements the man has made of late. It was easier when we had one enemy, the king, and knew what his motivations were. Now...Nathair may have more than a criminal trial in mind for your father."

"They tried to persuade him to craft weaponized candies."

Owen nodded. "But for who." It wasn't a question. He'd said it like he wanted Aini to think it out.

"To hurt you," she said, "the Dionadair?"

The red-bearded man slowly shook his head. "By now, they've guessed about his past work with my father. The Campbells know we're aware of the possibility of weaponized candy.

They know we'd be wary. Of course that doesn't mean they wouldn't try it. But..."

Thane stepped closer, his arm brushing Aini's.

Owen's gaze went to him, then returned to her. "We believe the Campbells want to use weaponized candies on the Scottish people."

"What?" Thane and Aini spoke together.

"After we realized who you are, Aini, and who your father is, we put out some...feelers. The Campbells are interested in a fear campaign."

"But why?"

"To persuade the people to rise against the king and back Nathair as an independent leader in Scotland." Owen pushed his wireframe glasses higher on his nose.

Thane made a grumbling noise. "What a load of cack. No matter what...interesting tactics he's using, Nathair can't possibly believe he can win against the king."

Vera laughed, and Aini fought the urge to cover her ears. "Is that not what *we're* doing here, Handsome?" Vera said. "The king *can* be beat and he will!"

The crowd shouted. It sounded like a blend of *Ha!* and *Muah!* Probably Gaelic, Aini thought.

Thane stepped back. "Yeah, well," he whispered to Aini, "Nathair is not as daft as this bunch. Mad, yes. Daft, no."

Owen's head jerked up and his hands fell to his sides. He'd heard Thane.

"My father won't help the Campbells use weaponized sweets against innocent people. He wouldn't even do it against not-so-innocent people. Like you."

Owen nodded. "Aye. Vera found one of our own father's diary entries that said as much about your father. Very against the whole idea, Lewis MacGregor was."

"Is," Aini corrected.

Vera glanced at her with pity pouring out of mascara-heavy eyes.

A fusion of frustration and anger buzzed through Aini. "He is alive. I'd know it if they'd killed him."

Owen stepped in and took her arm. Thane's nostrils flared and he looked at Aini like *Is this okay?* She shrugged and let Owen hold her elbow lightly, like an old man would.

"We do believe he is still alive," Owen said. "We have a plan. But first, we need information to shape that plan." He leaned closer, his voice a stage whisper, loud and soft at the same time. "Tell me, what did you see when you touched the Bethune brooch?"

Aini's heart solidified.

She should've been prepared for this moment. After all, she'd found the knife the brooch's vision showed. But still. Admitting her ability aloud, discussing it in front of three hundred or so strangers who may or may not—probably not—have her best interests at heart? One could even be a Campbell spy. A breath shuddered out of her. She could never really prepare for something as big as this.

"I don't know what you're talking about." Her words trickled out of her mouth when they should've marched, strong and defensive.

Vera's purple dress stood out in the crowd of brown, blue, and white. "Oh yes, you do. You know very well what we're speaking about. You wouldn't have the brooch if you were not meant to."

"Meant to?" Aini asked.

"It's the prophecy," Vera said.

Dodie came forward and grabbed Vera's arm in his meaty

hand. "She might've just found the thing." His curly, black hair fell over his heavy eyebrows. "She might not be the one."

Owen detached Dodie's grip on their sister. "She is. Enough of this, Dodie."

"What prophecy?" Aini leaned forward.

Neve and Myles gathered around Thane and Aini.

"Macbeth's Seer." Vera pointed at the knife, and cold perspiration slicked over Aini's face. "That's the old king's knife. Macbeth's knife. And I'd bet you saw the stone in your vision from the antiquarian's brooch."

Thane's eyes went wide and he staggered back a step. "My God. She's right."

"What's right?" Aini looked to Neve and Myles, who seemed as lost as she.

A ripple of whispers rolled through the crowd.

Owen held his hands wide, inviting the whole room to listen. "In the eleventh century, Macbeth, *MacBheatha mac Fhionnlaigh* —the real man, not the Scottish play—ruled Scotland. When threatened by a Scots leader who worked for the English—much like the Campbells do today—Macbeth hid a very special stone. Concealed it in the earth, deep, where no one would find it. That stone was the royal seat for the ancient Dal Riata Gaels. Every ruler from *Loarn mac Eirc* to Macbeth had been crowned upon it. It was called the Coronation Stone."

Neve gasped.

Aini wrapped her arms around herself. "A one-thousand-year-old legend doesn't have anything to do with me."

Owen stepped forward, his gait slow and regal, his hair copper in the overhead lanterns' light. "In 1819, my ancestor Angus Bethune and his spineless, betraying bossman, Donan Campbell," he paused to spit on the ground, "found the stone. They were antiquarians, relic-hunters. Angus Bethune hid it before that sleekit Campbell could give it to the English king and ruin Scotland's chance to free herself from tyranny.

"Donan Campbell killed Angus Bethune—knifed him in the back—when he found out, but not before Angus planted a trail, aided by Macbeth's ghost. Yes, he was a Ghost Talker and a Dreamer, seems like. In a dream, the ancient King Macbeth told Angus a Seer would rise. He said Angus must set a trail of visions embedded in artifacts, beginning with the brooch, that would lead the Seer to the resting place of the Coronation Stone, the rock that, when the true Heir to Scotland's throne touches it, will cry out and both its promise and its curse will free us from the English king and all in league with him."

As one, the Dionadair stood. They reached high and crossed their thumbs over their heads, faces solemn as gravestones. Every eye turned to Aini. These people, their hope, it burned with ferocity, a surety she'd never seen. Goosebumps rippled down her arms.

Neve made a sound like she'd breathed her last breath. Myles shook his head, and Thane paled, his glasses very black against his honey hair and fair cheeks.

The room spun. "Wait." Aini held up her shaking hands. "It can't be true."

She heard the unbelieving tone in her own voice. Felt it. On the surface, anyway. But the wild story rang through her bones like music she'd never heard before but somehow loved.

"Just give me a minute." She pinched the bridge of her nose, her heartbeat in her ears.

"Of course," Owen said quietly.

"Aini..." Neve edged closer, but Aini stepped away for space to think.

The whole thing came together in events, feelings, and visions, with the Dionadair as the good side in all of it. But they were rebels. Outlaws. People who threw rules back in the king's face. They were as dangerous as people could be.

But the king was worse.

He treated Scots like lesser beings than the English, prohibiting marriages without permission and laying out prejudiced taxes. The king had long ago abolished Parliament and taken away any chance they once had for a say in government. He was a tyrant. If he had his way, everyone like Aini, every sixth-senser, would be dead.

"It's because of this prophecy, isn't it?" she whispered. "This is why the king sees us—sixth-sensers—as abominations. He is afraid of me, of the stone, of the true Heir, the person who is meant to rule Scotland, the one the people would rise up and support."

Owen smiled sadly. "Of course it is, Seer. You understand it now, don't you?"

She put a hand to her churning stomach. Their theory, the story they'd told, drummed persistent and unrelenting through her flesh and bone. If she accepted this idea as truth, she'd forever be known as a sixth-senser, an abomination to the king, a person destined to die sooner rather than later.

Vera began to chant.

'Macbeth's Seer rises nigh, a stone reflected in his light eye, and he bumped the man upon the chair, ripped him up by the hair.'

Stepping back and holding his hands wide, Owen nodded. "Aini MacGregor, you are fated to free not just your father, but all of Scotland. You are fated to find our true Heir. You are the Seer."

Her blood halted in her veins, then sang and burned and made her want to scream. The Seer. It was crazy.

It is true, her blood whispered.

She sucked a breath as the crowd surged and cheered, a

moving tangle of smiles and bodies and hands lifted over heads. Thane stayed back from the rest, his fist on his mouth, thinking, overwhelmed, and she didn't blame him. She felt the same. The celebrating crowd crushed Neve and Myles into Aini's sides, their faces shocked, but joyful.

Neve squeezed Aini's hands tightly. Now Aini was not only a sixth-senser. She was not only an unintentional rebel. She had become the figurehead, the guide of the Dionadair.

The Campbells' greatest enemy.

CHAPTER 17
SEER

The excited voices, the chanting of the old song—all the sounds echoed off the barn walls and reverberated inside Thane's skull like alarm bells.

Aini was the Seer. Not just a Seer. *The* Seer.

She was the one the old stories said would find the Coronation Stone. Why had he never truly believed the legend? Rodric did. Nathair certainly did. He'd railed on about it at a clan gathering last autumn, his scarred face red in the bonfire's scattered light.

It really *was* more than a dream formed of whisky and Nathair's growing lust for power.

Head ringing, Thane's mind wheeled around and around. If there was one thing he could report to forgive all his recent shortcomings with his clan, this was it. If he was the Campbell to locate the Seer and destroy the fabled stone, he'd rule the clan. They'd flock to him like disciples. He shivered. What a thought. Rodric looking to Thane with respect? He shook his head. If Rodric respected an act, that act could simply, easily, quickly be categorized as pure evil.

As Thane shook his head to clear it, the Dionadair started ringing contacts on beat-up phones, heading through back doors with paperwork in hands, talking in groups. Two big men doffed boxing gloves in the cage to train. They were preparing for war.

Reporting this nest wouldn't be evil, would it? Even if it did please people like Nathair and Rodric. It was Thane's duty to his clan. To the good people in Clan Campbell.

But reporting Aini?

There she stood, so slight in her dress and open-front sweater. The woven piece of clothing swallowed her arms and hung below her knees. With that red ribbon in her ebony hair, she looked younger than she was. The skin on the back of her neck was smooth and he knew exactly how sweet that spot would be to kiss. To think of her taken by his clan...

Something stuck in his throat and he coughed. He rubbed his lip, the small scar on his thumb rough and familiar. He remembered getting that scar. He'd beat the sense out of a man who'd spoken against the king. It'd been up at his family's home. In Argyll. He'd been ten years old. In Thane's memory, his father was quiet, slick, and sure. Everything ten-year-old him was not, in his too-long arms and legs and squeaking voice.

"Hit him again, young Thane," his father had said then. "He's a traitor and you're doing the king's work."

After Thane had hit the man twice—the second sloppy punch hit the man's mouth and the traitor's tooth had cut Thane's thumb—Rodric and the others had hauled the man off to prison.

Eels swam in Thane's belly at the memory.

He blinked, pushed his glasses into his hair, and rubbed his face to clear the image away.

Now only Owen, Vera, Neve, and Myles made a loose sort of circle around Aini.

"I did not see that coming." Myles looked like he'd been hit in the back of the head, stunned and wondering how much pain was headed his way once his body caught up with the blow. "Of course, I'm not a Seer so…"

"Oh, Aini!" Neve grabbed Aini by the arms. "I can hardly believe it. It's amazing."

Aini stood motionless, until she turned and looked at Thane with coffee-black eyes. She needed support now, going through this madness. But all she had was him, the enemy, the wolf hiding in the trees. Thane grabbed his sweater at the chest and gripped it tightly, the loose weave distorting the curves of his fingerprints.

Vera snorted and swaggered up to Aini. "Think you can handle it, Seer?"

Aini's mouth worked, but nothing came of it.

Owen pulled Vera and Dodie aside. They spoke, heads together. Vera and Dodie joined a group at one of the many rickety wooden tables across the barn. The climbing wall stood behind them, covered in ropes like vines.

Owen waved Thane, Aini, Neve, and Myles toward the back of the barn. The wall there didn't sit quite flush with the rest of the wood. It was an exit. Or an entrance to another area. Thane didn't know where it led, but it was no place he wished to go. Not being a Campbell.

"What did you see when you touched the brooch?" Owen asked Aini. "Don't be afraid. We have several sixth-sensers here. Threaders. Ghost Talkers. No dreamers, yet… Sixth-senser skills are valuable to the cause. Yours, of course, especially so."

Raising her chin, Aini looked at Owen. "I touched the brooch and saw a stone. It looked like…like a seat. Someone had carved swirling shapes and circles in it. It's the Coronation Stone? The one that will announce the Heir when that person touches it?"

"Aye. It is." Owen rubbed his hands together. "It's mind-blowing. You've seen the stone in your visions." Throwing his head back, he laughed. "My siblings treated you terribly at the club."

Myles raised a finger. "Yeah, I expect a seriously beautiful *I'm sorry for punching your face* card from that thug you call a brother."

Owen pressed a hand to his chest. "Apologies, Myles."

Myles's head jerked back and he looked from Owen to Neve and back again. "How do you know my name?"

Owen raised his eyebrows. "As I mentioned earlier, when I guessed who this young lady might be, I released a few opera-tives into your part of Edinburgh. They told me you were Myles Smith, son of a successful plantation owner in the southern American colonies."

Myles's scowl could've melted the altered tablet candy hiding in Thane's secret bag. "Let's get back to this vision," he said quietly.

"I think I saw Angus, your ancestor, in the vision," Aini said, changing the subject. "He looked like you, Vera, and Dodie."

Nodding excitedly, Owen pulled on a thick rope, and with a snick of a mechanism, the uneven back walls slid to the side, revealing a rock passageway leading into the side of the hill. "He was the first of the Dionadair."

"What does that word mean anyway?" Aini asked.

Owen led the lot of them through the door and into a dimly lit, but large tunnel. Aini's gaze traveled over the dug-out passageway. She shouldn't have been too claustrophobic in this place, Thane thought. An elephant could walk through that passage. But what did he know of the phobia? He couldn't judge.

He squeezed his eyes shut. Where was his head? Here he was worrying over small things when they were about to stroll into a secret passageway with the head of the Dionadair. He'd gone mad, that's what this was. Thane had gone completely off his head.

"*Dionadair* means *protector*," Owen said. "We're protectors of Scotland and the stone." Owen blinked like an owl behind his glasses.

Cursing himself silently, Thane trailed right along behind Owen, Aini, and the rest. Every five feet or so down the passage, lights glowed—orange and inconsistent—from the rock walls. Scuffed beams lined the roof and made crude archways. Thane touched the chain at his throat. Quite the nest these Dionadair had here.

Aini looked over her shoulder at Thane, and he sped up to walk just behind her. If Owen tried anything, he'd be ready.

"There was a vision on the knife, too," Aini said. "It showed a wall marked with a spiral. The shape was reminiscent of the one on the Coronation Stone."

"The Waymark Wall," Owen said reverently. "When you find the wall and touch it, it'll give you the final vision and lead you to the stone. Where did you see it?"

Aini sure was giving away a great deal of information. Thane's mind whirred around the threats, risks, and the possibilities of this new world they'd been dumped into. The girl would be wise to keep some information back. He put a gentle hand on her shoulder and she glanced at him, a wrinkle appearing between the delicate slant of her black eyebrows. Turning slightly away from Owen, he put a finger to his lips. Her gaze going over his face, she began to scowl. He knew she didn't like being bossed about, but maybe she'd take his nonverbal advice anyway.

A droopy-faced woman in a dark shirt and corduroys came out of the back of the tunnel. "If you give us five minutes, we'll have the rooms ready."

Owen gave the woman a nod and she scampered off.

Chewing the inside of her lip, Aini kept quiet on Owen's last question about the location of the Waymark Wall. The way she was working that lip, she had to be making mental lists of what to do now. At least she'd taken his advice to keep quiet.

That Owen was wise. He kept his tongue as well, not pushing Aini to answer. He'd earn her trust backing away like that. Rodric could've taken a lesson from the man.

Aini sighed and nodded, as she'd come to some conclusion with herself. "I don't know where the Waymark Wall was in the vision. Near the ocean, I think."

Thane ground his teeth. She was going all in then.

Her eyes went bright like the time she'd thought of a new way to organize the lab stock. "What is our plan? So, what if I find the Coronation Stone, and somehow, the Heir? What then? It's not like the Campbells are going to simply hand my father over and make for the border with their tails between their legs."

She was right about that.

A daft smile slicked over one side of Owen's mouth. Thane was truly starting to hate that man. "They'll have to," Owen said. "They'll have no choice. Once we reveal the stone and the Heir, and Nathair Campbell's plan to poison his countrymen and blame it on the king, Scotland will rise behind us. We will force the Campbells out."

Thane pressed a fist against his mouth. They were getting a bit ahead of themselves. But his heart clanged inside his chest painfully. If the Dionadair were ready to go this far, and with Aini, Neve, and Myles in the midst of it, things were about to become very, very ugly. Thane paced a small circle as they waited on the corduroy woman, his feet hot in his boots and his palms sweating. If they knew Myles's name, they might know more. They might know something about Thane. The tunnel's ceiling was more than high enough for him to walk comfortably, even stretch, but Thane began to feel as Aini did in closed-in spaces. Like he was being buried alive.

He returned to her and touched her arm. "You all right in here? It's not that tight, is it?"

Her eyes shuttered closed and she swallowed roughly. Looking at the walls like they might bite, she whispered, "I'm okay."

She turned to Owen, who was watching Thane and her in a way that made Thane want to kick something. Someone.

"Where does rescuing my father come into all of this?" she asked smartly.

Thane crossed his arms and stood a bit closer to Owen, smiling at the head of height he had on the man.

"If we get their feathers up about a possible sighting of the true Coronation Stone," Owen turned a black and gold ring on his pinky finger, "it'll be easy enough to infiltrate their ranks and steal him back. They won't see this coming. It's their pride that'll make it doable."

Thane snorted and took up pacing again. It'd take more than Campbell ego to trip Campbells up. Maybe if the Dionadair had the weaponized sweets and could get the stone to roar in public —not that the thing most likely truly roared. Probably only a metaphor for something, but if the Dionadair could present it properly, they might have a chance at defeating Nathair. They'd still have a lot to deal with.

He stopped. His fingers unclenched, and a breath like a sigh or a cynical laugh floated from his mouth. He'd just been planning a revolution. A revolt against his own clan. Of course, if

Nathair truly did plan on trying to push the king from Scotland...

"What's your story, Moray?" Myles whispered. "You think these people are out of their gourds too? They do have a pretty boss hideout though." He elbowed Neve. "If you join the crazies, I'm in."

Neve whimpered and put hands on her head. "This is too much."

Myles rubbed her back.

Aini pressed her palms into her eyelids. "I don't know about all this."

"You'll have to trust me, Seer," Owen said quietly. "There's no other way out of this with your father alive and Scotland free."

"But...but why me?" Aini listed to the left.

Thane rushed to grab her by the arms.

"You need to sit down?" There wasn't a bench or anything in this stupid tunnel. Thane turned to Owen. "When are your blessed rooms going to be ready?"

Owen's mouth twisted into an ugly frown, but Vera was suddenly there, shiny as a beetle and blethering on with her brother about something. She held a walkie-talkie in one manicured hand and kept glancing at Thane.

Aini's lashes fluttered a little as a sad smile poured over her full lips. "Thank you," she whispered to Thane. "I just forgot to breathe for a minute."

"Let's not do that, all right?"

She laughed a little, and he forgot he was under a hill swarming with people who would happily murder him if they knew his real name.

"Agreed." She gave his forearms a little squeeze.

She had her weight under her again, so he released his hold, his stomach swimming. She was so brave and strong, but even the brave and strong needed backup.

Vera's gaze tore down Thane's body, and he tensed. "What is your story? You don't have the innocent look of the rest of these." She pointed to Aini, Myles, and Neve.

Myles mumbled an *oh please*, but Vera ignored him and ran a finger across Thane's chest. His lip curled. He lifted her hand off his ribs and dropped it, glaring.

A sideways grin pulled at Vera's lips. "We found out plenty of information about that one." She pointed to Neve. "With her many little brothers, alcoholic mother, and admirable work ethic."

Neve's eyes narrowed.

Vera licked her lips. "And we know all about Myles Smith. His plantation-owning mother in the Carolinas is a real horror story in the making."

Myles's eyes burned. He looked like a different person. "Shut up."

Vera laughed. "Don't get your knickers in a twist, colonial. It's not your fault mummy doesn't love you the way she should."

"Vera." Owen tilted his head, his voice warning his sister.

She crossed her arms. "It's only the truth."

"You soulless dog," Neve hissed.

Everyone froze.

Vera was the first to move again. "Ooo. The mousie has a mean bite, eh? Good. You'll need it."

Owen looked at the ceiling. "Forgive my sister. We've had our share of tragedy and it's sharpened our edges."

Myles whipped away from the group and strode farther down the tunnel. He couldn't know where he was going. Thane supposed the colonial didn't care. Just wanted to get out of here. Poor lad.

Myles tore back toward them. "You don't know anything about me."

Vera's face went from taunting with an eyebrow cocked, to sad, her eyes tipped down at the sides. "I'll not say another thing about it." She was a slippery one. Then she blinked at Thane. "But you. You've been naughty in your past. Shows in the eyes."

Thane's pulse slowed and his training kicked in. "I'm Thane Moray. I'm nobody."

Sneering, Vera said, "I doubt that. You can't go around looking like that and stay a nobody for very long."

She gave everyone except Aini a haughty look. With Aini, she seemed cautious, jealous maybe. Her eyes held questions.

"St. Andrews uni student," Vera said. "A friend named Bran, is it? And you're an orphan with an auntie near Glasgow? You don't dress like a Glaswegian."

Owen shook his head. "Vera, really. Stop."

Following Vera's touch, Aini's gaze was hard to define. Sucking a breath, Thane grabbed the woman's wrist and threw her hand away.

Aini stepped between them. "Enough about my friend."

"I agree," Owen said, eyeing Thane. "Aini wants to know *why her*. Let's focus, sister. Don't you have a little theory on that?"

"I do. I believe you're Macbeth's descendant."

Thane shook his head slowly.

"I'm a Threader," Vera said to Aini.

Thane's hands fisted. What would she see connected to him?

"Don't look so shocked." Vera raised an eyebrow at him, then at Aini. "Why do you think I've been the one to search for the brooch, to believe it was real? I see...connections from people to people, or people to objects. I saw the link, a slim silver line between you and the brooch, and assumed it was only a sentimental attachment like most have with a family heirloom. But no. You are Macbeth's Seer."

"This is all insane," Aini stammered. "Even if we find the stone, we don't know where the true Heir is that can supposedly 'bump' the king from his 'chair' as the song says. How are we going to, as you put it, *get the Campbells on the run*? Where does rescuing my father come in?"

"Exactly," Thane said before he could stop his mouth doing so. "You can't expect Aini to trust a band of cutthroat rebels, can you?"

Owen stared at the onyx ring on his own right hand. "Cutthroat."

"Aye. Tell me you wouldn't use weaponized candy yourself to take down the Campbells. You act like they're the only ones interested in new ways to control a group of people. What about that wall of guns you've got there in the barn? Unless I'm mistaken, those steely decorations do a bit more than make loud noises."

He knew he should shut his mouth, but the way that Owen wouldn't meet his eyes, the way they made themselves out to be saints all set to save Scotland—it was a load of bull.

Owen raised his head. "You wouldn't do what must be done to defend yourself? You'd let the kingsmen shoot you down, imprison your family and friends?" He nodded at Aini. "You'd stand by while they sentence the Seer to death?"

"I'd do no such thing, Dionadair," Thane spat. "I'm only saying you should avoid vague notions and be clear about your intentions and not pretend your plan does not involve violence. Because it does. It always has."

Aini put her graceful hands, one each, on Owen's and Thane's chests. Her hands were stronger somehow for their deli-cate beauty in this difficult place, but she could've saved herself the trouble. The fight had dissolved from Thane's fists and heart.

He was a Campbell.

He *would* have to stand by while someone sentenced Aini if it came to that.

The back of Thane's tongue tasted sour. His glare, aimed at Owen, faltered.

Owen cocked his head and a question crossed the man's eyes.

A line of sweat rolled down Thane's back.

"I won't help until you promise you won't try to...murder people," Aini said.

"The Campbells won't release your father," Owen said. "You'll have to take him back, and you'll only be able to do that if you help us take down the lot of them and reclaim Scotland."

"He's right, Aini," Neve said, her voice timid but steady.

Myles nodded.

"No," Aini snapped. "All we need to do is find the Waymark Wall, then the stone. Then we can leak the find to the Campbells to spook them and divert their attention from my father."

Owen turned and ran two fingers over his beard. "Yes."

Vera put a hand on his shoulder, but he gave her a look and she backed off.

"Yes," he said, louder this time. "It might work. After that, you can do as you wish, keep your father safe, and we'll find the Heir on our own and leave you to participate as you see fit."

Thane crossed his arms, his sweater pulling tightly against his skin. He might not have known exactly where he stood in this, but he knew very well where Owen was. At the center of a rebellion—not getting Aini's back.

"As she sees fit, aye?" Thane said, his tone woven to help Aini see the man's false front.

"Of course." Owen was a good liar.

Aini took a breath. "It's settled then."

Thane sucked a breath. Why did she believe Owen? She was smarter than that.

Vera's walkie talkie scratched and a voice carried through the tunnel. "Rooms prepared."

Thane wondered what the Dionadair had hidden while Aini and the others had waited with Owen in the tunnel. Maps of underground access tunnels the kingsmen hadn't yet found? Loot stolen from Campbell headquarters? Falsified papers and manufactured royal seals?

Owen and Vera led them to a large, dirt-walled room. Clusters of hammocks hung from the roughhewn ceiling beams. Several men and women polished guns and read books in the harsh white of overhead lights. A bank of filing cabinets stood on the back wall. Tiny, bronze keyholes stood out against the drawers' blue paint. On either end of the space, laundry lines suspended drop cloths that had been pulled back to reveal neat stacks of pants, shirts, and pullovers. Reed baskets overflowed with buckled boots, red-laced trainers, and steel-toed construction footwear.

The people in the room inclined their heads politely to Aini, their eyes bright with excitement. Wiping a rifle with a cloth, one man with a shockingly white mohawk smiled widely and said something to the people nearby. They nodded and went back to cleaning their portion of the Dionadair black-market arsenal.

Thane took a deep breath. They were obviously giving their Seer some space, but wished more than anything to ask her questions. Their gazes stayed on her as Owen led Thane and the others around the room.

"Sleep for a bit." Owen ran a hand over his beard. "There's food down the way in the kitchens."

"I can smell the bread," Neve said, raising her nose into the air.

Only the grease on the weapons reached Thane's nose. He felt simultaneously at home and nervous as he picked at a hangnail and kept to Aini's heels. This was her show right now. All he could do was hold on for the ride and hope they made it out of here alive.

Aini stopped abruptly in the center of the room. The big, overhead lamp shone down on her in strong beams, making a cage of light around her.

"I'm not resting," she said, her voice growing stronger. "My father is out there. With the Campbells."

Thane flinched, the truth nipping at his heels. He wasn't going to escape this thing intact. No matter how this played out, Aini would hate him and it would rip the best part of him in two.

She pulled a slip of paper from her sweater pocket. "I've thought about it. And I have a good guess on the Waymark Wall's location."

Owen clapped his hands together. "I'm as anxious as you, but it's obvious you need rest or you'll collapse before we've gone a mile. Sleep, and I'll have someone rouse you after just a few hours."

Thane wished he could sleep until this whole nightmare was over.

CHAPTER 18
WORRIES UNDER THE NIGHTTIME SUN

In the Dionadair's sleeping room, Aini sat on the very edge of a dilapidated sofa with Neve, who couldn't stop trembling. Owen's associates had just now roused them. Owen had let them sleep the rest of the night, and the entire following day. It was night again. She gripped the hem of her sweater and squeezed. They'd lost so much time.

Leaning his head against the wall, Thane slung one leg over the arm of the couch to sit. It seemed like a practiced sort of nonchalance. His foot wiggled, and he kept fooling with his thumbnail and touching that small scar.

Myles, who'd gone to the kitchen for them, walked through the entrance, water bottles under his arms and holding a loaf of fresh bread. He held a piece out to Aini. She surveyed her hands. Pretty disgusting. But there was no sink nearby. She wiped her hands on her leggings and reached for the snack.

"I know you're not checking the cleanliness of your hands while we wonder whether we're going to live or die in a rebel's secret hangout." Myles smirked.

"No reason to die from contagion in the meantime."

Myles smeared a hand over his face, and Thane chuckled, though sadness darkened his smile.

At the back of the room, two men in overalls played cards on a wooden crate.

"I can't believe we slept so long," Aini said.

"We needed it." Neve nibbled her piece of bread. "You may be part of a legend, but you're still human." She smiled weakly, and Aini tried to return one but failed.

Glad that she didn't feel trapped in the room, Aini breathed in and out slowly. The ceiling was high, and the wide entrance to the tunnel leading to the barn gave the illusion of an easy departure if necessary. But she did feel trapped in the situation.

Her best guess on the Waymark Wall's location was the ruins of St. Andrews. It was on the coast. She'd been there with Father once and remembered a green lawn similar to the one in the knife's vision. It was near Edinburgh, where the first Dionadair had hidden the knife. It made sense. If they made it to St. Andrews, she'd have to feel around the structure's walls, searching for a vision in front of everyone. She'd be all but admitting to the Dionadair that she really was this legendary Seer they were so excited about. There'd be no turning back after that. She'd be the Seer. Forever. Never again simply Lewis MacGregor's daughter. Not the upstanding manager of the most successful boutique candy lab in Europe. She could never go back to her old life.

Thane put a hand over hers to still it. She'd completely unraveled her dress's hem. His beautiful mouth parted and his eyebrows furrowed together, but he didn't add words to his gesture. Maybe there weren't words for this kind of thing.

Thane's watch was close to touching her, and she pulled back out of habit. She sighed internally. She'd already touched the watch and seen nothing. It didn't hold any memories. Even if it did, wasn't it about time she gave up avoiding who she really was?

She relaxed under his hand and took simple pleasure in the way his bare arm brushed hers, the way the gold hairs on his skin disappeared under his sweater's rolled sleeves, the movement of his iron muscles and sharp tendons, the fact that this strong arm was here to help her.

After handing out the supplies, Myles stared at the floor, his eyes unfocused.

"I'm sorry Vera said what she did." Aini hoped she wasn't pressing a bruise by bringing up his mother.

He shrugged. "I can't really get ticked off when it's the truth. My mother is not a nice person."

Neve reached a hand out and touched his knee briefly. "Even when you were little?"

"Nah." He shoved his hands into the pockets of his extremely wrinkled pants. "She shoved me off on nannies and servants. Said she never planned on having children."

Thane looked Myles up and down, a serious look on his face.

Myles moved his weight from foot to foot. "The nannies were fine."

Aini paused, not knowing what to say or if there's anything anyone could say to address that sort of twisted pain.

"May I ask about your father? Did she lose him and that's why..." She probably should've kept her mouth shut.

Myles rubbed the back of his neck. "He left right after I was born. Mom claims it's because of what I did to her waistline." He looked at Aini with a smile that wasn't happy but was better than the vacant look he'd worn a second before. "But my math tutor—God bless the patience of that guy—said it had more to do with a new blonde in town."

Neve made a Scottish kind of *hmm* noise. Thane nodded.

One of the men playing cards slapped the table and laughed as Vera and Owen entered the sleeping quarters. Vera wore a ridiculously tight dress in the same brown as her heavily lined eyes and more lipstick than anyone should ever even think about.

Walking over to Aini and the others, Owen slid on another out-of-style tweed jacket and clasped his hands together. "Dodie has the truck running. Are you ready, Seer?"

The reverence in his tone made Aini's stomach hurt, but she stood. "Yes, but I don't think we should travel with a huge group."

Owen frowned. "But if the Campbells trail you and realize what you're doing—"

"All the more reason to keep our party small. Just send..." Aini took a second to think: who was the least flamboyant of the group? Definitely not Vera. "Maybe Dodie. He's quiet, but big, in case it comes to a fight."

Thane agreed.

Owen glanced at Vera, who frowned but nodded. "Aye, then," Owen said.

Vera looked at Aini's shaking hands. "Sure you aren't scared, Seer?"

Aini pushed past Vera. "Not any more than I should be, Threader."

The woman laughed. "Maybe so. Maybe so."

THANE LEANED HIS HEAD AGAINST THE TRUCK WINDOW. THE glass cooled his temple but not his mood swings. He'd gone from shocked, to enraged, been mired down into guilt, and rushed head long into hope, only to burn up in cynical self-doubt again. In the seat in front of him, Dodie—silent and thick-skulled—turned the truck's steering wheel as they entered the town of St. Andrews. Thane knew these streets well, the slope and rise of them under the inky blue sky and between the whitewashed buildings. When it wasn't summer holiday, he took classes at the university as part of his feigned life as Thane Moray.

Beside Dodie, Aini cracked her window. The sound of sea birds and mildly frustrated traffic poured in through the space, and wind threw strands of hair like black ink across her soft, round cheek. Could he somehow escape his clan and be with her? If he were any other Campbell, maybe.

Myles leaned over. "Staring at her like she's an experiment gone wrong ain't going to win you any points."

Thane jerked. Then he closed his eyes. Forget points. When it came to any possibility of a relationship with Aini, he needed a whole new game.

"I can give you some tips, you know," Myles said. "There's this one move called the rub-behind-the-head that gets them every time."

Thane opened one eye to see Myles raising an arm so that his excuse for a bicep stuck out like a kid's bicycle tire.

"Best if you stop that," Thane said. "I don't want to jump you in front of the girls."

On the other side of Myles, Neve snorted. "Thane."

Thane straightened, going hot around the collar. "Sorry, Neve. I didn't know you were listening."

He'd thought she'd been asleep. Not that it was late. Just that they were all still exhausted. It was after eight, though the sun hadn't set yet, this being a Scottish summer.

Ahead, the crumbling ruins of the former cathedral and castle reached toward the heavy-bellied clouds. Windows—

empty of glass, but full of the darkening sky—decorated what used to be the cathedral's nave. Part wrought iron, part stone, a wall surrounded the worn architecture and the scattering of tombstones. Like a king's mantle thrown on an old man, a groomed lawn draped the decrepit grounds. The ruins grew even more hunched as they approached the flinty North Sea until they were indistinguishable from the rocky cliffs above the black sand.

Dodie parked along the street near an overgrown garden crowded with tree boughs cloaked in thick leaves. They all climbed out, except for Dodie, who stayed behind to keep watch.

"I'll join you if need be," he said.

Aini regarded Dodie with an appraising eye. She was probably wondering the same thing Thane was. What exactly would he do if there was anything to worry about? If anyone headed toward the group at the ruins, he wasn't the type to handle it with clever distraction. He'd most likely bash heads.

The briny air stuck to Thane's skin as they made their way down the curving street to the ruins. A ticket office sat in front, looking closed.

A small car zipped past while another vehicle parked up the street, across from a pub and not in Dodie's line of sight. The parked car spit out two kingsmen in black jackets and Campbell kilts. Thane whispered a curse.

CHAPTER 19
ST. ANDREWS

The kingsmen dropped out of sight, hidden because of the street's curve.

"I don't think we're going to get in the way you'd like, Aini." Thane cleaned the wet and salty condensation off his glasses with the edge of his sweater.

She raised a pretty eyebrow, her plummy lips pinched. "None of this is how I'd like it to be," she said, but she kept heading toward the dark ticket window like her body acted from rule-following muscle memory.

He leapt the ruins's fence and held a hand to her over the metal bars. "Just come this way."

Aini evaluated the top railing, the bottom, then examined his hand. She waved it off politely and climbed the fence, landing pertly at his side.

He couldn't fight a grin. "Don't look so cocky. You're not proving anything I didn't already know about you."

"You knew I could climb fences?"

"I've learned you're quite good at breaking rules when the situation demands it."

She made a noise.

Myles pointed and laughed. "You made that Scottish noise."

Neve put a boot on the lowest railing, it slipped, and she caught herself on the fence.

"Allow me, milady," Myles said. He got down on all fours. "Mount up."

"Really?" She took a pure beamer, her cheeks going bright red.

"Go on," Myles urged.

With a laugh, Neve stood on his back. Her foot pulled at his shirt and she almost fell, kicking the lad smartly in the ribs. Finally, she made it over with a hand from Thane and Aini. Still laughing, she apologized to Myles.

"No need to be sorry," Myles said. "Sometimes you have to show your mount who's boss."

He backed into the street and took off at a run. With a whoop, he jumped and did an awkward, painful looking shoulder roll to land at Thane's feet.

Thane pulled at his own collar, covering his face a little just in case. But it seemed the kingsmen had vanished. He grabbed Myles by the back of the shirt and hauled him to his feet. "Hurry, pal."

"You sure are more concerned about getting in trouble today."

"It's about time," Aini said, Neve at her side.

Thane strode toward the stone arch that led to the inner courtyard.

Myles began singing. "*Tails tied to trees too tall, goals gone, gore growing go...*" That stupid band he loved gave Thane the worst headaches.

"Shut it, Myles." Neve hurried past him.

"Just come on," Thane snapped, gently shoving Myles, the last of them, behind the arch and out of view. His nerves were raw as the sea's biting wind. "Tell us what we can do to help, Aini."

She was already crouched at the base of the stones, running a hand over the weather-beaten, vanilla-and-smoke colored rocks.

"Look for a spiral carved into the stone," she said. "It may be very faint." Mumbling to herself, she stood and dragged her palms over the wall and up over her head as far as she could reach.

"Should I lift you?" he asked, part of him forgetting all about kingsmen and prophecies and thinking only of her little waist and nice—

She turned, her cheeks red from either wind or shyness, he wasn't sure. "I'll finish looking where I'm able, then maybe...yes."

"All right."

Myles and Neve moved on to what remained of the cathedral wall near the cemetery. She said something to him and he hunkered down like an old man, making her laugh.

Thane wasn't seeing anything like a marking. Just stones and old walkways and empty windows. "Want me to lift you now?" he asked Aini.

"I suppose. Although wouldn't Angus Bethune stick with somewhat easily accessible spots?"

"You think getting into and out of Edinburgh's locked-up vaults was easy, do you?" The minute he brought it up, he regretted it, thinking of Rodric's attack. He clenched his fists so hard that his nails burned into his palms like brands.

"I'm sorry," Aini apologized. "It wasn't easy. And it's not your fault that person attacked me. You saved me from being hurt worse."

He sighed forcefully, so weary of all of this, strung so tightly he felt he might explode. "Let me lift you just a bit. To my height, at least. Then you can move on to where you see fit."

With her nod, he bent, one hand to the fine, soft grass. She climbed onto his shoulders, one leanly muscled leg on either side of his head. Her little boots were muddier than anything she'd ever worn.

As she sat on his shoulders, her legs warmed his neck and chest. She reached and touched the wall, her stomach tensed against the crown of his head. If Thane hadn't been concerned about the kingsmen, and wondering if he should come clean with Aini, this would've been a fine day.

"Am I hurting you?" she asked.

"No."

A minute later, she tapped his shoulder. "I'll get down now."

As he lowered her to the ground and they untangled them-selves, she looked at her hands.

"What if this is all a big mistake?" she asked quietly. The wind blew over her head and lifted strands of her hair.

He took her fingers in his. "All we can do is our best. Look for the Waymark Wall here. If we don't find it, look at another spot. When you feel you've searched all you can, then decide what to do next."

A sudden smile rose on her face like a sunrise. "Why, Thane. I think you just made a to-do list."

He laughed. "Aye. I think I did. You see the effect you have on me, hen?"

Aini leaned close, her shampoo and candy scent tempting. Her gaze brushed over his lips and he felt it like a touch. Her breath dusted his chin. Her small white teeth drew him nearer. What would her mouth taste like right now?

"Thane," she whispered with that mouth. "I—"

"Hey you all!" Myles called out.

Thane gritted his teeth. Aini broke away to see what the colonial was pointing to.

"Look at this!" Myles waved a hand.

Across the lawn, a metal railing and stairs led to a narrow opening in the ground. The stairs were slick and rounded from use over centuries. It looked like the entrance to a tomb.

Aini crossed her arms over her stomach. She seemed nervous. "What is it?"

Neve craned her neck to look into the tunnel. "It's a counter-mine." Her loose shirt whipped around her. "Protestants holed up here and defended themselves from Catholics in the sixteenth century. They dug these tunnels to intercept and demolish their enemies' mines—the ones dug to get into the place."

The railing cooled Thane's fingers as he entered the tunnel's damp mouth. After two steps, his boot slipped. He grabbed hold of the metal with both hands.

Aini shook her head. "I don't really want to go down there."

Neve sucked a breath. "I'm not claustrophobic and I still don't want to go down there. But they did open these up around 1800, so that's perfect timing for Angus Bethune to make his mark."

"Good thing you know so much, Neve," Thane said, looking back into the courtyard.

A flash of black and blue and green showed past the largest remaining section of the ruins. His heart leapt and practically hit his chin. Was it the kingsmen?

"You can do this, Aini," he said quickly. They needed to get out of sight. "We'll be right beside you. Just for a quick peek, aye?"

She inhaled and nodded, going in.

Continuing deeper into the dark tunnel, the rock remained like ice. Myles made a comment about snogging in slippery places.

"Do you know what people say of men who brag about their prowess?" Thane asked as Aini ran her fingers along the wall.

Myles took on an innocent look. "That those men are named Myles Smith and the bragging is as just as the day is long?"

Neve frowned over her shoulder. "That's a Mylesland answer."

"You know you want to visit, Neve."

"For what purpose?" Neve gripped the railing and looked up at the weak light on the ceiling of the tunnel.

The sea threw a gust of salty breath down the place as Thane tried to see the entrance.

"Mylesland has a fantastic library. Full of historical volumes."

Neve laughed. "Then I might consider the invitation."

"Of course the history is slightly skewed toward promoting licentious behavior. Only true libertines win in Mylesland."

"Libertines aren't necessarily licentious," Aini said. "They're simply fond of freedoms we can only dream about."

"Can you imagine having the freedoms the Dionadair want?" Thane asked, talking more to himself than anyone else.

"I thought you hated them," Myles said, nudging his way between Thane and Aini.

Thane swallowed. "I...I'm not sure how I feel actually." The lines between his real feelings and those he was using to maintain his role as spy were growing too wrinkled to smooth out.

Myles clapped hands over his mouth. "Seriously? Thane has no grouchy, superior answer?"

A growl rumbled in Thane's throat.

Neve eyed him. "You are a rebel of sorts like they are, Thane.

In the market, you stole those drinks because that man cheated Aini the week before."

Thane lifted one shoulder. "That doesn't mean anything."

"It does," Aini said, pausing to look at a rough spot in the wall below the railing. "You break the law, but only when you think it leads to justice. Or to help friends." She was thinking of Bran. If she only knew...

"But you hate the Dionadair." Myles clucked his tongue and ran two hands over the opposite wall, searching for carvings. "If they aim for justice for Scots—freedom to marry who they wish without permission, freedom to wear clan tartans even if they aren't Campbells, freedom to vote on taxation—why don't you love them as much as I'm beginning to?"

"I love them." Neve raised her chin.

Aini raised her eyebrows. "Neve, the rebel. I never thought I'd see the day."

Neve shook her head. "Sadly, I've no more drive to fight than a wee chicken."

They'd made it all the way to a black iron gate that blocked the tunnel's exit out of the ruins. Aini put a hand against the wall.

Her eyes went blank.

Thane began to take her arm, but held himself back. She was having a vision and he wasn't sure touching her was a good plan or not. What did it feel like to see things like that? Her lips moved once, twice. It was strange how Thane had once thought of sixth-sensers as people he would never understand. He didn't really understand Aini now, but he had realized such people were so much more than only their extended abilities. Aini was who she was, and then she was a sixth-senser. It didn't define her; the sense added another facet.

She gasped. Her knees gave out.

Thane caught her as she looked at him, her eyes alert again.

Neve and Myles hovered.

"Was it Angus Bethune again?" Neve bit her lip and pushed a fallen lock of Aini's hair behind her friend's ear.

Aini stood and brushed herself off. "It was a man in armor. He was choking on smoke...fighting someone he knew." She pressed her hands against her cheeks and inhaled deeply. "I need to get out of here."

Neve pointed to a spot on the wall. "There's a bit of metal embedded here. Must've belonged to some long ago Protestant or Catholic fighter." She shook her head as they hurried from the tunnel. "You are a wonder, Aini."

Cold air blasted through the passage.

Words slipped, barely audible, over Thane's ears.

"Ghost," he whispered, very glad he wasn't a Ghost Talker.

Myles whistled and looked around, wide-eyed. He looked a bit green around the gills. "I'm beginning to be a believer."

Neve smacked his arm. "Hush. Don't speak of it."

"Ghost or no ghost," Aini said, "let's go."

Neve crossed herself and hurried after her.

Then a real voice, not a ghost's, trailed through the tunnel.

Thane's heart tripped and he snagged Myles's arm. "Grab a girl. Let's see that snogging you've been going on about." He pulled Aini to him and gave Neve a gentle shove toward Myles. "Apologies, girls. But we're about to be caught."

Myles stuttered but eventually got out, "Ah. Gotcha." He laid a kiss on Neve.

Aini's eyes widened as Thane drew her face close to his. He dragged his mouth along her soft neck and was pleased to see chill bumps bloom along her skin.

"What are you doing?" she asked breathlessly, making Thane

feel like he was floating and he never, ever wanted to come back down to earth.

The stranger's voice said, "That's exactly what I wondered, lass."

It was a woman.

Squinting, Thane could only see her tall outline with the last of the late summer sunset behind in shades of blood and rust. Pulling away from Aini, he kept to a bend in the tunnel that the overhead lights didn't quite reach.

Aini spun, her cheeks going a bonnie shade of deep red. She looked to Thane, then to Myles and Neve, who weren't snogging, but stood very close together.

"Oh," Aini said, recovering. "We were...it was..."

Myles smoothed his shirt with big movements. "Just having some fun, miss. We'll move on."

"Come with me, please." Waving a hand, the woman started toward the entrance. She wore a black government uniform with red stripes down the sleeves.

They emerged into the dusk. Purple and blue battled for chunks of sky above the tombstones and the bones of the old cathedral and castle.

The gaunt-faced woman took out a walkie talkie and turned a knob. She was maybe fifty, fifty-five. "I'll have to report you. I am sorry."

Her nails were long and very red and gave Thane an idea.

GIVING AINI A LOADED LOOK, THANE LET GO OF HER ARM and approached the ruins guard. Aini immediately missed the warmth of his touch. This evening had been pointless. Frustrating. Longing for a shower, for a solution to all of this, for something other than wandering around and failing her father, she wiped her filthy hands on her leggings. She put a hand to her throat, wanting to feel the spot where Thane's mouth had been.

"Ah, now lass," Thane said to the guard in a sugary, deep voice.

Aini's insides melted.

Neve's mouth fell open.

"You don't have to tell anyone we were here, do you?" Thane strengthened his West Scots accent, and the guard smiled, which completely changed her face into something far more manageable. "We weren't doing any harm." He looked up at her through his black lashes. Two gorgeous dimples appeared in his cheeks as he smiled and angled his body toward her.

Aini pushed her sleeves up, suddenly very warm. That voice he was using...it was like a sixth-sense ability of its own.

"I bet," Thane went on, "that not so long ago, you yourself enjoyed similar activities."

Smiling, the guard pulled at the collar of her unattractive uniform. "Well, that's none of your business." A laugh pealed out of her throat.

Thane put a hand on his well-built chest and dipped his head, hanging a thumb on his trousers and looking like the most gorgeous thing in the universe. Those tattoos. Those glasses. Aini blew out a breath. Those arms. She knew she was being pathetic, but still. Still.

"Aye. Course not," he said. "But if you let us go, just this once, maybe we'll see you at the pub up the way later on tonight."

The guard's face lightened. "Oh?" She shook herself slightly and cleared her throat. "That's not, that's nothing I can..." She waved a hand. "Just go." An easy smile poured over her mouth then. "Go on, the lot of you. I was young once too."

Thane took her hand and kissed it slowly, his head bent like a knight.

Aini's heart clattered around like a broken mixer. It wasn't the most fun thing knowing she could've been conned by Thane too. Beauty was a powerful possession. Neve said Aini had it. Even if Aini could be convinced of that, she had no idea how to wield it like a weapon as Thane did. Thane, the Heart Bender, Drool Maker, Thought Swayer. She rolled her eyes at herself and almost laughed. What a sixth sense that would be.

"Thank you," Thane said, straightening.

He gave the rest of them a quick nod, and they were off, trotting back toward the truck before the guard could change her mind.

"Thane," Myles said as they climbed the fence. "You are my hero. In fact," he dug in his pocket, "I have twenty quid. Do you want it? I'll give you anything. I fully support the usage of male sexiness in times of need. And you, my friend, are a master of the art."

Thane glared at him and hopped off the pavement. "Shut your gob." He kept glancing down the road and at the painfully untended garden beside the truck.

"What are you looking for?" Aini asked, but he didn't answer as they made it to the truck and waved to Dodie.

Dodie pointed at a pub across the street. "Why don't we go in there and eat before heading home?"

The door opened, and happy music danced out along with the smell of something smoky and pleasant. Aini's stomach growled.

Thane opened the truck door. "We should go."

Dodie was already getting out, and Neve and Myles crossed the road.

Aini had failed and they had to eat. "Just for a quick meal. I have a headache and I want to get back to safety too, but..." She held out a hand toward the intoxicating drumming of a bodhran and a set of pipes' lilting tune.

Thane shut the truck door but didn't smile as he followed them to the pub.

Aini hoped the music would help her think.

CHAPTER 20
A REEL AND A STRAMASH

I n the pub, three stag heads large enough to impress Thane, who'd grown up surrounded by wildlife, decorated a wood-paneled wall. With their proud racks, the dead creatures presided over a group of musicians taking a drinking break. Tables of locals and tourists crowded around a dance floor. A man—with a nose that looked like it'd been broken several times—poured drinks for the patrons. The place smelled like everything had been doused in old ale and frying oil. Nabbing a seat facing the door, Thane sat at the closest table.

Myles dragged a chair out, making a racket. "I need a drink."

"You never drink." Aini peered around the room.

"Well, I need to start sometime, don't I? It fits my whole licentious behavior thing."

Neve sat beside him and put her purse on the table. "Don't let your idea of yourself rule you."

Myles blinked. "That was very wise, Neve. I...think I'll take your advice. I tried beer once and it really is pretty disgusting."

"I used to smoke," Thane admitted. "It was a stupid habit."

Dodie took a chair between Myles and Thane.

Smiling, Neve pulled a stick of something from her purse and slicked it over her mouth. Her lips looked no different. "But don't stop me when I order a whisky."

"A whisky?" Myles asked.

"I'm Scottish. It's like apple juice to us."

Thane nodded approval, and Dodie said, "Aye."

Thane snorted. That'd be the only thing a Campbell and a Dionadair rebel could easily agree on.

"Don't drink too much." Aini sat beside Neve. "We need to stay alert. Owen warned that we are being watched."

Cringing a little, Thane waved the server over. If he had to be miserable, he could at least do it on a full stomach.

Aini's phone rang. "...right. No, we didn't. Okay." Pocketing the phone, she scanned the pub with wary eyes. "Owen says we should go back to the townhouse for the rest of the night," she whispered across the table. "He says it will keep...certain people from wondering what we're up to."

The man with the bent nose appeared with a notepad to take their order.

"What's that smoked haddock soup you're always wishing you had?" Myles asked Thane.

Thane pushed his glasses up. "Cullen Skink."

"That is not a good name for something you want to put in your mouth."

"Suppose not. But I'd have thought green was not a good color for your melon either." Thane pointed at Myles's hair.

"Shows what you know."

"You're the envy of mold spores everywhere, colonial."

Myles started to frown, but then laughed loudly, startling a bonnie, older woman at the next table.

Everyone ordered, and Thane sat back and kept an eye on the door.

The musicians began puttering around. A bald man drummed a round, skin bodhran with a small stick. A woman wearing a yellow snochterdicter as a headband perched a fiddle on her shoulder, made the instrument whine twice, and turned the small knobs at the end of the fingerboard to tune it. Another member of the group, a man with ears far larger than God should've given him, strummed a guitar. Then they started a reel.

"The Riverside Rant," Neve said.

"My sister likes this one," Dodie said.

Everyone looked at him.

"Hey," the man said. "If we're going to be around each other, might as well be civil."

"It's not that," Aini said. "I just didn't realize you cared much for conversation."

Myles glared at him. "I'd like it better if you kept quiet."

"Get over it, pal. This is a war we're in. When you don't seem to be on my side, I'm going to plow you down. When you're with me, I'll do all to keep you standing."

Myles threw Dodie one last mean look, then turned his attention to the music, pretending Dodie wasn't there.

Following the rhythm, Myles banged his knuckles lightly on the table. Neve smiled and watched the fiddler like she'd never seen one before. Aini's delicate fingers moved and curled an inch above the table in some imagined pattern.

"Did you ever think of being a dancer like your mother?" Thane asked.

The server handed him a hot crockery bowl. Aini took her own bowl of the same soup he'd ordered.

"No. I love being at home. The candy making business suits me." She smiled like a memory had touched her.

"I didn't mean to make you sad," he said quietly.

Myles made up lyrics to go with the band's music. Neve laughed and spilled a little of her whisky.

Aini looked at Thane, the corner of her mouth tucked up. "You didn't. I just remembered having competitions with Mother to see who could spin the fastest without growing dizzy." She frowned. "I've always been angry with her. For the divorce, for leaving Father. Even when we were having fun and getting along, there was a part of me that stayed angry. She'd see it sometimes when I snapped at her or chose Father over her, but she never said anything. She could've told me. I might've been on her side. I wouldn't have blamed her when I missed Father. I might've understood when she was demanding with him about petty things. She was hurt by all this too."

"Are you angry with your father?"

She swallowed. "I should be, I guess. But no. I know who he is, in spite of the secret part of his past. My life is so different from what I thought it was. I was blind. Even though he's still an amazing person, Father isn't the innocent I thought he was. And Mother wasn't the cold, bitter person I'd believed her to be."

The whisky fuzzed Thane's thoughts, and a memory of his recurring dream blinked through his mind. His fingerprint, and the feeling of falling and rushing forward. How his skin turned black. He wished he could call his mother, check on her. Beg her to go to Great Uncle Rabbie's for some invented reason until he figured everything out. He knew something bad was headed his way if he continued on like this, riding the line between his clan's demands and this girl's needs—his heart's needs.

The music had pulled in couples from around the tavern. The people lined up, crossed their arms, and walked circles around those next to them.

"Even I know this one. Strip the Willow," Myles said. He

lifted his soup bowl with both hands, downed what remained, and pushed away from the table. He held a hand out to Neve. "Care to take me for a spin?"

Neve shot the rest of her drink. "I believe I do. Or the whisky does. But I'm not of a mind to argue it just now."

They walked to the start of the lineup. Myles linked his arm in Neve's and tugged her around, stopping at the second couple and dropping his hold on her. She took up the next man's arm. Myles wiggled his eyebrows at a portly woman and shimmied. Thane sighed, jealous of his easy nature and more jealous of his ability to shrug off his troubled childhood. Why couldn't Thane throw off what he'd been born to? Why did it feel like his childhood, his family, grew over him like unbreakable vines, tight and tightening still?

Aini dabbed her mouth with her napkin. "We should dance, too. I feel terrible. I can't think. A good reel will help."

Thane didn't feel like dancing. Not even a little. But that smile she was giving him...

"All right," he said, standing. He nodded at Dodie, who kept his seat and chewed a toothpick.

Snagging Aini's hand, Thane pulled her into the reel. They both knew the steps, their feet and hands turning and moving in time.

A look of surprise showed on Aini's glowing face. "You're a great dancer. I mean, club dancing is one thing, but this?"

"I've all sorts of yet undiscovered talents," he said.

She missed a beat, then continued.

He tore his gaze from her curving neck and soft-looking face. "I'm sorry. That sounded..." he stuttered.

Spinning once under his arm, she came up against him. Her chin tilted. Her mouth was so close. "It's the whisky, isn't it?"

"It washes a person's manners clean away." A strangled laugh came out of him.

She grinned like a devil, and they joined everyone in making a circle, surrounding one dancer. The man in the center did an impressive jig, then returned to the edges of the crowd.

Thane gave Aini a little shove to the middle. She eyed him, grinned again, and began to dance. Taking the hem of her dress, she moved slowly, toe, toe, heel, heel, following the slow driving beat. The musicians, by now on their feet with the rest, built their tempo, challenging her. She moved her feet behind and in front of one another, moving faster and faster, spinning every fourth time, and giving a great leap at every one of the violin's high notes. Eyes closed, she became a piece of the music.

Thane couldn't take his eyes off her.

Her arms were lines of low and high, her fingers moving beautifully, and her feet punching staccato drum beats on the wooden planks of the floor. She began to spin, round and round, like a top.

The song came to an end and the room erupted into applause. She opened her coffee eyes, a lock of sweat-wet hair over her face and a real smile stretching her lips.

Aini MacGregor was definitely going to be the death of him.

Here he was gawking at her when they had a true storm coming down on them any minute. Rebels. Kingsmen who he had to avoid to protect his cover. Lewis in Nathair's hands.

The dancing broke into a mess of blethering and couples goofing around. Thane and the others headed to the bar to get water. Thane wiped his face with his sleeve, then peeled his lightweight sweater off. He'd left the bag of chemicals and candy under a cot at the Dionadair barn, so wearing only a T-shirt wouldn't be a problem. There was nothing that needed hidden.

As he leaned on a wood post waiting for Aini to order, a

couple of guys started mouthing off at the barkeep. They downed another shot of whisky and said something pure awful about the keep's mother.

Though the keep went about his job, this show of patience wouldn't last. The lads should've kept their tongues, considering the size of the keep and the look on the man's face. He didn't look like one to take it in stride, not with that cricket bat he had stored near the cash register. The only sport that bat had seen was the kind that ended in blood and bruised ribs.

The pub door opened.

The kingsmen walked in.

Thane swore under his breath.

One man with a shock of black hair was familiar. He'd been to the Bluefoot. Through the smoke and crowd, he squinted right at Thane. Preparing for the possibility that the kingsman—who'd obviously recognized him—would fail to retain his cover, Thane shook his hair down over his eyes.

"Forget the order," he said into Aini's ear. "Grab Myles. I'll get Neve. We're leaving."

Aini turned and saw the kingsmen too. "Okay. What about Dodie?"

"He'll get out. He knows what to do."

As the first kingsman dragged the other to the bar, Thane and the others made their way behind the crowd, nearer the door.

The barkeep and the guys were still arguing.

Back at the table, Thane waited until the keep had his back turned. Then he picked up his whisky glass and hurled it over one punk's shoulder. The glass hit the keep in the back of the head and crashed to the floor. A man and two women shouted as the keep whirled around, the bat already in his hands.

"Whoa!" Myles raised both arms and laughed.

The keep swung it at the guys. "Get out!"

They tried to argue it, pointing back in Thane's general direction. "We didn't—"

The keep swung again and this time, the punks had to duck. The bar erupted into a full-fledged fight.

Thane gathered everyone up and slipped out the door, the black-haired kingsman trying to get to them but blocked by the stramash.

In the street, they ran to the truck. Dodie drove them quickly out of town.

Dodie squinted, eyeing the motorway. "We'll have to get rid of this vehicle."

Neve was breathing too fast and Myles looked ready to faint.

"Aye," Thane said. "Dump it soon as we're within Edinburgh proper and we'll cab it the rest of the way. Neve. Myles. You're fine now. It's all right. How's the head, Myles?"

"I can't believe you just started a bar fight." Aini's eyes narrowed at Thane.

Out the window, night blurred by. "It was going to happen anyway."

Dodie shifted gears and the truck groaned.

Aini hugged herself, fingers pinching into her skin. "I have to think of another place to look for the Waymark Wall."

"We'll figure it out," Neve stammered.

Aini nodded, but Thane could tell her heart wasn't in it. Thane squeezed his eyes shut and laid his head against the window. After all they'd been through, could she be convinced that he'd see her through this somehow? Could he even make such a promise?

He lightly knocked his head against the glass. He wanted to make that promise, wanted it to be true. But the whole thing was so tangled and dangerous. Maybe if he could talk some of the other Campbells into backing him up instead of Nathair. Putting his elbows on his knees, knowing full well he was crazy for even thinking it. The minute they were at the townhouse, he had to send a message to Rodric. Further silence would be seen as disobedience. He'd mention the blinding powder that could be teased into gas form—the stuff he'd developed—and the negating tablet. Maybe if he could manage it, he could get Aini and the others to make a batch of the gravity-reducing hard candies and he could alter the mix to make the effects more extreme. He could report that too. That would keep his clan off his back until he figured out what to do. It was a mess that was certain.

The quiet of the rest of the drive was punctuated only by Myles's occasional bursts of song.

"For fire fight for friends, run ragged rings round reason, 'tis too tame to talk, touch, win wildly, wearing wounds wound with worship..."

Wearing wounds wound with worship. That line pretty much described Nathair Campbell. The chief of Clan Campbell, Earl of Argyll, wore the scar on his neck like a badge of honor. Anytime someone spoke up against him, he pointed to the thing like it was a holy relic and asked them what they had given of themselves for king and country.

A shudder wrapped around Thane. Outmaneuvering his clan was not going to be easy.

CHAPTER 21
FULLY LOADED

"No." Aini slammed a hand on the lab table the next day. The cool metal sent a chill over her. "I won't let you do this."

Thane paced the floor. He looked like he was going to be sick, but she wasn't going to ease off. Dawn's orange fire glowed through the high, leaded glass window, shining over him like a broken, unmoving lighthouse beam.

She'd discovered that, while the rest of them had slept, Thane had reworked the formula for Father's gravity-reducing hard candy, but it wasn't only to accomplish a punchier grape-lavender flavor. He wanted it strong enough to lift a person clean off the ground and keep them floating freely like a bird for a half hour.

"That is a weapon," she said.

The scent of burnt sweetness fit Aini's mood rather well.

"It wouldn't hurt anyone," Thane said.

Aini pointed a finger and stubbornly ignored his looks. It didn't matter that he was like something she'd dreamt up as he grabbed one of the low, black wood beams that crossed the ceiling. His slightly wrinkled, gray T-shirt shifted. The movement revealed the fine slope of his strong arm and a peek of his hipbone above his low-slung cotton pants. She looked away, staring instead at the colored sugar on the far wall.

Neve walked in, still braiding her hair. She paused and took in their scowls. "Surely Aini, at this point in our lives—with rebels and corruption and visions—you're not as worked up about paperwork, are you?" She must've heard part of their arguing. "So, what is it?"

Myles, nibbling an orange, came up behind her and frowned at Aini. "I wonder. Is there specific paperwork for a sixth-senser working in a candy lab?"

"Shut up, Myles," Thane and Aini said in unison.

Aini spun her mother's ring around and around her finger, its edges cutting.

"Don't you understand this at all?" She quieted her voice to keep it steady. "Father was taken because he refused to do exactly what Thane wants to do. Weaponize candy. Push its limits. Use it to alter people in ways that could truly affect lives." Spinning, she faced them and crossed her arms. "I will not go against my father's idea of right and wrong with regard to crafting sweets. This is HIS business. Not mine. Not yours. HIS. He spoke against the Campbells, risking everything, to fight the idea of stretching the effects of his sweets. I will not betray him now. Especially since I'm the worst possible kind of child he could have."

A sob tried to choke her words, but she forced it down and set her jaw.

"No, you're not," Neve said, her own chin trembling.

Thane's mouth turned down and he cocked his head at Aini. "Don't say that, hen."

"You are definitely not the worst," Myles said. "Not great, but not the worst. *I'm* the worst child someone could have. You should've seen my graduation. They're probably still cleaning the paint out of the dean's hair."

They all argued quietly against the fact, but it remained a fact. For a candymaker—a job you had to specifically apply for—to have a sixth-senser in the family? A mistrusted abomination? It didn't matter that Father had stopped helping the Dionadair. He was doomed because of Aini and some prophecy. She shook her head. A sick twist of fate.

Neve stepped around the table and stood beside Aini, her face pale. "Your father was against this. But that was before they ignored his right to a trial, to justice. He was against it before they hurt him. Before they kidnapped him."

"So, now you want me to make crazy concoctions so we can fight against them?" Aini said.

Shoving his glasses into his hair, Thane leaned on the table. He pressed his hands against his face. He really did look ill.

Neve raised her chin. "I do."

Aini's mouth fell open. She turned to Myles. "And you?"

He laughed and spit an orange seed into a napkin. "You know I do. If we're going to go up against those Campbell kingsmen, I want to go in fully loaded." Pretending he had some kind of enormous gun, he blasted the list of the king's rules hanging on the wall.

Fury rising, Aini jerked the stove's knob and turned the heat off. "No. We're not making anything. This lab is closed." She marched to the light switch and threw the room into darkness. "If I do this, Father will never be able to craft sweets again." She waved a shaking hand at the mixer, the rainbow of ingredients along the wall, the taffy puller, and Father's desk. "Our whole way of life will be over."

Thane stood tall, his face all lines and sharp angles. "It already is, Aini."

Her stomach lurched. "No," she whispered. "If we can spook the Campbells with a picture of the stone," she said, louder now, "and distract them and help Father escape, they might give up their plans for him. They might let us—"

Neve and Myles stared, their eyes sad and deadly calm.

They didn't believe it could happen. Everyone thought her life, their way of life, was actually over. It was all over.

Head spinning, Aini ran to her room. She refused to cry or rage in front of anyone anymore. Sitting on the bed, hands clenching the duvet and heart hammering, she suddenly wanted everything of Father's around her. She wanted to see him in everything. To somehow keep him close. Her heart clenched. She wanted to see him in a vision.

Rushing from room to room, she gathered his things. Dodie woke from his temporary bed on the couch and asked questions she ignored. She collected Father's favorite dark blue coffee cup, a keychain he'd bought in the Dominion of New England—where he'd visited her and her mother—and a tumble of chemistry and math volumes. Back in her room, she poured them onto the bed. Over and over again, she brushed fingers along each item of rough crockery, silver-plated metal, worn cloth, and leather.

None held a vision.

She started to drop onto the bed to forget this stupid idea—she needed to think of where else the Waymark Wall could be—but then she remembered she'd hidden the brooch under her floorboard. Maybe there was a place she hadn't touched yet, a sliver of memory left, one little vision.

The slat came up easily and there was her diary.

Her stomach dropped. The brooch was gone.

"Thane!" She didn't know why her mouth called for him when they'd just argued.

He banged into the room, his face worried, his glasses hanging from one hand. "What is it?" His tattoo of the chemical formula for salt had been splashed with purple food coloring.

"The brooch. Someone stole it."

Thane swore in Gaelic. Aini echoed the sentiment.

Myles stuck his head in, eyed her stash, and whistled like a bird. "What's going on in here?"

"The brooch is gone," Thane said. "I'm going to question Dodie."

The very man came to the door. "I heard you. And I don't have the Bethune brooch."

"Did the Campbells come here again and take it?" she asked. "But they didn't touch anything else."

Thane swallowed. "Guess it's all they needed."

Myles whistled low again, and Aini suddenly remembered the birds in the knife's vision, the ones on the island.

What if the island wasn't just another separate thought like the sight of the stone was? What if there was an island near the castle ruins, near the Waymark Wall?

She knew of one island in the area, one that fit the bill. It was covered in birds, which would explain the strange white color in the vision. She'd been a fool. This made sense. This had to be important.

"For now, forget the brooch. The candy. I have another idea about the Waymark Wall."

CHAPTER 22
A DOISTER

They left Edinburgh in a rush, met with the Dionadair on the motorway, and headed to Tantallon Castle, another jumble of ruins on the North Sea. Aini's palms tingled as if they somehow knew the Waymark Wall was there, waiting for her. Or maybe the stress had finally broken her and this was simply the beginning of her end.

Dodie agreed that the Campbells probably took the brooch. Somehow they'd learned she had it. What else they knew was still a mystery and that was no good. If they made it to the stone first, that would be the end of the road.

Dodie's lumpy form sat behind the steering wheel, Vera beside him, and Aini was squeezed between Thane and Myles in the back seat. Neve was on Myles's right, all of it making for a really tight fit. It didn't help the discomfort of the situation that Vera kept bumping her knife hilt on the roof, and Neve's nervousness was spilling out of her in the form of random historical tidbits.

Wind kicked last year's leaves into the cloudy sky as they

sped down the curving, narrow country road. Another truck drove in front of them, puffing foul exhaust through the open windows.

"Tantallon," Neve said, blinking too quickly between words, "is a castle of *enciente*, meaning it has a curtain wall. Forty-nine feet high and twelve feet thick, if you can believe it. Walter Scott wrote extensively about the castle in one of his poems. It's the one that everyone quotes. *Oh what a tangled web we weave, When first we practice to deceive!*"

Vera turned suddenly. Aini thought for a second she might cut out Neve's tongue, but she held up her phone, a serious look on her beautiful face. "Owen sent a message. A scout in Edinburgh says some of the Campbells are meeting to discuss something. Said even Nathair will be there. They know, Aini. We need to get to the wall and to the stone before they do or the game is up."

Icy fingers curled around Aini's throat.

His foot bouncing on the floor, Thane rubbed his knees. His tattoos blurred in the darkening truck cabin.

Vera made a call. "Gavin, take the tail." She was talking to the truck in front. "Call Tom Hunt. Tell him we'll be in his territory in twenty minutes."

Thane bumped into Aini as the truck moved down a hill. His hand pushed against her thigh. "Sorry," he said, his gaze shifting across her face.

She couldn't tell what he thought now. Fear? Anger? Regret that her mess of a life had snared him? It was impossible to tell. He'd retreated into himself since they realized the Campbells had the brooch. Or maybe because of their argument about the candy.

Leaning over Myles, Neve smiled. "You'll find it. You're fated for this."

"I wish I had your faith."

Vera sighed. "I wish our Seer wasn't such a wee feartie."

Thane raised his head. "She's not a coward. It's only that she cares about the people around her."

Vera stared Thane down. "Oh, and I don't care? Why do you think we're out to throw the Campbells and the king down? For the money?" Vera laughed loud and batted her thick black lashes. She slammed a fist against her chest. "My parents were shot to death." Tears shone in her eyes. "And I'm risking my life for my countrymen. I do it every day."

"And you put your cause before those you love," Thane said. "It's pointless to fight against the Campbells. You're leading us all to the slaughter."

Heart drowning, Aini shuddered. Didn't he have any hope in her at all?

Myles shoved a tiny apple into Aini's hand. "Ignore them and eat, sweetheart." He produced another like a magician and gave it to Neve. "You too, love."

Aini held the apple, turning it in her hands. They had to quit bickering. They needed to be a team if this was going to work. She had to be strong enough to bind them together in this madness. But they kept on arguing and shooting glares at one another.

She put a hand on Thane's back and eyed Vera. "Please, stop. We're in this together, for the moment anyway. There's no purpose in fighting right now."

Thane twisted. His nostrils flared out and in. "Are you ready to do as the Dionadair do and risk all? Because these people, they're not putting your father first. I can tell you that."

Vera snorted. "You think the Campbells are just going to hand him back? He's good as dead if we don't take all of them down."

The truck bounced, sending Aini's apple to the floor. Myles retrieved it and traded fruit with her.

"Please," she said. "I need to think. To remember the vision so I can find the wall."

"Aye. Of course," Thane and Vera said in unison.

Sighing, Aini put her head in her hands.

Neve whispered, her tone joking but her words shaky. "For a lady so lovely, Vera sure can give a mean growler. What a scowl."

Peering at the expression Vera directed at Thane in the rearview mirror, Aini laughed shakily, agreeing, then closed her eyes to try and bring every detail of the vision to mind.

Thane's mouth was suddenly at Aini's ear, his soft lips moving and making her breathe unevenly. "Take this," he said and handed her something small.

It was a square of tablet, the sugar and butter candy Father altered to negate the effects of the golden taffy. "Why?"

Keeping an eye on Vera, Thane handed a piece of the tablet to Myles and Neve too. "Just keep it. Eat if I ask you to."

Neve stared at it.

"What are you up to?" Aini asked.

Thane shuffled on the seat and adjusted the hidden bag under his sweater as Vera swore at Dodie. Myles shrugged and slipped the candy into his shirt pocket.

"I'm just making sure we have an escape plan if we need it," Thane said.

"Escape from who exactly?" Myles asked.

Aini studied Thane's serious face. "He's worried about the Campbells. But how will this help—"

Vera had stopped fighting with her brother. She turned. "What's this you're blethering on about?"

"Nothing," Neve and Aini said.

Thane rolled his eyes.

Vera sniffed. "Right," she said, but she did drop it, thankfully.

Aini pretended to cough and stored the tablet in her bra, wondering what Thane had in mind. Especially considering he hadn't shared the plan with the Dionadair. She didn't like this. Not one bit. Too many variables clashed around, too many things not planned out or reasoned properly. What she wouldn't give to spend a week figuring this all out and writing a proper list, a plan of attack.

DODIE DROVE THEM INTO A PARKING LOT FRAMED BY TALL grass. Thane, Myles, Neve, and Aini piled out of the truck. The moonlit ruins of Tantallon Castle loomed past a tourist shop and a mown field.

"Go on ahead, Seer." Vera locked the vehicle's loading doors and nodded to Dodie. "My brother and I'll keep watch. Our other truck will be here soon."

Tantallon was a child's sand creation made real in the starlight. Below lacy clouds, a curtain wall of red sandstone reached across the headland, a gatehouse at its front. Aini shivered. It was just like the vision. The North Sea hissed at the cliffs beside and behind the old castle.

"That's the Douglas Tower," Neve whispered as they walked through the clipped lawn. Grass snicked at their shoes. She pointed up to the left. "Seven stories. Circular, originally. There's a pit prison down below."

Myles looked at his feet and smiled. "I'll stay near you, Neve. Don't be so nervous. There aren't any Campbells out here as of yet. Plus, we've got two truckloads of black market, gun-wielding rebels on our side even if they do show."

Neve sighed heavily and put her hand in the crook of his arm. "You do know how to sweet-talk a lady." She rolled her eyes.

Taking a breath of the briny air, Aini studied the uneven line of the ruins. A far-off noise hovered in the air like someone plucking poorly tuned guitar strings. Sea birds. Beyond the castle, an island sat in the waves. The moon lit its sloped face as well as the water that rolled around the island's base.

Aini pressed her fingers into her eyelids, picturing Father the last time she'd seen him. His bushy gray eyebrows. His salt and pepper beard. His sparkling, smart eyes surrounded by new wrinkles that made her want to take his hand and ask him about his day. In her mind, he called her *squirrel* again, the childhood nickname she'd earned by climbing the maple in front of the townhouse. Her throat convulsed, but she pulled air in through her nose.

They passed through the time-chewed gatehouse.

"Look for a spiral in the stone," Aini said. The wind was chilly and salty. She pulled her sweater more tightly around her. "I think it was at the base of a wall inside a room. I'm going up."

"I'm coming with you." Thane's voice was low and strained.

A retort rose inside her mouth. She wanted to tell him she was fine on her own, that she'd be all right, but he looked like he needed the company and his worry had just washed his tone in acid.

Myles and Neve walked through the open grass of the courtyard toward the shell of rooms near the sea cliff.

With Thane, grouchy but quiet at her back, Aini found a stone, spiral staircase, much like the one leading to the tower lab. They wound up and up and up. These ruins were huge. Desperation weighed down her shoulders and eyelids.

They reached the summit of the castle. The parapet stretched along the top, a slim road of stone and low wall, overlooking the courtyard. Myles and Neve's silhouettes moved far below Aini, and farther still, the North Sea's waves shifted. The wind tugged Aini's hair, and water crashed beyond and below, its surface as silver as the dress she'd worn to King John's birthday masquerade last year in London. The king had accidentally brushed her arm during one of the dances that night, and his smile had given her chills. Pushing the memory away, she ran a hand along the base of the wall. Thane knelt beside her and did the same.

"When did you start seeing visions?" he asked, his words nearly lost in the wind and his hair flying around his head. He took his glasses from his pocket and slid them on.

"My visions...um...around my sixteenth birthday."

"Does your father know you're a sixth-senser? Tell me the truth. Please." Thane moved into a crouch to examine the middle row of stone.

Touching the gritty top of the wall, Aini stood, stepped closer. Dust and grime from centuries ago fell away where she rubbed the stone.

"I couldn't tell him. I was afraid it would somehow get him in trouble. And I was afraid of what he would think of me."

"So, you lied to keep him safe and to maintain his high regard for you." There was no questioning tone in his voice. "Because you...you love him."

Aini glanced at him out of the corner of her eye. The wind threw his hair sideways. The moon danced over his shoulders, across his glasses, and the line of his crouched shape. What was he getting at?

"I hated hiding my ability from Father," she said. "He would've loved me anyway—I know that now—but he was terrible about keeping quiet when it came to any kind of surprise. At Christmas or with things in the lab. I was afraid kingsmen would question him and he wouldn't be able to keep my secret." She laughed, but it wasn't funny at all. "Guess he kept the secrets he really needed to."

Thane gaze went to hers. "We all have secrets."

Her breath caught in her throat. "I'm not mad at him for hiding his past. Not anymore. He's a good man. He took care of me. Spent so much time and money to travel overseas to visit me every month. He never said a mean word to Mother, even during the divorce. He did what he thought was best for us."

Thane reached out a hand and touched her cheek, and she shivered under the wonderful heat of his skin.

"To have you think like that of me..." he whispered.

The wind gusted, and rain drifted down in a cold, misty sheet, covering the castle grounds.

One hand running along the pitted wall, Aini pulled him to the staircase. Halfway down, they ducked into a small, circular chamber. A glassless window opened to the fields out front and the grassy lawn beyond the gatehouse. With bobbing flashlights, the Dionadair waited in clusters. Her neck and shoulders tensed.

Myles and Neve ran into the room, their hair hanging wet over their foreheads.

"Find anything?" Myles slicked his green spikes back.

Talking over the search so far, the four of them scoured the walls as the rain lashed in through the window. The wind howled once, loud and long, around the ruins.

Vera appeared in the doorway. "We need to go. The wind's rising. There's a doister coming."

"We can't go yet."

"What's a doister?" Myles asked.

"A big storm. A nasty one," Neve said.

Aini's head began to pound. If she didn't find the wall tonight, the Campbells would track her down. The Dionadair would be destroyed, along with her only chance at getting her father back.

"I'll just go look at a few more places." Aini tore past the rest of them and ran down the stairs.

The only room they hadn't collectively checked at all was the rectangular space that used to serve as the great hall, where people had once feasted and drank by the massive hearth.

The roof was long gone. The hall stood open to the churning clouds overhead. Rounded supports protruded from the walls where thick beams once ran side to side. The place looked like the rest of Tantallon, the skeleton of something that had once been powerful, protective, a shield against the storm of armies and intrigue.

With the rain increasing, Aini worked her way to the base of the closest wall. The salty water lashed out, fogged the stones in front of her, and flavored the moisture that ran into her mouth.

Thane ran up, rain streaming down his face and sticking his sweater to his strong chest, revealing the edges of the bag he'd hidden beneath.

"We need to go. The storm is—"

A gust ran fingers through her hair and yanked out her scarlet ribbon. The slip of fabric flew through the storm, catching the diffused moonlight, until it snagged the nearby corner where the back wall and the outer met in a triangle of darkness. She couldn't stand the thought of leaving it out here in the cold rain near the crashing ocean. A hard shiver rocked her and she fought a sob, Father's face in her mind, bleeding and dirty.

She raced to retrieve the ribbon, and crouching, curled her hand around the soft fabric. Her fingers brushed a curving indentation in the sandstone. She pressed a hand fully against the wall.

It was a spiral.

The wind kicked up, and the stone bones of Tantallon's ancient great hall cooled her flesh. Everyone else ran into the great hall and crowded around her. Excitement buzzed through her veins.

A looping shape had been carved into the base of the open room's back wall. She traced the curve and remembered her vision of the Coronation Stone, the one imprinted on the brooch. As her finger dragged into the heart of the spiral, Thane's furrowed brow, the rain falling sideways around him, Myles, Neve, Vera, and the ruined castle walls—it all shimmered and disappeared, leaving the world gray around the edges.

A man's face appeared.

Angus Bethune, the first of the Dionadair.

Angus raised his chin. His palm lay against the spiral in the wall. Closing his eyes, he pictured the black stone with its metallic flecks. The Coronation Stone. A hollow sat in the stone's center, more circles and spiraling shapes decorating its exterior. Over the stone, a shape came into focus, a black and white space surrounded by churning movement.

The island.

A bird darted to the crashing sea. The air was thick with briny mois-ture. A stone building sat against the island's rough terrain. Inside, there was a small, underground room lit by candles. A chapel? There. Seer. Seer! *Angus called out.*

The earthen floor of the small room grew hazy, but there, somewhere, was the stone. Sitting, waiting like a beast in hibernation. Power hummed around the ancient throne like the black rock was alive, breath-ing, ready to strike. Tear our land from the wrongful king! You are the Seer. You have the gift! *Angus shouted. His words became unintel-ligible, his brain flying through pictures. Emotions like colors streaked the scene.*

Murky yellow fear, blue truth, green trust.

Faster. Faster.

A shout tore out of Aini. Thoughts brushed along her mind too quickly like she was running through a forest and any minute she'd slam into a tree. She shook her head, and at last, the vision faded.

As she tilted to the side, nausea squirmed in her middle, but a sense of joy soaked through her, waiting for the sick feeling to pass.

Her hope roared to life.

The man from the vision—Angus Bethune—had been so sure, so very sure, about her role to play as Macbeth's descendant, the Seer. His faith lifted her to her feet. The strength she'd felt in the Coronation Stone poured steel into her limbs and steadied her.

Maybe the Dionadair, with her help, really *could* succeed in their quest to free Scotland. She could find the stone, find the Heir, and take down the Campbells and the king. But before the rebellion, and so much sooner, maybe Father would be in her arms again.

"Aini."

She whirled around and Thane stood there, waiting. The wind whipped his hair, and his eyes matched the tumultuous sea beyond. The darkness that had always hounded his features cleared. He smiled, and her heart surged. It was a real smile, like he somehow realized what this vision had meant to her.

"You truly think this can be done," he said over the weather. "You can change everything."

Myles and Neve stared, wide-eyed. Vera, Dodie, and several other Dionadair surrounded them, awe coloring their faces.

"I...I do," Aini said, shocking herself. For a breath, she imagined a Scotland with a good ruler and a Parliament, a place where people had a voice.

Vera took a step forward and held out a hand. "Let's get you out of this weather, Seer."

The rain unleashed its wrath then and came down in lashing whips. They splashed into the muddy courtyard. The storm nearly obscured the island from the vision—Neve had called it Bass Rock. Aini kept glancing at it as they hurried through the towering gatehouse and sped toward the trucks' yellow headlamps.

The rain tasted bright and salty on her tongue and the world was suddenly sharper. Like everything they'd been through shone in stronger contrast.

CHAPTER 23
REVELATIONS

Back at the Dionadair's barn and underground facility, Aini squeezed rain from her hair. The wind howled through the double doors until Dodie latched them tight.

"Did you see it?" Neve asked. Her clothes hung on her like a wet rag.

"I did," Aini said, turning to Owen, who'd come from the entrance to the tunnels. "It's on Bass Rock, the island off the coast near Tantallon. It's in a chapel. Some sort of buried chapel."

"I know about that place!" Neve said. She began telling Myles about some saint and the history of the island.

Thane came up and took Aini's hands, warming them. Wonder had replaced the darkness in his eyes.

"It's amazing," Aini said. Everyone had gone quiet and turned an ear toward her. "The Coronation Stone has this...power to it." Goosebumps ran over her skin.

A tentative grin spread over Thane's mouth. "I cannot

believe I'm saying this, but if we can get it and find the Heir... things might truly change."

Thane cupped her chin, his eyes light gray and brimming with concern. The circles under his eyes said he needed rest, though he was nearly buzzing with energy. Or was that her?

He leaned in and spoke near her mouth, throwing shivers down her neck and chest and shoulders. "I'm proud of you. None of what I've been worried about will really matter if—"

Owen clapped his hands together once, shattering the moment between Thane and her. "If you'll follow Vera to the sleeping quarters," he said, checking his phone, "she'll find you some dry clothing." He addressed the teeming mass of Dionadair. "Once the storm has passed, we head to Bass Rock!"

As they made their way through the tunnel attached to the barn, Myles whistled a southern colonial tune, punctuated with lines that rhymed with Neve's last name Moore.

"I only wished my sweet faced Neve would give me more, my heart is sore, my Neve thinks I'm a bore, to love me be a chore!"

Thane muttered something about strangling, then looked over his shoulder at the circle of light coming from the main tunnel they'd just left.

"Hey, if this doesn't go the way we want it to or if the Campbells find this place," Thane whispered, his lips grazing Aini's cheek and making her mouth go dry, "eat that tablet I gave you and get Myles and Neve to the truck. Dodie leaves the key in his. Go toward a port city. Get out of Scotland."

Any warmth she'd found faded fast. Her teeth chattered from both fear and her wet clothes. "How can I do that? It'd be—"

"Mr. Moray," Vera said, her voice singsong and falsely sweet.

Aini spent half her time hating that woman and the other half deciding whether she should be her next hero. "It's not polite to share secrets in front of others."

"You need to teach your wandering hands about manners before you can do any preaching on the matter," he spat back.

Myles and Aini laughed as they came to the sleeping quarters.

Vera snorted. "You are a spicy one, Thane Moray." She pointed to a rack of hanging shirts, coats, pants, and dresses at the back wall. "Grab something to wear. All of you."

Securing some dry clothing, Aini and Neve went behind the hanging drop cloth on one side of the room. The guys found their own screened area on the other. Aini pulled a sea-colored long shirt over some dark blue leggings, and after grabbing a pair of unmatching but clean socks, put her damp boots back on since there weren't any shoes available in her size.

Neve threw on a green v-neck T-shirt and some trousers that were several sizes too big. She latched a belt on and found a pair of men's black boots. As she tugged the laces, her copper brown hair fell over her eyes. Aini thought about how much Neve had been through for her and Father.

"Think your brothers are doing all right without you to check up on them?" Aini straightened her heavy hair over her shoulders.

"Suppose they're getting into all sorts of trouble." Neve grinned, but there was a gravity to the look. "Clive's old enough now that he can make sure everyone has food on their plates."

Neve was risking so much. "Thank you for being a great friend. It sounds stupid, but thank you for staying by my side. I couldn't do this without you. Or what you know about Scotland."

Neve raised her head and smiled, her front teeth too large,

but somehow pretty anyway. "Scared as I am, I wouldn't miss this for anything, Aini. Don't doubt that for a second. I have a question though." Aini nodded, and Neve's eyes took on a faraway look as she sat up. "Did you see the Heir in your visions?"

It was a good question. "No."

"Could it be you?" Neve bit her lip.

"I'd know it, wouldn't I?"

Neve shrugged. "It's not like there's anything to go by."

An alarm blared through the room, a shrieking, piercing wail. A cold sweat spread over Aini. She and Neve traded a panicked look and hurried out from behind the screen.

The Dionadair shouted at one another and ran into the tunnel, cocking shotguns and shouting directions.

Hair still dark and lank with rain, Thane and Myles emerged from their own screened spot. Thane wore a slightly baggy pair of brown pants and an ivory shirt that was only buttoned half-way up. Aini noticed he'd removed his silver chain. Maybe he'd lost it. The edge of his secret bag showed.

Dressed in mostly black, Myles hopped on one foot, tying on his second boot.

"Someone has breached their perimeter," Thane said.

The breath went out of Aini.

The Campbells.

Thane waved for them to follow him into the tunnel. The lights along the bare rock walls flickered. The alarm screamed, searing Aini's ears.

"Do you think it's the Campbells?" she asked, panting as they ran.

"Well, it isn't Owen's granny coming to call." The orange lighting made him look sick. "Just when I'd thought maybe life could be different," he hissed under his breath.

The entrance to the barn was closed. Owen came flying up from behind, a rifle in his arms. A scream and several loud bangs sounded behind the door. The whites around Owen's eyes were bright in the low light.

"Stay here," he said, jerking the entrance open.

The barn was in chaos.

Faces twisted in anger, kingsmen in Campbell kilts poured in through the double doors. Swords and clubs swung in quick arcs from their hands. Guns fired. The Dionadair swelled and met them with fists and knives flashing. Shots blasted off the barn's towering wood slat walls and rock foundation.

A rush of people flowed out of the tunnel, pushing past and shoving into Myles and Thane. Owen grabbed a man with a dragon tattoo peering out from the neck of his shirt.

"Get the rest of the guns down. Find Dodie," Owen ordered the man. "I'm here!" he shouted at Vera, who'd hitched up the mini skirt she now wore and was scaling the shelves of weapons, reaching for a bronze-handled rifle.

"Then get to it!" she screamed back, her face wild.

Thane spun toward Aini, Myles, and Neve. His voice was loud and steady despite the horror behind him. "Eat the tablet I gave you. Here's more." He fished some from his bag and handed it to Myles. "I'm going to blind everyone else. Though it'll be uncomfortable, you and only you all will be able to see. Keep to the walls and edge your way out the doors. Remember what I told you, Aini."

Her lungs seized up. Noise and fear battled for space in her brain.

Myles's and Neve's gazes followed the action left and right.

People were everywhere.

Thane pulled a flat, glass container and a fold of paper from his hidden bag. He crouched in the corner where the earth met the wall of the barn and tugged the cork of the container out with his teeth.

"This is a spin on Lewis's golden taffy made into a gas. It'll give you time to escape this mess."

Aini looked over his shoulder, her curiosity overpowering her anger that he'd once again gone against her in this. "But it's powder."

"It is until I mix this in." He held up the fold of brown paper. "Then it'll become a gas. It's some of the Cone5 and a five to six ratio of—"

"What about you? You act like you're not running away with us."

"I'll make sure you get out alive."

She grabbed his shirt.

Ignoring her, Thane shook the package into the container and immediately a cloud of yellow snaked from the glassware. He coughed. "I'll find you. Don't worry."

"No way, man," Myles said, bouncing on his toes. "We're not leaving you."

Neve agreed.

Thane met Aini's eyes and something dark crossed the gray of his irises.

"I will worry," she said. "No matter what you have up that sleeve of yours. Why don't you just come with us?" Her heart was breaking. This was supposed to be the beginning of a new life for everyone, not a horrible ending.

Across the barn, near the double doors, a tall man in a muddied kingsman jacket and a Campbell kilt raised a huge handgun.

"Traitors!" the man shouted. A scar puckered his neck like a gruesome smile, but otherwise he was a fairly handsome man with wavy red-blond hair and broad shoulders.

Aini's stomach turned. It was Nathair Campbell, the king's head of security.

"Death to the traitors!" he shouted.

A strangled noise came from Thane's throat. As he stared at Nathair, he fell back and gripped the wall. "It's him."

The vial crashed on the stone, and the yellow haze curled quickly into the air, spreading into the barn. Aini helped Thane away from the smoke he'd created.

Neve gripped Aini's arm hard. "That's him. Chief of the Campbells. Earl of Argyll. The King's Deathbringer."

Myles pulled at them. "Let's go." He looked at Thane. "You're sure about this?"

Thane nodded tersely. "Get Aini out of here. She can't be in the same room as that man."

Aini didn't even get a last look at Thane as Myles dragged them into the barn. There were too many people moving, fighting, shouting, pushing. Thane's chemicals whirled around the room like sickly ghosts. Every man and woman shrieked as it touched their faces. Dionadair and kingsmen alike put hands to their eyes, blinded and running into one another. They struck out with weapons and pulled triggers, some killing and maiming. Swords and axes hit tables, walls, and people before clattering to the floor.

Shaking, Aini took the lead and shepherded Myles and Neve along the left side of the barn toward the fighting training cage near the exit.

At the cage, a kingsman, his eyes rolling as he tried to see past what had to be a blinding, glaring rainbow of colors, swung a club at a Dionadair, way too close to Aini's head. She dodged the thing, the fighting cage's barbed metal biting into her back and her heart pounding.

Through the press of bodies, they eked their way to the double doors and into the predawn light.

Outside, three kingsmen knelt by strange boxes. Their kilts partially blocked Aini's view.

"They say a chemical's been released," the first one said into a walkie talkie, not noticing them. His associates swore and spoke into their phones and to one another. "No one can see," the first one said to them. "That yellow fog—it's screwing with their vision. Call for the false retreat. Then raze the front section." The second man held a black box with a red handle. "Explosion on my count. Are you clear?"

Aini's knees shook. Explosion. They were going to blow something up.

The men shifted as more kingsmen with streaming eyes rushed from the barn, some Dionadair trailing them. Thane's concoction blossomed into the air and dissipated.

"Retreat!" the man shouted as they rushed toward Dodie's empty truck. "Soon as you see the chief clear the entrance, raze the barn."

Thane is in there.

Aini ran free of Myles and Neve, with nothing in her mind but buzzing and white and panic, she dove at the man with the black box. She hit him hard, her cheek bruising against his shoulder as more yelling rose around her. Then all the noise and movement was swallowed by a flood of golden light. As she fell to the earth with the kingsman under her, the ground beneath the three-story barn erupted into the air. Splinters big as a man. Foundation stones. Sprays of dirt. Bodies. Everything in sight shot into the dawn.

She landed, ears throbbing, and jumped off the kingsman. Myles was near, on his knees, Neve at his side and lying on her stomach. Her hands shielded her ears.

Surprisingly, most of the barn's other side still stood, but the front area near the doors was nothing more than a pile of rubble overrun with kingsmen and Dionadair, scrambling up to continue their fight or holding bleeding comrades. Moans and screaming came from the rubble as the yellow haze dissipated.

Thane.

Aini tore toward the damaged barn.

At the first cluster of wooden debris, a man shouted, "Aini MacGregor!"

She froze.

The man was partially covered in broken wood planks and dirt, his body trapped beneath one of the barn's doors. Reaching from the rubble, his hand snagged her ankle and she screamed, pulling with everything she had. His fingers dug painfully into her boot and the skin underneath. He held on, the scar at his throat vivid despite the mud and dust.

Nathair Campbell.

The man who had led the public execution of rebels last month. The Campbell who seemed to be going mad. The one who gripped his own countrymen by their throats and squeezed money from them and their businesses, who had ordered so many innocents shot to death or imprisoned for life in the famed cells under Edinburgh. The memory of the boy crying on market day blazed through her mind. He'd lost his parents to a ridiculous law about Subject Identification Cards all because of the king and his beast, this man, Nathair.

And Nathair controls the men who have Father.

Keeping his hold on Aini and blinking repeatedly, Nathair used his other hand to dig beneath the stone, into his pocket. He tossed something at her. A roll of rag cloth. It fell to the ground at her feet. With Myles and Neve shouting to come on to the truck, she unwrapped the cloth. But she couldn't understand what she was looking at. Flesh. Pale and blue and streaked with blackened blood.

A finger wearing a ring. The MacGregor ring.

Gasping, she dropped it, and the ring fell away from the flesh. A rushing sound filled her ears, bile rising in her throat. She braced herself on a boulder and bent to vomit. It was Father's finger. His. Finger.

The ground dropped away, and she took hold of the boulder with both hands.

"Is he still alive? Is my father still alive?"

"Aye," Nathair hissed, working his way out of the debris to stand.

The earth stopped rushing away and she managed a breath.

"You should look to what side you choose, girl. I don't think you'll enjoy losing." His words rose and fell unevenly, his body swaying and his head cloaked in blood.

"Father," a low voice said.

Nathair and Aini both whipped around.

Thane stumbled out of the boiling mess of fighting and bleeding men and women.

A cool rush of relief ran over Aini. Blood masked the left side of Thane's face. Like a wraith, his cheekbones were sharp in the sunrise, and his eyes were deep and dark, but he was alive.

Nathair held his arms open wide, a twisted look on his face. "Son."

The word cut Aini at the knees.

Shaking, weak, choking, she met Thane's gaze.

Regret blackened the light in his eyes. A shiver rolled through him, and he clenched his hands and threw his head back as a vicious shout of frustration and rage erupted from his throat.

He launched himself at Nathair, fisting his hands in the man's shirt and jerking him roughly. Nathair shoved Thane back, but Thane drove at him again. Shouting unintelligible words, he rained down wild strikes. Tears mixed with the blood streaming over the line of Thane's jaw. His shirt absorbed the wet and clung to his chest.

Aini was frozen. Neve and Myles were suddenly beside her, but she felt no relief. It couldn't be true. She shook, worked air into her lungs. The trees, grass, the mess of the explosion, the people—hurting and shouting—spun once, fast, around her, before she could focus on Thane and Nathair again.

Though he was unsteady on his feet, Nathair dodged most of Thane's blows. Staggering, he ripped a silver chain from his neck. "You left this at the MacGregor house." It was Thane's necklace. "You should not forget who you are, son."

Tearing it from Nathair's large hand, Thane threw the chain to the earth. The silver dropped to the ground like a piece of the morning moon had fallen from the sky.

Aini choked out one word. "Why?"

Nathair smiled. "Because I told him to."

Chest heaving, Thane's rage took him again. He was a lion, his strikes quick, strong, vicious. A hit to his father's stomach. A knee to the groin. Two elbows aimed at Nathair's temples. Nathair's eyes dazed, and he fell at Thane's feet.

Myles and Neve seized Thane by the shoulders and dragged him back a step. His shirt ripped down the back as they pulled him away.

Aini's stomach reeled. Her fingers were numb.

A terrible smile tore across Thane's face. "I'm as terrible as him. As the lot of them."

Jerking away from Myles and Neve, he laughed like a madman, wiping tears and blood from his face. His torn shirt hung loose and showed his shoulder, the tendons and muscles moving beneath his skin as he looked at Father's ring in the mud. He closed his eyes, his black lashes making lines above his cheekbones.

"To think I believed all this could change...I've always been a Campbell." He punched a fist against his chest. "That's all I'll ever be. *Ne Obliviscaris*. Forget Not. That's our dear clan motto. Forget not how we beat you down until you're bleeding and begging to serve us."

He performed an exaggerated bow, almost seeming drunk, stumbling but catching himself on another pile of rock.

"I tried to tell you, Aini. But I should've known. How could you care for a man who has a part in this? I'm a fool. A spy. I'm the worst thing that's ever happened to you."

"No," she whispered. "Bran is working for them, but you, you're my father's favorite, like a son..."

Aini's world fractured into a million pieces. Was anything she believed actually true?

Scooping up his Campbell necklace, Thane rushed toward the damaged fencing surrounding the property. A black horse trapped in the space between a fallen section and a tree shied from him, but he caught the animal and threw a leg over its back.

Myles ran after him. "Thane!"

Thane pushed his heels into the horse. "Yah!" His voice cracked, and he rode toward the dawn's light, the sun making his bare shoulder and tangled hair glow. The horse's hooves kicked up chunks of earth as they disappeared down the road.

The fight went on around Aini. A shot rang out and something stung her ear, but she didn't flinch. Father's finger lay in the grass beside the MacGregor ring.

Myles and Neve put hands under her arms.

Myles pulled Aini toward Dodie's truck. "We have to get out of here."

Neve shuddered. "I never would've guessed Nathair's own son...right in front of our faces. There was something odd about him, yes, but this? I never thought the genius lab rat could be *that* Thane!"

"Wait!" Aini pushed away from them, running to Father's ring. She cupped it in her palm, then returning, clambered into the truck.

Though she'd already played out the vision embedded on the ring, memory brought it back, clear and beautiful and sharp as glass. The vision—a memory so important to Father that it had sunk into his signet ring—had shown the day she was born. Her mother, sweating and smiling, held a red, newborn Aini. She screamed like babies do, her face scrunched in a fierce scowl. Father took her into his arms, his face glowing, and Aini's crying stopped.

Aini suddenly felt far away from where she was. Her mind took her...somewhere else, a place foggy.

White.

Numb.

Then the truck bumped harshly to the right, and the daze slipped away. Myles was behind the wheel, silent and eyes narrowed. Dirt covered Neve's knuckles as she stared out at the road. There was nothing in front of the three of them but ruined plans and the coming crash of grief.

CHAPTER 24
CREATURE

Thane slid from his horse under the broad branches and clustered leaves of an English oak, maybe five, six miles from...everything. He was in a bracken and weed-strewn fallow field beside long, flat runs of barley and something green and short. Blood slugged through him as he moved his fingers slowly in and out, fisting and unfisting. Dried red flaked from his knuckles. His father's blood.

Thane's eyelids shuttered closed against the struggling dawn. He pictured a finger in the grass and mud. Stomach roiling, he dragged a hand over his sore face and swollen eyes.

What was wrong with Father? What had they all become? But it was a question he already knew the answer to. They had become people Aini could never forgive. Shouldn't forgive.

Exhaustion lay over him like a lead blanket. His last thought he had before sleep pulled him under was of his mother. Her eyes, pewter like his, always smiled even when her mouth did not. His mother was scarred, her spirit lashed and beaten into submission by a love she shouldn't feel.

Almost every Monday morning of Thane's childhood, his father went to London and his mother took him from their Georgian mansion, Inveraray Castle, and out to the wishing well, hidden among the clean-scented pines and dense oaks outside of town. He remembered reaching a hand toward the arch of carved stone that stood over the sacred spot. The air smelled like it did here in this farmer's field, green and good. She'd picked him up, her hands gentle on his sides. When she nodded toward the spring bubbling from under the earth, he'd made a silent wish that every day would be Monday. Now the king had taken the very day's name away.

His dream came to him then.

It showed his hand, five fingers, then the palm, then closer and closer, until the dips and swirls of his ring finger's print were walls, valleys, canyons. The flesh darkened, blackened, grew sharp and strong, and Thane was lifted by a thundering storm and driven through the curves, flying, rushing, the sound like one thousand drums.

Eventually, the sun's white light chased the confusing dreams and tender memories from Thane's mind, and he lifted his aching head, his hand going to his ribs. The dull pain didn't crack him apart like a true break. It only made him slow in rising to his feet. A cut pinched at the side of his head, but it wasn't serious. He pulled a twig from his hair and rolled his tongue around in his mouth. Thirst almost seared away the pain in his body and his heart. Almost.

Past the oak's wide-reaching and dappled shadow, the horse he'd ridden snapped up grass with velvet lips. Bracing himself against the tree, Thane stood. The summer breeze blew across the bare skin of his shoulder. When had he torn his shirt? Everything was a blur of violence. Fists, fury, and shouting.

But it had also somehow freed him.

All his life, a creature with burning eyes and grabbing claws had lived inside him. He'd thought the creature to be a sense of justice. But now, no. He knew better. It was his father's growing need for power, his madness. Nathair had nurtured the creature with nights by the hearth spent repeating why Campbells were special and owed fealty. The creature knew the names of generations of Campbells, MacArthurs, MacIvers, Burnes, and MacConochies, and Orrs. It was well versed in the wrongs done them by the Dionadair. And what Campbells did about it when they found the rebels.

Thane put a hand over his chest. His heart beat slow and sure.

The creature was gone. The crippling fear and anger absent.

He only hoped Mother would understand.

Taking the horse's loose reins, he searched the saddle bag for water, ale, anything to wet the desert of his mouth. A hawk's sickle shape soared high, swooped low to the golden grasses, and rose again to search for prey, ready to strike. Thane's fingers tightened on the reins. The ragged leather twisted in his grip. Even with the creature exorcised, his father would always be there, watching, waiting, wanting.

Mounting the horse, running a hand down the animal's warm, ebony side, he made a promise to himself. A secret promise.

Swallowing disgust with what he had to do, he took off at a gallop toward the road to find a town, a train, any path back to Edinburgh.

CHAPTER 25
MY ENEMY'S NIGHTMARE

Aini sat at a wide table in a stranger's kitchen, looking out the window at a dead tree. Owen had caught up with them on the motorway and detailed the loss of lives, injuries, and how the Campbells had reportedly left the area to regroup, their bruised leader shouting orders to go after his son. A widow—mother to one of the rebels—had offered her house to the Dionadair, so they'd holed up here in borrowed blankets, cots, and hammocks, not far from the site of the violence. They wouldn't be staying for long, Owen had said.

He and Vera were talking to Aini about Thane, his loyalties, and their fears. Really, they were talking *at* her. Toying with the bandage on her ear—it turns out, a bullet had just missed her—she was still processing, picking apart every moment she'd had with Thane.

"But he never told you a thing," Vera said.

Neve was quiet beside Aini, her hand gently perched on Aini's knee. An anchor Aini needed to keep from drifting into swells of hopelessness.

Owen's voice was careful. "And he was responsible for that blinding gas, aye?"

Aini stared out the warped window panes, the dead tree's branches black and twisting toward the sky.

What was real?

Thane had handed her Macbeth's knife with his head bowed in the exact same manner he'd used when conning the female guard at St. Andrews. So that one, that moment she'd thought they'd had, was false. A lie. A stage direction in his play.

But their kiss. That had been real. The blood had risen to his cheeks. And the way he'd looked at her... Not even Nathair Campbell's own master spy and son could fake that. Could he?

The memory of Father's ring and severed finger washed the tree and the window from sight. She put her head in her hands.

Father.

She wanted to drive a knife through Nathair's chest. She wanted to scream, hit, to destroy. Gripping her hair, she stared at the table's deep grain, seeing veins and blood. Anger was more than a feeling. It was a person she'd become.

How could Thane have been part of kidnapping him? The way they'd been in the lab together, trading ideas... Father had loved him like a son.

But he didn't really know anything about Thane.

She'd shared so much about her childhood. Her unjustified anger with her mother. The divorce. How she'd been angry with Father, but how she finally understood his choices. Her parents had been doing what they felt was best for the people they cared about.

Father had lived to make up for what he'd felt was a wrong choice. He'd gone out of his way to visit Aini and her mother in the colonies, month after month, year after year. Every time her mother demanded he reschedule a trip for some invented reason, he went along with it.

Her mother had been trying to protect her. She'd left her new home of Edinburgh to live in the colonies to keep Aini away from rebels and what she viewed as stains in her father's past. She'd endured what Aini had: the pain of not fitting in anywhere.

Aini had tried to keep her sixth sense a secret to protect her father, Myles, Neve, and Thane, worrying they would go to prison just for knowing her. She'd struggled every day not to touch rings, watches, bracelets, treasured books, sentimental gifts at Christmas and birthdays. She'd been called *cold* more than once as she clung to rules and structure to protect herself and everyone around her, to keep from invading their privacy, to shelter them from suspicion if she were ever taken for questioning. She'd held herself back from hugs and close friendships, from spontaneity, to live a safe life.

But while she'd shared her pains and confusion, Thane hadn't told her a thing. She knew about Bran. That awful pub. But that could've been a lie. She didn't even know where Thane was from or who his mother was. And his father...she supposed Thane was from Argyll. If he was the Earl of Argyll's son, he'd grown up at Inveraray Castle, a sprawling estate where he'd have been treated like some sort of Campbell prince. But had he? Pain had always shown in his eyes, a shadow that had haunted him until he'd started to believe Aini really could find the stone and the Heir.

And when Father had spoken kindly to Thane, listening to his hypotheses and working with him, Thane had seemed so unaccustomed to the behavior, so maybe he hadn't been treated like a prince. Maybe Thane had been mistreated growing up. It was a guess she'd made long ago, why she'd never been jealous of their close relationship. Nathair had no doubt expected a lot from his son, educated him, taught him to fight, paid for amazing schooling and fine clothing, but he maybe hadn't loved him in a healthy way. Did that excuse Thane's betrayal?

No. No, it didn't.

Aini pressed her fingers into her eyelids, angry tears burning out as Owen and Vera murmured a blend of kindnesses and opinions. Neve's stillness and quiet comforted far more than anything they could say or do.

Thane had never reported discovering the Dionadair. If he had, his father's presence wouldn't have sparked such surprised rage in him. Thane had fallen against the tunnel's wall, stunned, when they'd first glimpsed Nathair in the barn. The angry side of Aini demanded, *It doesn't matter.* He'd lied, hidden who he was. He'd had so many chances to tell her.

This was how her mother must've felt when she found out Father was working with the rebels. Aini wondered if he'd told her, or if she'd discovered it on her own.

Aini pressed a fist against her chest. It just hurt so much. *I'm sorry, Mother.* She squeezed her eyes shut. If only Aini could've known, realized why her mother had never answered Father's questions with more than a few words, why she handed the phone to Aini immediately when he called. The pain on their faces when they were together—it all made sense.

Now, the kind widow who'd invited the Dionadair in pulled a pot of oniony stew from the stove as a Dionadair with shaggy brown hair ran up to the table.

"Someone's left a package," he said to Owen. "Found it at the end of the road. Near the turn off."

After glancing at the door, Owen looked to Aini, and a frisson of fear jarred her spine. He was thinking the package contained explosives.

During the Campbells' attack, they'd lost five people and

more than twenty were seriously wounded and being treated at an underground hospital near Stirling.

Thane could've reported the Dionadair right after they'd run into them at the club. But he hadn't. The attack on the barn had nothing to do with him, aside from the probability that another Campbell had been watching him, an operative that *did* report everything to Nathair.

Vera threw her legs over the table's rough bench and started toward the door, the kitchen light shining off her midnight hair.

"Wait," Owen said, hurrying to follow.

Aini watched, buttoning and unbuttoning the mandarin collar of her blood-stained, sea-colored shirt. Standing, she tied her hair into a loose bun and put Owen's pencil through it. She ran a hand over her forehead and swallowed, her throat raw from crying on and off. Her phone sat in the waistband of her leggings, still quiet, still with no word from Thane. She wasn't sure whether she wanted a call or not.

Gritting her teeth, she closed her eyes and tumbled questions around her mind. Over and over and over as she trailed Neve to the front room.

One second, her anger with Thane blistered her skin, not caring for any cool reason. The next, she was sad, anxious, longing to have Thane here so they could spill out all their fears and worries and see what withstood the flood.

Two things bore down on her shoulders, heavy and unrelenting. One: Thane was still missing. She had no idea whether he'd go to Nathair, or if he was off on his own, hating himself, or maybe even dead by his own clan's hand for attacking their chief.

The second item that weighted her was that Thane wasn't just the son of a Campbell, which would've been bad enough. Thane was the son of their chief. No wonder he'd never come clean. If Aini hadn't seen his fury after the explosion at the barn, the idea of him going against his own father, a man everyone in Scotland feared now more than ever, would've been very, very difficult to swallow. But the way Thane's eyes had burned with the knowledge that he couldn't change his blood, and had been trapped with his father's mad schemes, had shown her what she needed to know: though he'd started his assigned task—it had to be spying on lab work and developing weaponized candy—as a firm Campbell follower, he'd changed.

No. Yes. Maybe. No. He was who he was. He lied again and again.

Owen and Vera had the mysterious package open and inside the door. It was a wooden crate loaded with crumpled newspaper and bags of round beads.

Aini blinked, rolling Father's signet ring around her finger. It clicked against her mother's wedding band. "Those are my father's cherry drops."

Crouching beside the crate, Owen adjusted his round wireframes. "And why are they on our doorstep?"

Vera opened one of the plastic bags and lifted a drop. "What do they do?" She began to pop it in her lipsticked mouth, but Aini knocked it from her fingers.

"Normally, they're aphrodisiacs."

Vera wiggled her sculpted eyebrows and went for another.

Aini put a hand on hers. "Normally. Nothing about right now is normal."

Nodding, she pulled her hand back.

Bending, Aini looked through the crate. Under the five one-gallon bags, a square of lined paper showed scrawled writing. Slanted. Slightly looped. Thane's hand.

She snatched it up and held it under a green glass lamp on a side table, tracing each letter with a fingertip. She could see him in her mind, holding the pen too tightly like he always did, his knuckles white. His tongue touched the inside of his bottom lip as he concentrated. His hair curled slightly around the frame of his glasses.

Neve looked over her shoulder and read the note. She let out a breath. "Aini, you know what this shows."

"What does it say?" Vera said.

Aini had to laugh at herself, her throat tight, because she hadn't even read it yet. She'd only pored over his handwriting, the little bit of him she had there in her hand.

"It says, *If we don't become his worst nightmare, none of us will dream again.*" She shivered. "It's from Thane." She folded the paper into a neat square and cupped it in her palm.

Owen was beside her in a blink, his hand out like she might share the note.

Her mind brought up the memory of Thane's face as he fought his father. Tears dragging through blood. The necklace, thrown to the mud and grass. A wrenching suck of breath as he saw Father's ring on the ground.

"Thane wants us to somehow use these," Neve pointed at the crate, "against the Campbells."

"We can't trust that git," Vera snapped.

Neve glared even though Aini thought Vera was so, so right. "You're not the only one with an opinion," Neve snapped. "You don't even know him. Nathair Campbell is his father! Can you imagine the childhood Thane probably had?"

Owen rubbed his nose, then put his hands behind him. He walked toward the kitchen and back again, giving Neve a look. "Pull the claws back in, Neve. Vera is right and you know it. He's Nathair's own son, for God's sake. We won't trust him. Not ever."

"If Thane had a chance to alter these cherry drops, we should use them." Neve's voice didn't sound like her own, the words cracking like dry branches and whipping around the room. "No matter what you think of him." She glanced at Aini. Neve's eyes flashed with a quiet strength and a silent question. *Do you agree with me?*

Out of the corner of her eye, Aini saw Dodie bend to pick up the drop she'd smacked out of Vera's hand. "Dodie, don't!"

He pushed it into his mouth and chewed. "What's that?" he asked before falling promptly to the pine floor.

They rushed to him.

Vera put his head in her lap and lifted Dodie's eyelid. "Brother!"

Owen tried digging the drop out of Dodie's mouth, but Aini pulled his hand away. "I wouldn't touch the inside of his mouth right now. Not if he bit the candy and released its gooey center," she said, sitting back on her heels.

"They're not aphrodisiacs anymore, and that's for certain," Vera said snidely. "Wouldn't want a man in my bed snoring like this lout is." She pressed a gentle hand on Dodie's cheek and smiled. "But you think he'll be all right, then?"

"I do." Aini hoped. "Thane put a man at the Origin to sleep with something that acted that quickly. Maybe it was the same sort of formula, a sleep agent or some sort of paralyzing concoction."

Owen called three men over, who took Dodie away. "Watch over him," he called out as Dodie's caretakers disappeared down the dark hallway. "Ring me if he seems troubled at all."

They resumed their spots at the kitchen table. The room smelled like stew and the hot lemon water the old woman had used to clean the wooden surfaces.

Leaning forward, Owen folded his hands. A new scab covered three of his freckled knuckles, but the lean muscle and taut tendons seemed to be working fine.

"Why do you believe Nathair's son—"

"Thane."

Owen pressed his lips together. "Why would *Thane* send us a crate of weaponized candies?"

"Because he's on our side," Vera said, oddly quiet.

Owen probably looked as surprised as Aini.

"Exactly." Neve crossed her arms.

Vera shrugged and picked at a nail. "Neve is right. The thing didn't explode on us, and he left that note. The only thing that makes sense is that the lad is as Neve claims. A good man. A man for Scotland. A man for the Dionadair." She paused, pondering something. "I saw a golden thread between our Seer and him at the Waymark Wall. Sparkled like pure gold. I'd thought it was only because of who you are to Scotland," she said, looking at Aini, "who you are to him, to everyone, but now I think...I think it's because he loves you."

He loves you. Aini's hand went to her chest.

Here was truth: it didn't matter what Thane had or hadn't done. She cared for him. Her heart couldn't be bothered about evidence. It raged, beating for him and nothing else mattered.

She was an idiot. She could never forgive him. She was doomed.

"I don't trust him," Owen said.

Aini fisted her hands on the table. "Me either."

Neve inhaled and exhaled slowly. "He gave us this gift, this weapon to use for our side."

Owen looked over his glasses at Aini. "I thought you wanted nothing to do with such a thing. You were completely against using your father's creations to fight."

Aini swallowed, her mind and heart warring. "I don't. But at least they don't kill anyone. They're not so bad, I suppose. Unless this is a trap Thane has set."

Vera snorted. "Oh, so it's all well and good for the Campbells to off our lot, but killing them would be bad?"

A bitter taste covered Aini's tongue. Her head pounded. She wanted Thane here, to ask him questions. No, she wanted him gone so he could never lie to her again. Her thoughts whipped through her head, beating her with stinging truths and unbearable feelings. "I'm going to bed."

Vera opened her mouth, but Owen gripped her wrist and shook his head. She settled down as Aini and Neve stood.

"I suppose you need some rest, Seer," Vera said without any vinegar.

"We can talk when you're ready," Owen said as Aini and Neve walked toward the hallway.

"Fine." Aini's legs were jelly. She felt like she had sand in her eyes and down her esophagus. "Give me four hours. Then I'll be up and ready."

"Five."

"Okay."

"Okay," Vera said back in a faked northern colonial accent like Aini's.

AFTER WASHING HER FACE IN A BIG, WHITE PORCELAIN BOWL and doing her very best not to disturb all the other sleepers in the front room, Aini sat on her assigned cot. Neve snored lightly two beds down, blanket tangled in her legs already. Aini's pillowcase had a foul, brown stain so she flipped it.

A square of paper the size of her thumbnail flittered to the floor.

Across the room, Myles snorted in his sleep and she jumped. Heart racing, she picked the paper up. This wasn't Thane's writing. It was blocky and full of sharp edges. She squinted to read the tiny print.

We'll trade your father for the stone's location. All offenses wiped from the records. Meet at the bend in the road. One hour. It can be over tonight. Done.

Her heartbeat was loud enough to wake everyone. She pictured Father reading Robert Burns by the fire, his salt and pepper beard illuminated by the flames. She imagined him being hit across the face and dragged like a criminal from the MacGregor townhouse steps.

Sliding the note into her bra, she lay down, eyes wide open.

A Campbell operative had sneaked into the widow's house, past the guards, through the hammocks and cots, and somehow found her pillow.

They'd known exactly where she was going to sleep.

The note's words ate at her. *It can be over tonight.* She took a slow breath. Another. She could have Father safe in her arms, could see if he was recovering from his awful wound, could go with him back to Edinburgh and lock the door on all of this.

On all these people.

But five people had given their lives for her, for this mad quest. More would probably die from their injuries. Nathair might agree to protect her and her father, but what about Myles? Neve? Owen and Vera and Dodie? If he knew she was here, he knew they were as well and was most likely assembling another attack right this second.

She rolled onto her side and pressed a fist against her mouth. Another slow breath.

In. Out. In.

Then she climbed out of her cot and headed for the door.

Her fingers rubbed together, remembering the feel of Father's wool suit jacket as he walked with her to the train station. She inhaled, thinking of his soap and shoe polish scent. She bumped a cot as she grabbed the side door's handle. The tenant shuffled in her sleep and drew her knees up under a thin blanket. Aini opened the door and walked into the pale light of a Scottish summer night.

A guard with wide-set eyes adjusted the black gun at his belt. "Do you need something, Seer?"

"Just...need some air. I'll be right back."

She was only going to talk to the Campbell messenger. If they had Father, if she could just see him for a minute... Her boot hit a dark spot in the dirt drive, and she stopped.

Blood.

It was from earlier when they'd moved a man still bleeding, a man who'd missed the truck to the safe hospital. She remembered him from the sleeping quarters in the hillside. His white mohawk hair style had contrasted with his quiet, polite smile.

What was she doing? If they had Father there, they'd only use him against her. To murder her friends and the rest of the Dionadair, the people who risked everything to fight against Nathair's mad quest for control.

Even if the Campbells did release her father, were he and Aini supposed to go back to their lives with the knowledge that the kingsmen could scoop them up at any minute and put them to death for treason or whatever infraction Nathair cared to invent?

Aini looked up. The stars shimmered, fighting to shine in the fading blue sky. Before Thane, before the slaughter, before meeting the Dionadair and seeing their passion, she could've made peace with a life lived in determined ignorance. Safety for safety's sake. A quick memory of the vision she'd seen in Thane's necklace poured over her thoughts. The cold edge to his father's movements, the pain in his mother's face, the twisted loyalty Thane felt as a child.

Aini couldn't allow Nathair to win. Not this time. No matter what.

Father wouldn't want her to fight. He'd left this life to keep her in his life, to try and make amends with her mother.

Dizzy from lack of sleep, and the pull and stretch of fear, she tugged her hair free and let it drop over her shoulders. Taking a shuddering breath, she raised her hands to the sky and crossed her thumbs. Maybe the Campbell messenger would see her and know her decision.

She wanted the Scottish people to be free from Nathair. She wanted her father to be free from Nathair. She wanted Thane to be free from Nathair.

Back at the farmhouse, she nodded once to the guard and went inside.

Owen was waiting beside her cot. "So, you're finally ready."

"I am," she said, her blood hot in her veins.

CHAPTER 26
IF ONLY FOR A FEW MORE MINUTES

Under a flint gray sky, five Dionadair trucks shed their hiding places on the old woman's farm.

"If it doesn't confuse them—though I think it will —it'll surely keep them busy," Owen said, helping Aini brush straw from a truck's hood.

Aini bent her head and climbed inside. Myles and Neve went around and scooted across the seat. Vera and Dodie sat up front with Owen.

The first truck to leave, recently tarped and covered in branches behind the barn, headed to the townhouse to see if any Campbells were stationed there. Another Dionadair vehicle, that had shared the barn with a dozen operatives and five cows, drove south as a mere distraction. Maneuvering out of a struggling orchard, a third truck carried the Dionadair's finest fighters toward the Campbells' holding cells beneath the Signet Library in Edinburgh's Old Town, just down from the townhouse. They were going after Father.

Aini put a hand over her aching heart and said a silent prayer.

Let him be okay. Let this all work out. Please. Let me have my only family back again.

That wasn't quite right though. She had more than her father. Her friends had become family too. Myles and Neve sat beside her in the cabin's back seat, their faces pinched with worry. Aini laid her cheek on Myles's shoulder, breathing in his paint and cotton smell. He patted her hand and Neve leaned over. She gave Aini an encouraging smile, her front teeth over her lip.

Their truck, and the one going with them, bumped out of the farmhouse's dirt drive and aimed at North Berwick.

They were headed for the stone.

"When do you think we'll hear from the Signet cells team?" Aini took a small bite of another of Myles's quietly procured apples. A real breakfast wasn't really happening on a day like this.

Vera sipped an aromatic dark roast from her travel coffee mug and answered for her brother. "We'll hear from them when there's any development."

Myles picked at some paint under his thumbnail. "As in, when they find Lewis?"

"The poor man." Neve looked out the window.

Aini flicked a glance at Myles and forced another bite of the tart apple down. "Yes, when they find him. If they fail, the Campbells aren't going to let them give us a ring to chat."

Neve made a little noise and Myles shut his eyes.

Wishing for a message from Thane, Aini took her phone from the wide, military belt she'd borrowed from Vera. It had a good sized pocket and a place for the Macbeth knife. She felt better with the weapon at her side even though Owen had only given her two, one-hour lessons on the ways to use it yesterday. She'd probably hurt herself more than any attacker.

But at least she wasn't going down without shedding some enemy blood.

Rolling hills, clusters of painted buildings, and roads smaller than the one they were on made up a patchwork of faded green, white, and black beyond the truck's windows. The landscape had probably changed little since Angus Bethune set this trail of artifacts, guided by Macbeth's ghost. The roads, of course, were different. The billboards too. But the growing things were most likely much the same and the lay of the land.

"We have a tail," Vera said, leaning over Owen and looking at the side mirror.

Owen slowed and moved into the next lane on the wide motorway. Myles, Neve, and Aini moved to see. In Owen's mirror, a black sedan nosed out of the mild traffic and took a place three cars behind the truck of Dionadair traveling with them.

"They've been with us since we entered the motorway." Vera bent and came up with a pistol. She cocked it, and Aini's heart clicked like it was preparing itself too.

Her hands began to sweat. She hoped it wouldn't come to a battle. She didn't want to see more blood. Bile rose in her throat. The metallic smell of broken people still haunted her. Surely they could do this without anyone else getting hurt. Maybe Nathair Campbell would realize what he was doing wasn't going to win him more power, that the Dionadair would always find a way to protect their loved ones from his ruthless plans.

Passing through the small, cobbled town of North Berwick, they approached the docks. Boats, red and white, bobbed in the choppy water along the rugged coastline.

Myles, Neve, Dodie, and Aini followed Owen, Vera, and ten other Dionadair heavies down the long, wooden dock to a middle-sized fishing boat. A gust of wind blew across the Firth of Forth, a slice of the North Sea, and sprayed Aini lightly with salt water. Eyeing their boat's tall mast and the netting strung along the side, Myles leaped onto the craft and helped Neve board. Aini grabbed the side of the boat as it dipped in the water. She jumped onto the deck with fairly steady legs, but her mind was still with Thane and wondering whether they'd been followed.

Dodie started the boat's engine as Vera and Owen untied their lines from the dock. They started into the leaden slab of ocean, Neve's hair and Aini's tangling together in the wind. Aini pulled her borrowed, light wool sweater higher at the back of her neck. The red fabric was soft under her fingers and she wondered who had originally owned it. Were they dead now? And how did they die? Or was this simply a loan from Vera or another Dionadair, maybe one of the operatives who'd volunteered to drive the distraction truck in the opposite direction?

Myles rubbed a hand over Neve's back and Aini's. Aini smiled, and he gave her a wink. Half of her wished they weren't there, but the other half was so glad they were. She'd told them about the Campbells' offer and filled them in on Thane's message too. They had a plan for those cherry drops that had put Dodie down for four hours. She didn't like it, but it was better than having a bloody shoot-out, because every single Campbell could have a gun. The Dionadair only had as many as they could scrounge from the black market. The king was a much better provider.

Promising rain, a blue fog curled around the rocky cliffs of Bass Rock Island as they approached its southern side. White plumed gannets soared above, every so often tucking their ebony-tipped wings and diving from impossible heights into the water like spears thrown from heaven.

As the boat sidled into a small, walled-off harbor, a mother seal hissed like a banshee. Dodie stood with one foot on the prow, ready to throw a rope around a weather-beaten post.

Looking through the salt-crusted windows of the cabin, Owen lifted the lid of a storage trunk and removed three hunting rifles, one hulking shotgun, and a few shovels. He handed them out to Vera and the other Dionadair before they tied up and climbed out of the craft.

A modern staircase made a jagged line up the face of Bass Rock Island. A lighthouse rose like a white mushroom from the blackened decay of a former fort, and a rectangular stone building perched to the left, about halfway up. Plants reached over its moss covered walls and through its missing roof. The empty, round window on the end reminded Aini of the Waymark Wall's vision.

"That ruined stone building is the chapel." Neve pointed, then grabbed a tire secured to the side of the boat to steady herself as she disembarked after Myles. "St. Baldred's. It was built on top of his monastic cell in 1542, if I remember right."

Anxiety tremored through Aini's limbs as she gripped the worn edge of the boat and made her way onto the dock. The stone could be right there.

"So," she said and coughed as they started up the rough stairs, "you agree that this is the place to look."

Neve nodded. "What you described, the hollowed-out chapel and the earthen walls...it says monk's cell to me. I've studied a great deal of history."

"As if we could ever be ignorant on that fact," Myles said, giving her a gentle elbow.

She smiled and pulled her sleeves over her hands.

"I just wish I had your faith," Aini said, hurrying to catch up with the Dionadair, who'd almost made it to the rectangular chapel ruins.

Dodie held a shotgun over one shoulder and a shovel over the other. Vera sauntered up the stairs with a rifle tucked behind her arm. Holding his own firearm, Owen kept checking on Myles, Neve, and Aini, his glasses reflecting the scant light.

Gannets, yellow-tinged heads tucked against the weather, nested close enough that Aini could've touched a chick's fuzzy white crown if she'd wanted to.

Myles clicked his tongue. "What'll these crazy Dionadair folks do if the stone roars for one of us?" He ran fingers upward through his hair, making it stand up like grass. His gaze landed on the back of Vera's head, his eyes worried.

"There's only one written record mentioning the roaring and the curse," Aini said. Neve had told her about it.

"What curse?" Myles asked.

"It's pretty vague." Her legs ached from the steep stairs. "Neve, didn't you say the record mentioned that anyone who went up against the true Heir to Scotland's throne—meaning the one who makes it shout or roar—would have some sort of punishment?"

"The history books make no mention of the curse." Neve kneeled to retie her boot. "But the texts on legends and myth give an archaic, brief description. It's the power of the old to protect their own, or something of the sort." She straightened and they continued on.

A cold breeze floated through Aini, raising bumps along her forearms.

Neve crossed herself and said something in Gaelic.

A whisper tickled Aini's ear, and she heard something that sounded like her name. Her palms tingled. "Did you hear that?"

"No, but I doubt the message was for me, Seer." Neve frowned at the air around them. "And I think you can add Ghost Talker to your sixth sense resume."

Myles looked from Aini to Neve, to the Dionadair, then shivered violently.

Yes, Aini's mind said. Neve was right. She'd heard words in Greyfriars kirkyard. Whispers had followed her when she toured the old battlefield of Culloden with Father as a child.

"But everyone hears ghosts a little bit."

"Aye, but only Ghost Talkers can hear all of it and understand the meaning." Neve swallowed and kept her eyes on her feet.

Neve had been fine, excited even, about Aini's Seer ability, but this... "Why do the spirits make you so uneasy?" she asked Neve.

"It's like having a multitude of stalkers, isn't it?" Neve slowed her pace. "You'll hear them whether you want to or not. They can follow you anywhere."

Myles grimaced. "They can? Like even into the toilet?"

Neve scowled at him. "You are a piece of work, you know that?"

"A fine piece." He winked and she rolled her eyes.

Aini's thoughts swamped their conversation, muffling everything else. She hadn't had any trouble with ghosts trailing her so far. Would she now that she'd begun to really use her sixth sense? Would it all grow stronger? Become even more problematic?

The path went left and led to a view over the wide waters of the Firth of Forth, back toward Tantallon. Red against the plumes of cloud and mist, the castle ruins where Aini had found the Waymark Wall seemed to hang on the edge of mainland Scotland. Under the Douglas tower, grass lay in patches on the northern side of its rocky seat over the shoreline.

They neared the chapel ruins, and a gannet flew from the space where the roof used to be. Aini leaned back to watch it disappear into the cloudy sky, almost wishing she could escape along with her.

Owen and his band stopped. Some brows were furrowed with curiosity. Vera wore a challenging look, like she wanted Aini to prove her status as the Seer. Dodie twisted his hands around his shovel's wooden shaft. The scent of green things and the tang of a coming storm cleared Aini's head.

Lightning blinked, far off, and she headed into the former chapel. Thick grass caught her boot as she moved toward the center of the hollowed out structure. Untangling herself, she said, "We need to get into St. Baldred's cell." She pointed down. "It's here. I...think."

Everyone with a shovel took up digging into the weeds and earth. Myles shed his shirt on a nearby sapling growing in what used to be the aboveground chapel's floor. Aini couldn't seem to stop praying silently.

AFTER AN HOUR OF TAKING TURNS WITH THE SHOVELS, THEY found a slab of rock.

"I've found it!" Dodie jabbed his shovel underneath the hard surface.

With help, he wedged the slab up. Squirming creatures and musky-scented ground fell away from the edges. Dodie and Owen pulled the slab to the side, and it thudded to the grass near their dirt-caked boots. Owen rolled his sleeves higher, the storm lifting a few of the red curls on his head, and wiped his face on an arm. A square of black yawned where the covering had rested. Aini hugged herself as Dodie directed his flashlight into the hole to show a set of earthen stairs leading into darkness.

"I'll go first," she said, nodding thanks as Dodie handed her his flashlight.

The gathering steel clouds argued and sent a blast of thunder over them. A movement at the chapel's door made Aini pause. Owen said something sharp. All the Dionadair, except Dodie, Vera, and him, disappeared over the walls and into the tangled brush and waving trees surrounding the chapel.

Aini's skin went cold. "What is it?" She looked from Owen to the others. Dread climbed onto her back, a heavy, clinging thing.

In the gloom and kicking gusts of wind, Campbells poured through the opening wearing their kingsmen jackets, muddied boots, and bright blue, green, and black Campbell kilts. Next to a beast of a man wearing a flat cap, Bran and Thane appeared.

Aini's heart hung useless in her chest.

Thane wore the same kilt as the other Campbells. His face was unreadable. Bran's eyes were slightly closed and the corners of his mouth turned down. Wearing plain trousers, he didn't seem to belong. What were they doing here? Was there a plan they had in mind or had they simply returned to following Clan Campbell orders?

Lightning washed the clouds and the coming storm boomed, almost covering the sound of guns being cocked and shouts of warning from both sides.

Neve spoke in Aini's ear. "He's not with them. Remember that. He has some reason for being here, dressed like that."

Myles took a step closer. The saint's cell at Aini's back breathed ancient air.

"This is not your business, Campbells," Owen said to Thane and the big man.

The man laughed. "Now that our good earl is at home mending," his eyes cut to Thane, "everything in Scotland is my business, Dionadair. My name is Rodric Campbell and I'm leading the clan. I speak for Nathair."

Rodric looked at Aini like she was something dangerous.

Probably the same way she'd been looking at him. Like if he stared long enough, he'd glimpse claws at the ends of her fingers or horns coming out of her head. He crossed himself. She glared at his hands. They'd killed people, she was sure of it.

"Seer." He spat and adjusted his flat cap. "The stone rests somewhere down in that hole, aye?"

"I'm not telling you anything, kidnapper, murderer."

She felt Thane's gaze on her. She glanced at him, but his blank face told her nothing. He wore what the rest of them did, a black kingsman jacket and the Campbell kilt, his muscled legs showing above his boots.

Rodric's lip curled. "You are as naive as they come, Seer." He turned to Thane. "Bring the chemist."

Myles caught Aini's arm as her knees gave out.

Thane nodded obediently and left through the arch.

Owen looked to Aini, and she pulled her arm gently from Myles and stood on her own. Owen gave her an almost imperceptible nod and trained his gaze on Rodric again.

"I suggest you lower your weapons before anyone gets themselves hurt," Rodric said.

None of the Dionadair lowered anything.

Thane returned, gripping a hooded man's sleeve.

Father.

Aini realized she'd yelled his name. She closed her mouth, feeling all the blood drain from her cheeks. His head was covered in a burlap bag, his hands were bound with twine, and a dirty bandage covered the hand now missing one finger. Rodric took a silver pistol from another man and pressed it against Father's leg. Aini's stomach rolled.

"Aini," Father said. His voice was Christmas morning, oatmeal with honey, warmth and safety and promise. Tears leaked from her eyes, not caring at all that she wanted to appear as a leader and failed.

"If I shoot him here," Rodric said, his knuckles white as the blink of lightning overhead. "He'll die slowly."

Dots floated in front of Aini's eyes. She jumped in front of Owen and the others, and pushed their rifle barrels down.

"Here," Rodric aimed at Father's gut. "Well, let's just say he won't like how that one goes. And neither will you, Seer, considering the shade your face has taken on. I did give you a chance to do this a nicer way."

Vera and her brothers flicked a glance at Aini. She hadn't told them about the message under her pillow. Only Myles and Neve.

Aini cleared her throat and traded a look with Thane, whose hair curled into the wind and whose eyes matched the rising storm.

Did he have a plan? How many different ways could this go?

He pursed his full lips and tilted his head a little, just a small movement that seemed to say *It's your decision.*

She'd known this outcome was a possibility. That if the Edinburgh team couldn't secure Father, and the Campbells found them here, her father and the rest of them would be at the Campbells' mercy—a thing no one seemed to think existed. But she couldn't just give the word to fight and throw Father's life away. She couldn't do it. Not like this. Not unless there was no other way to go.

"I don't even know if the stone is in there." She pointed to the rectangular square of black in the ground.

Rodric's eyes narrowed. "Then take a peek, aye?"

His hand shook. He was scared of the stone, wanted nothing to do with it. How could they use that fear?

"Fine. But my father stays whole and alive."

"Or what?" Rodric laughed again.

She gritted her teeth and Thane closed his eyes, one hand still holding Father's arm. The big, horrible bully was right. She had nothing to hold over him if the stone was here. He could take it and, as Owen explained, destroy it and ruin Scotland's chance to find the one meant to rule, the one the curse would protect, the one person who could fight the Campbells and the king and their cruelties.

Strangely, Aini wished she could hear a spirit's voice, something to encourage her to move forward, a word saying everything would somehow work out. But the only cool wind to blow across her face came from the storm that quickly approached over the hills and sea water.

To keep Father alive, if only for another few minutes, she turned, walked over to the earthen stairs, and descended into the ground.

CHAPTER 27
AND THE EARTH TREMBLED

Aini's heart slammed against her chest as she made her way down the stairs. Clicking on the flashlight Owen had given her, she breathed in the smell of wet dirt. The side of the chamber was smooth stone and dirt. Someone, presumably Baldred, had rubbed the earth's body to a level, sloping shape, creating a domed cavern. In the damp air, the light painted the long room the pale shade of bones and the dusky blue of bruises. Shapes and shadows moved in the corners. The stone? Other things Baldred kept here? Ghosts?

"Wait," a deep voice said from the top of the stairs behind her.

Her pulse surged in her throat. She spun and shone the light upward. Thane stood there, a tattooed hand on the wall as he climbed down, his kilt swinging as his knees moved. A prickling sensation spread across her back, a mix of fear and desire, her blood glowing in her veins.

She took a tentative step. No one stood directly at the entrance behind him.

Thane ran a hand through his hair as he studied her face. "Rodric sent me down here. Doesn't seem to care much if either one of us dies from whatever horrible thing he thinks will happen. But...he can't hear us now."

Aini's lungs wouldn't expand. Her throat wanted to scream at Thane. Her arms longed to pull him to her.

He took a step. "Aini, I don't know how to tell you, how I...I know you hate me and you've every right to feel it, I—"

"Don't explain. Just apologize." Anger and the pain of betrayal heated her skin and thinned her voice.

"I'm sorry." His eyelashes shaped black rings around his stormy eyes. Mist dotted the edges of his glasses. A jagged crack marred one lens.

Without realizing what she was doing, Aini touched his face. It was slightly stubbled and warm. His lips parted. "I don't hate you," she said, swallowing confusion and wonder and fear. "I should. But I can't seem to do it. You had better be done with lying." Tears heated the corners of her eyes.

Sighing, he covered her hand with his much larger one. "I should've just told you. I should've never obeyed my father as long as I did." Dropping his hand, he turned toward the stairs and his fingers curled into fists. "I have no excuses."

"You aren't back on their side. You're here..."

"So I could follow them to you. To unhinge their plans. To work from the inside one last time."

"Why did they take you back? You fought your father, their leader. How did you make them trust you again?"

Thane stared at the wall, beyond Aini's head. His lips were pale and bloodless. "I did something—" He squeezed his eyes shut. "They had to see me do...I did a horrible thing."

Aini didn't want to know. She'd had enough of this. If Neve trusted him, if her own heart trusted him now, maybe that was enough. She laid a hand on the drape of soft wool tartan over his jacket, waist to his shoulder, and kept one eye on the cell's opening. Why did she want so badly to forgive him?

His father was a monster, a murderer, and a liar. He was obsessed with power, mad, a man who didn't care about the people who he was meant to lead and protect. Thane couldn't possibly respect the man's decisions, his clan's decisions. He had to see how wrong Nathair had been for so long. Especially after he'd executed those rebels and sixth-sensers without even the ruse of a trial citizens were supposed to get. It was plain; there was nothing anyone could say to defend his horrifying abuse of power. Why had it taken Thane so long to see it and act against it?

But Nathair was also Thane's father, the most important man in his life so far, the one who'd been there since he was born, at every milestone, there for every decision. Nathair, head of Clan Campbell, had been there when Thane had learned to walk, talk, to ride a bicycle, maybe, and a horse. Maybe the man had taught him to drive. It was a lifetime of habit and a twisted normalcy.

She assumed Thane had fought hard against the normal drive to stay devoted to one's father. In some ways, he had gone against Nathair.

It couldn't have been easy to go against your own father. It would be heart-breaking, frightening, overwhelming.

"Get on with it!" one of the Campbells shouted down, fear of the stone soaking the voice.

Aini's father had sided with the Dionadair and she'd still followed his trail. Granted, she now believed the rebels were the answer for Scotland's problems. Or, at least, the start of a powerful conversation between the people and those who ruled them. If Father had been on the wrong side of things, how far would Aini have gone along with him? If he thought what he was doing was right, it would still be near to impossible to cut him out of her life. If he was mad like Thane's father surely was, it would feel even worse. The urge to talk him out of his madness, his wrongdoing, would be hard to turn away from. The desire to do as best she could to smooth the situation would be a powerful thing.

She'd never truly understand what Thane was dealing with, how it felt, but one thing was certain—it had to be truly terrible.

His light eyebrows drew together. The crack in his glasses blinked in the uneven light.

"I forgive you," she whispered. Her chest ached with the truth and pain of it. "I know you're with us now."

He swept her wind-tangled hair from her cheeks and cupped her jaw in his warm, calloused hands. "I am with you. I don't know what we're to do now, but I'm with you and Lewis and the foolish Dionadair all the way now."

Her chest pressed against his as they breathed the same air, warm and getting warmer. They'd been through so much that no matter what was going on, she wanted so much to disappear into the brush of his thumb over her lip, the touch of his mouth, the hard lines and muscle of his body leaning into hers.

"Aini, I've been so..." He dipped his head and lightning flashed close, thunder ramming through the space and making them pull apart.

But she had to touch him, to know he was all right. She had to feel those lips on hers.

Lifting onto tiptoe, she tugged him to her, and kissed him hard. He started to draw her into his arms, began to say something, but a strange hum from the back of the cell had her dragging him farther in. The flashlight ghosted over the walls and the shapes toward the back.

"Do you feel that?" Thane asked, rubbing a hand over

his arm.

A buzz ran over her skin like electricity. Everything else was forgotten. "Yes."

A wide, wooden chair squatted along the wall. The seat section, mostly disintegrated, had fallen to the earth below support frame. A table with roughly shaped, square legs sat beside it.

The hairs on the back of Aini's neck stood on end. "Either we're about to be hit with lightning or that's..."

And there, in the very back of the saint's cell, black and covered in carved spirals, was the Coronation Stone.

For a breath, Aini's heart stopped.

The ancient royal seat was really here. She'd found it. Her pulse stamped against her wrists as her heart started up again, loud in the dirt-walled chamber.

The white-blue of the flashlight illuminated the carved swirls and circles in the stone's surface. Made of rock dark as the night sky, the stone stood hip-high and looked like a shapeless hand, curved and hollowed to serve as a seat.

"The carvings," Thane whispered, "the swirls, they remind me of my dream."

She glanced at him.

"Ever since I was a wean," he said. "I've dreamed of my fingerprint. The pattern grows dark like...like rock. It's...it's the stone I've been dreaming of."

Shock held her as she took a step toward the ancient artifact. "Then you're a Dreamer, Thane." She felt like she was in a dream now. "You have a sixth sense. All this time, you've had one too."

The stone heated the air. Waves of its buzzing energy filled the cell. The power hummed in Aini's fingertips and through the blood pulsing in her veins.

They stood beside the Coronation Stone, close enough to

touch. Shivers flew up her back.

As a Seer, she wanted nothing to do with touching the thing. She could get lost in the centuries of emotions embedded on the stone. Her hand was wet with the air's moisture and her own perspiration, and the flashlight tried to slip from her fingers. She gripped it tightly.

A wash of close lightning brightened the entrance to the chamber.

Thane's whole body leaned forward, toward the stone, his eyes wide. "My God," he said reverently.

Before he could touch it, he pulled his hands back and exhaled slowly. He studied the bare skin below his rolled up and muddy sleeves. Goosebumps raised the blond hairs on his forearms.

"He—Rodric—he," Thane said, his voice flat, "he wants you to touch the stone. He wants to know what you see."

Aini's shivers rose again and spread so that her skin matched his. "What about the curse? What if it's more dangerous than we think?"

His eyebrows lifted, but his mouth still turned down at the corners. "It won't hurt you. The curse will only hurt those who go against the Heir. I'll do it first. Or together. We'll do it together."

Thunder growled outside, and rain lashed through the opening.

Someone outside shouted, and Rodric's order to one of his men echoed into the chamber. Then Rodric himself pounded down the stairs. He pulled his flat cap lower to hide his eyes, then motioned to the stone with a handgun.

"Get on with it." He stepped toward Aini.

"You're afraid of the stone, aren't you?" Aini said quietly, watching his shaking hand and the gun gripped in his meaty fingers.

Thane glared. "Rodric, I—"

"I knew you hadn't gone back into the fold," Rodric spat. "You worthless traitor. Rabbie believed you. But me?"

Thane got between Aini and Rodric. "I'll die before I let you touch her again."

"Still angry about the fun in the vaults, aye?" He snorted. "Save your hero crap for a girl who's not good as dead." He raised the gun.

Realization lit Aini's memories of the Edinburgh vaults. Rodric had hit her in the vaults. It hadn't been a mugger. It'd been this older Campbell, who obviously had some further conflict with Thane.

Thane cut him with a string of Gaelic words.

Out of the corner of her eye, she saw Thane reach across the stone. She twined her fingers in his. Lightning poured white and blue into the room.

"For Lewis," Thane whispered. "He'll kill him if we don't do this. We'll do this, then figure out what to do."

Aini nodded. "For Father."

She slammed their linked hands onto the humming stone.

Wind blasted around them. It kicked dirt into the air, knocked the flashlight to the ground, pressed Thane's kilt against his legs, and turned his jacket collar up. The earth rumbled, shook, and the supernatural storm tossed Aini's hair around her head.

A sound like a lion's roar vibrated from the stone and smashed against her eardrums.

The stone chilled Aini's palms, and a vision wiped the cell's close quarters from sight.

A whirlwind of colors—orange and green and blue and gold and iron and bronze—spun through the air around the stone, slowing to become pictures. Men in all kinds of patterned clothing—white tunics, plain shirts and dark cloaks—touched the stone, then sat and raised their eyes to their people.

Voices echoed in her mind, a tangle of sounds she didn't understand. Then, slowly, the words crawled out of the noise, clear as a bell.

The spirits' mouths moved, calling out their names. Kenneth Mac Alpin. Donald I. Constantine. Malcolm. Dubh and Culen. Macbeth. They were bearded and old, wide eyed and young, muscled, thin. Every one sat tall, straight, and possessed the fire of purpose in their eyes.

They were ghosts. And they were kings.

Aini yanked her and Thane's hands from the stone. As quickly as the tempest had begun, the chamber quieted. Her hair fell back onto her shoulders, and Thane's collar settled against his neck. From outside, lightning flashed.

Both of them were in a terrible situation. But one, *one* of them was directly, inseparably lashed to a political storm to rival any in their country's history. A tempest of powerful men and women, desperate to curl hands around money, people, farmland, cities, towns, and businesses.

She spoke first, her chin shaking. "You're the Heir. The wind and that noise, it all started when your hand touched the stone." She didn't want it to be true for him, but it had to be true, because she knew it wasn't her.

"Your hand was on it too," he said.

Rodric had fallen. He swore, found his feet, and ran up the stairs, shouting orders Aini didn't hear.

"You're *the Seer*," Thane said. "It only makes sense. You're the Heir, Aini."

She shook her head so hard it was in danger of falling off. "I'm less than half Scottish."

"You think any one of the line is fully Scottish by blood? Course not. They're all married into English, German, French families. What matters is...the stone has called us."

It did feel that way. Like the kings had set a quest at their feet. Because of Thane's bloodline—Campbells did hold a tenuous line to the old rulers, as did many clans—but also because of who they were. Seer and Dreamer. Merlin and Arthur. Hearts ready for sacrifice.

Thane pressed a fist against his mouth and studied the stone. The fallen flashlight and the storm's intermittent waves of white and silver cast a haunting light over both man and throne. It had to be him with his broad shoulders, quick mind, and high cheek-bones. His tartan completed the picture. Thane had been through so much. A military upbringing under a madman's hand. Life-threatening situations when he had to make split second decisions. A moment when he'd had to go against everything he knew—father and clan—to become the man he wanted to be. And he'd grown a good heart and a brave soul throughout his struggles.

The Coronation Stone has chosen well, Aini thought.

Outside the entrance, gunshots blasted through the rush of rain.

Leaving the stone, they ran from the cell to see a fight already in motion. The bulk of the Dionadair—who'd concealed themselves at Rodric's arrival—worked in pairs, grabbing Campbells from behind and bringing them to their knees. One of the two would hold a gun to the Campbell's head and the other would grab him by the hair and force a cherry drop down his throat. The Campbells fell one by one, paralyzed with Thane's concoction.

Myles and Neve were back-to-back, brandishing a gun and a knife, their faces ghostly as they held off two Campbells with wild movements. The Campbells circled Myles and Neve like wolves do their prey.

Bran traded punches with a Campbell who kept shouting, "Traitor!" Blood ran in two thick rivulets down Bran's chin, but he smiled anyway and threw another fist.

Thane put a gun in Aini's hand and cocked one of his own. "Stay beside me," he said. "Please."

Rodric had Father and was dragging him away from the fight, toward the arched door. He fired off two rounds into the fray. Owen jerked, hit.

"Brother!" Vera shrieked and fell with him to the mud.

At her scream, the other Dionadair lost focus and ran to their leader. Some shouted for Aini; others were captured immediately by Campbells who hadn't been dosed with the sleeping agent. At the shoulder, Owen's shirt was black with blood and his cheeks had gone white.

Aini scraped at her throat, feeling like she was suffocating.

"It's over!" Rodric shoved Father to the ground, and Thane and Aini took off at a run toward him. "Rabbie," Rodric growled at a lanky man with deep-set eyes, "destroy the stone."

Bran stepped over the Campbell he'd knocked out and started toward Rabbie, but Rodric pointed the gun at him.

"No, Bran. You've shown your colors. Get over there with the rebels where you belong."

Bran held up his hands and joined Vera and Dodie. He bent and felt Owen's pulse as he whispered something to her. Vera shot curses at Rodric. She took a wad of cloth from another Dionadair and pushed it into Owen's wound.

Rabbie hefted a massive canvas roll from his back. He pulled out five sledgehammers and handed them out. The men pushed past Vera and Dodie and Owen, who moaned and tried to lift an arm. They stormed into St. Baldred's cell.

"That abomination must be eliminated," Rodric said, sounding so much like Nathair had during his announcement on the square. Then, Aini hadn't understood why the king called sixth-sensers abominations, why he drove his head of security to destroy them. But now she knew. He was afraid—terrified of the possibility of a Seer finding the true Heir and the people who would support that Heir.

Myles waved his knife to drive back the Campbells surrounding him and Neve. The Campbells dodged Myles's knife and the taller of the two kicked at the gun in Neve's shaky hand. Hair tangled around her face and nose running, brave Neve managed to keep hold of it.

The weighty ping and smash of sledgehammers battled the increasing wind's howl and the cracking thunder.

"You're going to smash the Coronation Stone?" Aini shouted up at Rodric. "Aren't you afraid of the curse?"

"My dear uncle Nathair is the curse you should fear. His will crushes through my hand. That is the real threat." A feral smile creeped over his mouth. He held a hand out toward Owen, whose lips were blue, glasses fallen to the ground beside him and his siblings. "Isn't that right, Dionadair?" He spat the word into the rain, full of arrogance, but his eyes gave him away as he glanced toward the saint's cell. Fear flickered in his gaze. Perhaps that's why he wanted to destroy it. He thought that would end its power.

Hands trembling, Aini worked the burlap bag off Father's head. He looked up at her, one of his eyes swollen shut and bruised to a purple she could see even though the storm had blackened the sky. She cradled his head and wept over him, her stomach sucking and pulling as she cried, in relief, in rage, in absolute terror. A line of dried blood divided his gray and white beard. Dirt stuck in the lines of his forehead and the crow's feet at his temples.

"Aini." He coughed.

Thane went to one knee and, pushing wet hair out of his face, pulled a knife from his kilt belt, then cut Father's hands free.

"I didn't want you here," Father said to Aini, his voice a croak. "This is my fault." He was shaking his head as the rain poured down, sticking their clothes to their skin.

"It's my doing, Mr. MacGregor," Thane said, his face dark as the sky.

Father put a hand on Thane's knee. "No, son."

The Campbell nearest Neve launched forward and ripped the gun from her. The second slapped Myles's knife away.

"No!" Aini shouted, fear scratching through her bones. Why wasn't the curse doing anything about this?

"Hold them. Hold them all," Rodric ordered as one of his men cocked Neve's gun and pointed it at the Dionadair. "They'll meet our firing squad for this. It'll make for a braw show."

Myles, veins sticking out on his forehead, struggled against the Campbell who had an arm wrapped around his neck. Neve whimpered and stomped her captor's foot. Holding her by the arm, the Campbell smacked her across the face and split her lip open wide. Aini's stomach rolled.

Rodric tapped his gun against his own head. "Nathair has a fine plan for a show in Edinburgh. Remind the people who is in charge in Scotland and who they should pay fealty to."

Fury raged inside Aini, a storm of her own, made of blood and heart and refusal to bow to the Campbells, to the clan who'd maimed her father and ruined her life.

"It's not your fault," she said to Father. She stood, water shucking off her leggings and dripping from the loose ends of her hair.

Thane leaned toward her. "Aini...what are you doing?"

"I'm not going to let this happen." *For Father. For my country.* "I will not let him win."

Tucking his gun in his belt, Rodric crossed his arms like there wasn't a man bleeding, maybe dying, not ten feet away. "And just what are you going to do about it, Seer?" He spoke casually, but terror flickered in his black eyes.

Her heart lodged between her ribs like a knife. "I am exactly as dangerous as the king thinks I am." She flew toward the cell.

"Aini!" Thane's and Father's voices followed her down the stairs.

Vera called out, "Seer, wait!"

Their work lit by a battery floodlight, the men inside lifted their hammers and drove them into the throne, breaking Aini's heart in a million ways for a million reasons. There were pieces of the ancient throne everywhere. Then as the men hit the center, a large crack etched down the black, glittering stone. A corner of the stone fell away and tumbled toward Aini. The men didn't turn, didn't seem to hear her above the noise, as she lifted the rock. One spiral marked the piece, its edges like a giant's fingerprint.

She tore out of the cell and into the storm.

Lightning poured over Rodric, his boot now on Father's chest, and two of his men pointing guns directly at Thane.

Campbells restrained Dodie, Bran, and Vera.

Owen lay on the ground, partially covered in Dodie's coat and shivering.

The wind rippled kilts and the ends of jackets, grabbed at hair, and threw sounds of hammering and crying and thunder around like leaves. The air smelled like steel and blood.

"I'll not settle for a cousin who knows nothing of loyalty," Rodric said, his voice broad and curling with his West Scots accent. "I'm the son Nathair should've had and it's time I rid him of you for good."

"Thane!" Aini shouted and her voice cracked, her throat on fire. She threw the heavy piece of the Coronation Stone.

Squinting, Thane spun, his kilt twisting above his boots. He caught the piece.

Everything happened at once, but slowly, like in a dream.

The dirt under Aini's boots began to quake. Growing in strength, the Coronation Stone's tremor knocked her to the sharp bracken and sucking mud. A frigid wind whipped through the chapel's skeleton walls, stinging her cheeks. Crackling like a fire, a blue-white haze oozed from the stone, and Thane's face went slack as he held the stone tight, arms shaking. The pale fog formed the appearance of men with stoic faces, beards and crowns, long shirts and draping robes that snapped in the wind.

They were the ghosts of the kings of Scotland—ancient Celts, the Gaels, the men of Alba.

With gray hands like claws and eyes empty but burning with purpose, the ghost kings rose. Aini smelled woodsmoke, pine, and a deep, complicated scent like sage or cloves. Their voices filled her ears. Pleading, asking, retelling old tales.

She stood tall, wind tearing around her. The urge to speak to the ghost kings pressed against her mouth, but what could she say? Only the truth and a request.

"They want to kill Thane Campbell," she said to them, her throat aching and her heart in pieces. "He is the stone's chosen ruler. Protect the Heir!"

The blue-white light sighed and brightened. Gunpowder flashed, orange and blinding, from the Campbells' guns.

Surrounded by the kings' twisting light, Thane didn't fall.

The spirits grew, unfolding from the stone, their draping tunics and tartans fluttered over their seemingly solid bodies.

Scrolled metal decorated the nearest king's belt. The blue glint of an ethereal light flashed from another's simple crown. Which one was Macbeth?

The ghosts opened their mouths as one, releasing a sound like a broom dragged across a dry floor. They rushed forward and swamped Rodric, Rabbie, and the rest of the Campbells, engulfing them in milky blue, their odd, magic scent increasing, overpowering the salty sea and the metallic flavor of the rain. The men's guns splashed as they hit pewter puddles on the ground. Shouting, Rodric and all the Campbells in the chapel, except Thane, grabbed their chests and pulled at their shirts and jackets.

They collapsed, white-faced and still.

The ghost kings faded into shining dust and disappeared into the biting air.

The curse of the Coronation Stone had worked its magic. Rodric and the rest had tried to kill Thane, the Heir, and they'd paid the price. *The power of the old to protect their own.*

Blinking and ears ringing, Aini scrambled to Father. Thane lay the piece of the stone down and they helped him to stand.

Black lines of makeup marred Vera's face. "Thane Campbell." Her voice shook. "You are the Heir and we, the Dionadair, promise to serve you."

Vera, Dodie, and the rest of the Dionadair crossed their thumbs over their heads as the storm pulled its ashen cloak from the island.

Bran took a knee as the sun battled its way out of the clouds. "I swear fealty to you, Thane Campbell."

Thane's throat moved in a swallow. "I may be the Heir, but I'm not the chief of Clan Campbell."

Bran smiled sadly. "I think you'll need to claim that too if this is to work."

Thane's eyes shuttered, then he looked to Aini, his face grave. Tentative joy and relief flew through her like birds and she drank in the sight of him, strong and able, and of Father standing tall too. Whatever must come next, it was over for now.

It. Was. Over.

CHAPTER 28
SWEET AND SOUR

"**D**on't think you're getting my side of the room just because of all this," Myles shouted over at Thane. Aini slapped him because Neve wasn't there to do it. Neve was checking on her family. "What?" Myles frowned and stacked some card stock at his desk. "He can't have everything."

Aini shook her head and joined Thane at the taffy puller. He gave her a sideways grin that turned her bones into butterflies. Last time they'd made taffy... Aini's gaze went to his parted lips.

"Don't lose focus over there, squirrel," Father said. "It's a lot more expensive now that it's loaded with more Cone5."

Cheeks going hot, Aini forced her eyes away from Thane's broadening smile. "Of course not, Father."

The taffy was finished aerating. As it dropped from the puller's silver arms and onto the tray, Thane and Aini used plastic scrapers to remove every last bit from the machine. Who knew when they would have access to the candy lab again? Probably never. Tears burned Aini's eyes, but she willed them away. They'd won the first battle. Now they had to prepare for the next. That involved moving whatever they could into the Dionadair safe house on the outskirts of Edinburgh, where Owen was healing with the rest of the rebels. There was no time for sentimental tears.

"The hard candies are ready," Father said, closing the small, purple treats up in a tin. "These will make some brave soul float like a leaf in the wind."

They hadn't decided how exactly to use these intensified sweets. But using candy to improve abilities seemed the best way to help the Dionadair and fight Nathair. Poisoning people could be done in more efficient ways. The rebels had a full armory. Aini hated that she had to consider such things now. But this was war, not a party.

Aini had suggested eating intensified altered candies to form a sort of improved team of operatives. She hadn't realized the idea would result in her being in charge of said team. "I hope that's not the one I end up using," she admitted quietly to Thane.

He chuckled. Sadness still pulled at him, darkening his eyes, but he smiled easier now. "It would be good to see an area from above in a pinch."

"Then you do it."

"Maybe I will."

"I think I'm going to be the one eating the taffy." She'd had another idea late last night when they'd returned from Bass Rock. "Maybe the Cone5 will allow me to see more spirits, to communicate with more of them."

"Ah. Good thinking."

"We'll test it when we get to the safe house. Vera said there's a cemetery nearby."

"We could test it when the rest take the first load. The house will be ours."

His voice sent good shivers down her back. She tried to breathe evenly so he wouldn't know how much he affected her. It was embarrassing how he could melt her with a word.

"Maybe," she said.

His eyebrow twitched near the frame of his glasses and that grin appeared again.

"All right," Father said. "Myles. Help me take these tins downstairs. Bring your supplies. The lorry should be out front. You two, finish wrapping that taffy, please, and meet us there." He threw a stern look at Aini, then said something under his breath. Even patient Father had his limits.

The second Myles and Father were gone, Thane threw the taffy and scraper down onto the tray, took Aini's face in his sticky hands, and covered her mouth with his. Aini fell into the warmth of his lips, the strength in his chest and stomach against hers. She ran her hands into his hair, not caring one bit that it would make the ends stand up and everyone would know exactly what they'd been doing. He said something into her neck, a piece of that old poem, and she couldn't stop smiling, her lips stretching and her hands smoothing the back of his skull. His scent had changed. Still the clean cotton of his clothing was there, but something like sage, like magic, cloaked him. She pulled back to look at his eyes, the steely gray of the cold North Sea, swirling with power and pull.

She raised an eyebrow. "I told you that you were the Heir."

A little laugh escaped him. "Aye. And I see that, though you're fine with breaking rules now, you've not lost your love of being right."

Lifting her chin, she smiled. "No. I have not." She chewed the inside of her cheek, not wanting to ruin the moment, but needing to talk about what was to come. "You have to go to Inveraray and claim your place as Chief of Clan Campbell.

And Nathair will have something to say about that when he is well."

He swallowed and looked away. "I suppose I must try. We need the clan behind us against him and against the king, if it comes to that. It will be a fight. A terrible fight. I'll need you with me. As Seer. The clan will want to hear about the kings you spoke to and how they followed your commands."

"They weren't following my commands. They were fulfilling the curse."

"I disagree, hen. Regardless, do you think they'll rise up to help us again? Or is the curse a one-time thing?"

So, he didn't see it. In addition to the magic scenting the air around him, a very subtle aura of blue light shone around him since that night on Bass Rock. "Look." She turned him toward the mirror beside the lab sink.

"I don't see anything but how you messed my hair to prove you've had your way with me." The corner of his mouth lifted.

"The blue light around you? You can't see that?"

He shook his head. "No."

"I thought everyone could." That was going to make convincing Clan Campbell he was the Heir and deserved total respect much more difficult. "Maybe you'll see the aura if you eat some taffy? The clan could see it then, if they ate some?"

"Another good idea. But," he smiled down at her, "I think we've time for a wee kiss first. Don't you? What's saving my life if I don't do my best to enjoy it?" His sad smile widened into something brighter as the late night sunset turned the lab's high windows purple.

"I'm not judging, but how can you smile like that when you know war is coming and we're going to be in the thick of it using experimental candies and ghosts to stay alive?"

"I've had a rough go of it so far. I'm not complaining. I just...

now that I have someone who understands me, who likes me despite who I am and what I've done."

She turned his chin so he faced her. "And I do. I forgave you. For all of it. And I hope you can forgive me."

"What for? You did nothing wrong."

"I lied to everyone for a very long time."

He nodded and ran a palm over her shoulder. "I can't let the bad things that will happen ruin what time I have with you. Nothing in life is safe, permanent. I know that much at least."

Aini's heart squeezed once, twice, then she pressed her mouth to his. The tip of his tongue swept gently across hers and a fever rode down her back and into her thighs, making her knees weak. This humble, brave man was hers. For now, anyway. She was determined to soak in every ounce of sweetness while they had this time together. Thane ran a palm up the back of her head and tangled his sticky fingers in her hair.

"Got you back," he whispered, chuckling.

She grinned and caught a glimpse of his tattooed hand as he traced a thumb, just barely touching, over her cheek. Soft, gentle. He dipped his other hand to her lower back and eased her body against the strong lines of his.

"I'm glad you've decided to go claim your place with your clan," she whispered, amused that her voice sounded so husky.

"Aye? It'll be dangerous."

"Yes," she said, "but I'll get to see you in a kilt again."

Taking his top lip between her teeth gently, she kissed him thoroughly, inhaling his new scent. A rushing, lovely heat twisted through her veins and filled her with happiness, and legends, ghosts, and revolutions took second place in her heart.

Get the next book in the Edinburgh Seer series today!
Go HERE to get The Edinburgh Heir!

THE EDINBURGH HEIR

Will Aini and Thane persuade the Highland clans to support them against Nathair? You don't want to miss the new altered sweets, wild concoctions, stolen moments in green glens, and dangerous missions in the next book in the series.

www.ingramcontent.com/pod-product-compliance
Lightning Source LLC
Chambersburg PA
CBHW031059270626
47155CB00027B/2828